Whiteout

DYAN LAYNE

ISBN: 978-1-7364765-7-4
ASIN: B0CCSZLFBT

Cover photography: Michelle Lancaster, @lanefotograf
Cover model: Eric Guilmette
Cover designer: Lori Jackson, Lori Jackson Design
Formatting: Stacey Blake, Champagne Book Design

Dear Miss Dalton,

On behalf of our client, your presence at Dalton House is kindly requested.

She'd been summoned. By the grandmother she never met. After missing twenty-one years of her life, why did she want to see her now?

Please make arrangements to travel before the arrival of winter weather in the Sierra Nevada.

Breanna had questions. Grandmama had the answers. But classes, friends, and parties came first. The week of Thanksgiving break would have to do.

Mountain roads can be treacherous when the snow comes.

And the snow was coming. Now. She met him in a roadside diner—Sinjin. Her dark savior. Her rescuer from the storm. Trapped together in a remote mountain cabin, he taught Breanna what she needed from a man. He warned her to be careful. And when the snow stopped falling, he was gone.

Do let me know when to expect you, Miss Dalton.

I'm looking forward to meeting you.

Sincerely,

Derek St. John, Esq.

Derek St. John, Esq.

ST. JOHN, MAYNARD & ST. JOHN,
ATTORNEYS AT LAW

Playlist

Stream the full playlist on Spotify here:
https://tinyurl.com/WhiteoutonSpotify
Or on YouTube here: https://tinyurl.com/WhiteoutonYouTube

Burden of the Sky | *Whiteout*
Bad Omens | *Like A Villain*
Otyken | *Storm*
REDZED | *Blizzard*
Sleep Token | *Dark Signs*
Tommee Profitt (feat. Laney Jones) | *Be Careful*
Yeah Yeah Yeahs | *Heads Will Roll*
Kings of Leon | *Closer*
Deftones | *Digital Bath*
Palaye Royale | *Closer*
Anya Marina | *You Are Invisible*
Ghost | *Missionary Man*
Toothgrinder | *The Shadow*
Sleep Token | *Hypnosis*
Greg Puciato | *Through the Walls*
Marilyn Manson | *Sweet Dreams (Are Made Of This)*
Valerie Broussard | *A Little Wicked*
Spiritbox | *Circle With Me*
Outrage X GorillaT | *Deceit*
Mick Mars | *Right Side of Wrong*
Merci Raines | *The Devil is a Gentleman*
Memphis May Fire | *Somebody*
Yeah Yeah Yeahs | *Burning*
Bachman-Turner Overdrive | *You Ain't Seen Nothin' Yet*
First Aid Kit | *Out of My Head*
Alice In Chains | *Right Turn*
VV | *Echolocate Your Love*

Bryce Savage | *Curiosity*
Tommee Profitt (feat. Fleurie) | *Midnight Oil*
Margo Price | *Been To The Mountain*
NOTHING MORE | *Déjà Vu*
Evanescence | *Haunted*
First Aid Kit | *Walk Unafraid*
Godsmack | *You And I*
Sleep Token | *Give*
Carol Kay | *Ain't Gonna Stop*
No Resolve (feat. Kayla King) | *Kiss from a Rose*
Sleep Token | *The Summoning*
Sleep Token | *Chokehold*
NOTHING MORE | *IF IT DOESN'T HURT*
Queens of the Stone Age | *The Way You Used To Do*
Robot Koch, John Lamonica | *Nitesky*
Ghost | *Phantom Of The Opera*
Mikey Ekko | *Who Are You, Really?*
In This Moment | *I Would Die For You*
Deftones | *Passenger*
Bachman-Turner Overdrive | *Let It Ride*
Lisa Marie Presley | *You Ain't Seen Nothin' Yet*
Bring Me The Horizon | *DArkSide*
Burden of the Sky | *Whiteout (Acoustic)*
Palaye Royale | *Fever Dream*

Author's Note

The first nine chapters of **Whiteout**, which are included here, were originally published in Billionaires and Babes, the BABE2023 Charity Anthology, but that was only the beginning, a prologue if you will. The rest of the story lies within these pages.

Whiteout contains subject matter that may be sensitive or triggering to some readers and is intended for mature audiences.

Happy reading!

Dedication

For my Aussie babes. I started this one for you, after all
And my sweetie-pie, Jalina, who napped beside me while I
wrote this book.
I love you.

whiteout noun

Definition: a surface weather condition in a snow-covered area (such as a polar region) in which no object casts a shadow, the horizon cannot be seen, and only dark objects are discernible

also: a blizzard that severely reduces visibility

Whiteout

Chapter One

Five hours.

That's how long she'd been driving already, and Breanna hadn't even reached the state line yet. Maybe she should've stayed on I-5 instead of cutting over to Route 39, but that's the way her GPS sent her, so she took it. Cranking up the tunes, she passed Klamath Falls and grinned. "Seventeen more miles."

With her Spotify playlist blasting, she excitedly waved goodbye to Oregon as the 'Welcome to California' sign appeared. The state of her birth, though she would be nowhere close to her family in LA. She hadn't even told her mom she was making the trip. She'd only worry. Besides, just hearing the name Dalton made Sarah Benjamin sad. It surprised Breanna she got to keep her dad's last name.

Bad blood between her mother and her late father's family. Namely, her grandmother, Valerie Dalton, whom Breanna had never even met. She'd never met Shane Dalton either—not that she could remember, anyway. He died when she was just a baby.

So when she received an official-looking letter from St. John, Maynard & St. John, Attorneys at Law, on her grandmother's behalf, requesting her presence at Dalton House, it aroused her curiosity. What did Valerie Dalton want? Breanna doubted it was a desire to meet her son's only child after twenty-one years. But it could be, right? The woman had to be in her seventies now. Maybe she'd had a sudden change of heart in her old age.

Yeah, and maybe shit doesn't stink.

The correspondence, signed by one Derek St. John, said little. No clue why she was being summoned. He only stated he was following the wishes of his client and advised Breanna to plan to get there before the Thanksgiving holiday—and the arrival of winter weather in the Sierra Nevada. Mountain roads can be treacherous when the snow comes.

Did he think she was an idiot?

Chrissakes, just because she was a California girl, didn't mean she'd never driven in snow before.

After marinating on it for a week, she left word with the lawyer's secretary to let him know when to expect her. The week of Thanksgiving break would have to do, and too bad if Derek St. John or her grandmother didn't like it. Breanna had friends to see, parties to go to, and classes to attend. Okay, she was on the flexible undergrad track for her BA in English. If she wanted to, she could log into lectures on her laptop, comfy in her pajamas, from the sofa in her apartment—or from anywhere, for that matter, but the old lady didn't need to know that.

Her gaze flicked over to the snow-capped range of peaks to the east. Overcast, the midday sky looked dreary, but the clouds weren't ominous. *Yet.* She'd be fine. But Breanna still had five hundred miles, some seven hours of driving left before she reached her destination, and her ass was already numb.

A hundred and forty miles later, her bottom screaming at her to get up and stretch, gas gauge down to a quarter tank, she got off the highway. Refuel. Restroom. Coffee. There was no time to waste if she wanted to reach Dalton House before dark. Estimating she'd only need to make one more stop after this one, Breanna stood in line, Styrofoam cup in hand, rubbing circulation into her aching backside with the other. As long as the weather held, and barring any unforeseen hazards on the road, she should be good.

Her ass protesting once more, she sat back down behind the wheel, burning her tongue on the steaming hot battery acid that passed for gas station coffee. *Yuck.* Breanna grimaced into the cup, her phone vibrating on the center console.

"Hey, Kay," she answered.

"Just checking on you. You there yet?"

Kayleigh, her closest friend at college, and her roommate, was a worrywart. An old mother hen in a twenty-year-old body. She was the girl who forbade the consumption of jungle juice at parties—especially those held on Greek Row, cockblocked the fuckboys, and forced her to eat something besides cheap ramen noodles for dinner. And Breanna loved her for it. God only knows just how many bad decisions she'd saved her from.

"Hell, no." She expelled some air, tipping her head back against the seat. "Just made it to 395."

"You're not being safe." Breanna could just picture Kayleigh shaking her head. "You should stop. Get a room and rest for the night."

"No, I'll be fine," she assured her. "It's only a few more hours."

"Stubborn." Kayleigh sighed through the phone. "Have you even bothered checking the weather, Bree? They're predicting—"

"Snow. I know." Swallowing a sip of the putrid battery acid, she glanced up at the sky. "I'll be there long before it gets here, so don't worry, okay?"

"Yeah, I bet that's what the Donner Party said too, and look what happened to them."

"So dramatic," Breanna said, chuckling at the historical

reference. "I think it's pretty safe to assume no one's going to be eating me—dead or alive."

Kayleigh giggled. "Well, should that lawyer guy or Grandmama serve fava beans and a nice chianti at dinner? Run. Fast."

"Will do." And she started her car. "I'll text you when I get there."

The cloud cover grew more dense the farther she drove. No longer merely overcast, the sky appeared heavy, saturated in a deepening gray. Breanna wasn't too concerned, though. According to her GPS, Dalton House was less than an hour away.

Like a good, obedient girl, she exited off the highway as the robotic British male voice instructed her to. She preferred him to the Siri-sounding woman. A checkpoint was set up on the road in front of a mom-and-pop store. Coming to a stop, Breanna lowered her window.

"Evening, miss."

She tipped her chin. "Hello."

"You're gonna need to get chains on those tires before I can let you through. We're expecting a doozy of a storm. Can't have you getting stuck out there on the pass."

"But—" *It's not even snowing yet.*

"Sorry, miss." He pointed toward the little store. "Hank's got 'em if you're needing some. Seventy-five bucks and he'll put 'em on for you too. Have you back on the road in a jiffy."

"Okay, thanks," Breanna assented, raising the window. "This is some bullshit. Hank must be raking it in."

Figuring she might as well top off her tank before heading inside the store, Breanna pulled up to the gas pump. A cold gust slapped her in the face as she exited the car, making her clench the unzipped jacket tightly around her middle. Trees danced on either side of the road, their naked branches bending

4

to the will of the wind in the thickening darkness. Gazing heavenward, the slate-gray altostratus ominously churned.

Triggered by a familiar tickle in her nose, she sniffed the air. The scent of an approaching storm mingled with sweet benzene. Breanna zipped her worn, black leather bomber, and winding a scarf around her neck, made her way across the small parking lot. Bells attached to the door clanked into the glass as she wrestled with it, a sudden squall pushing her inside.

It was as if the passage of time had forgotten this place. To her left was a small diner with a checkered floor, red vinyl seats, and an old-fashioned soda fountain. To her right, a counter with rows of penny candy—cost twenty times that now—and a cash register. In front of her were several aisles of grocery essentials and sundries.

A balding head popped up from behind the counter. "Need something, miss?"

"Yes. Yes, I do. Chains." Behind her, the door burst open again. Breanna shivered, tingles creeping down her spine. "The officer at the checkpoint told me to see Hank."

"That's me." Pointing a thumb backward at his chest, he cracked a crooked grin, revealing a crooked front tooth. "I'm Hank."

"Can you put them on for me?"

"Be happy to." His head bobbed. "Where's your car?"

"Right outside," she said, handing him the keys. "The white Miata."

Breanna heard a snicker at her back. A voice, smooth and deep, muttered low, "Figures. Damn girly car."

She whirled around to find six feet of rugged man standing behind her. Bearded. Suede coat lined with sheepskin. A black Stetson on his head. Dark hair brushed his shoulders. Eyes the color of whiskey. "Yeah, well, I *am* a girl."

"I can see that." Smirking, he dropped his head to the side and winked.

Probably drives one of those big-ass pickup trucks to compensate for having a tiny dick.

Flustered by the stranger's boldness, Breanna turned back to Hank. "How long will it take?"

"Not too long," he assured her. The crooked grin fixed on his face, he bobbed his head to the left. "Why don't you get yourself a cup of coffee while you wait? Have a piece of banana cream pie. My wife makes it. Best damn pie in the world, trust me."

"Can't pass that up, now can I?" She smiled at Hank, side-eyeing the tall, dark, imposing stranger. Brushing past him, Breanna took a seat on a vinyl-covered stool at the end of the counter.

Sweet on her tongue, she licked thick, whipped cream from her lips. Hank did not exaggerate. The pie was chef's kiss, and the coffee sublime, especially after the gas station sludge she'd been existing off of.

Rubbing his hands together, cheeks reddened, Hank came behind the counter as she washed down the last of her pie with a sip of coffee. "You're all set, miss."

"Great, thanks." Breanna handed him her credit card.

He just held it in his hand, staring at it. "Dalton, huh? You any relation to Valerie?"

"Yeah, she's my grandmother. Why? You know her?"

Tucking his tongue into the corner of his lip, Hank nodded. "Well, I'll be goddamned. I had no idea. You'd have to be Shane's girl then."

"That's right."

Brows cinching together, his eyes flicked to the windows behind her. "It's startin'. Best get you on your way."

The bold one sat in a booth. Hat on the table, a mug of

coffee poised at his mouth, he shook his head. "Suicide. Chains or no chains, she's gonna slide right off the mountain in that thing."

Standing up from the stool, Breanna sniggered. "It's just a few snowflakes."

Slowly, he swiped his tongue across his lip and grinned.

"And every storm starts with just one."

Chapter Two

Illuminated beneath a lone lamppost, snowflakes flitted in the wind. Still sniggering, Breanna tossed her jacket onto the passenger seat and got behind the wheel of her 'girly' car. *Asshole.* Okay, the guy was nice to look at, which she found disconcerting, but he had a helluva lot of nerve. Like his opinion mattered. How was she any of his business, anyway?

Figuring it would be better to text Kayleigh before cell service became spotty, and so she could concentrate on the road, Breanna tapped out a quick message letting her know she'd made it. So what if she wasn't exactly there yet? She was close, regardless.

As soon as she switched on her headlights, the door to Hank's store opened. Plowing his fingers through thick, dark hair, the man from the diner pulled his hat back down on his head. He paused in front of her car, and dipping his chin, the corner of his mouth rose. Breanna watched him walk over to a Ford Raptor. *Knew it.* Then she put her car in gear and slowly drove out of the parking lot.

With a thumbs-up, they waved her through the checkpoint. Here, on the valley floor, the driving surface was level, the snowfall light and pretty. Releasing the tension in her shoulders, Breanna turned on her playlist and settled in for her journey up the mountain.

She imagined the surrounding vista was breathtaking in daylight. Lights twinkled from the village ahead. Dark, majestic peaks, soaring ten thousand feet into a pink-hued sky—its color a warning—loomed in front of her. A real doozy of a snowstorm was waiting, all right. She only hoped she reached the summit, and Dalton House, before it unleashed its wintry fury.

The foothill village, a testament to a bygone era, was small and quaint. Gas lampposts. Old buildings, the year of their construction etched into the brick, lined either side of the four-lane road. Vintage-looking script painted on storefront windows. A couple of older gentlemen walked into a bar. Other than them, the sidewalks were empty.

Breanna came to a stop sign at the edge of town. The road ahead narrowed from four lanes to two, before curving to the right. No longer level, it felt like the pavement beneath her tires tilted in that very direction. Flakes of snow melted on her windshield, the air outside thirty-four degrees. She turned the wipers on.

A sign of fluorescent yellow warned motorists the pass lay ahead. Steep drop-offs. Narrow shoulders. Eight percent grades. She read aloud to herself, "Use caution. Alternate routes advised."

Yikes.

And below that, a rectangle of green and white. "Dalton Pass Road." *Dalton? What the hell?* "13 miles to summit. Elevation 10,264 feet."

She bent her neck to look at the sky. The surrounding mountains appeared to shoot straight up into it. Releasing a breath, she turned off the music and pressed her foot to the accelerator. "I can do this."

Following the curve to the right, Breanna took it slow. Nestled into the side of the mountain, a lone dwelling appeared on her left. Then up, up, and away, with her fingers curled tightly around the steering wheel, she cautiously began the brutal ascent.

The higher in altitude she climbed, the lower the temperature dropped. And the harder it snowed. Flurries tumbled out of the sky, whirling in front of her headlights. Thirteen miles never felt so far away.

"Ten," Breanna muttered to herself, clenching the wheel steady on the switchback. She'd made it three so far.

As much as she wanted to go faster, she didn't dare. One glance to the right and her heart was in her throat. No shoulder to speak of. No guard rail. Nothing but a hairpin drop-off into a chasm far below.

"*Suicide. Chains or no chains, she's gonna slide right off the mountain in that thing.*"

Perhaps she should've heeded the stranger's warning. How many vehicles before her had done just that? Now that Breanna was driving on this death trap of a road with her name on it, she understood how easily it could happen. One small miscalculation could have her slipping over the edge, careening into the void. And certain death. She didn't want to even imagine it.

Reciting a *Hail Mary* in her head, she white-knuckled the wheel, traveling at a snail's pace. At this rate, it would take another hour to reach the summit and Dalton House. And the weather was worsening by the minute.

The clock told her it was well past dark, but all she could see was white. Powerful gusts blasted her windshield with snow faster than the wipers could clear it. Breanna couldn't just stop. In a white car, she'd be invisible—a sitting duck. There was no place to pull over or turn around to go back to the village and wait out the storm. With no choice other than to keep going, she was fucked.

Her breath locked in her lungs, panic speared at the walls of her throat. Battery acid coffee churned in her gut. Beads of nervous sweat erupted on her forehead, trickling down her skin. Every foot forward, a blind walk on a tightrope with no safety net.

"In three hundred feet, turn left," the British voice instructed her.

Driving in a snow globe tossed in a blender, Breanna couldn't see three feet in front of her, never mind three hundred.

"Turn left."

"Left where?" Like she expected the voice to answer.

If Breanna missed the turn, she'd be even more fucked than she already was. The map displayed on the screen showed here, so.

It's now or never.

She cut the wheel to the left.

"Fuck!"

Lifting her head from the steering wheel, Breanna couldn't be sure how long she'd been sitting there. Seconds? Minutes? Hours?

Snow blanketed the windshield, but the car's interior wasn't cold, so not very long. Something warm and wet tickled her forehead. She swiped at it. Blood smeared her fingers.

"Don't panic," Breanna told herself as she searched for her phone.

Finding it on the passenger side floorboard, she prayed for a signal, not that she expected to be so lucky.

"No bars." She tossed her phone to the seat. "Course not."

Think, Bree.

Just sitting here in the car wasn't going to help. She had to assess the situation, at least. Breanna shrugged into her jacket, and winding her scarf around her neck, went to open the car door.

No go.

"Dammit."

It wouldn't budge, forcing her to crawl over the center console to the other side. Pushing the passenger door open, crystallized ice pellets cut into her face like a million tiny daggers. Breanna pulled her scarf up over her nose, feeling along the side of the car until she reached the windshield. The car, buried under snow, seemed wedged into the mountain.

Leaning over the windshield, Breanna flipped the wipers up, so they wouldn't freeze to the glass. What the fuck was she doing that for? If she didn't get her ass back inside the car, it was her they'd find frozen.

In May.

After twenty feet of snow melted.

And now she was wet and cold, shivering inside her useless, girly, white car. She turned the hazard lights on. Another car would surely come along, right? But how would anyone be able to spot her in this weather? The snow was coming down in thick, sideways sheets, drifting with the ferocious winds, and rapidly accumulating.

That's when it hit her. She could die here. On a road named Dalton. Sitting in her car all alone.

"Fuck that."

She'd watched one of those survivalist shows on National Geographic once. These guys got caught in a snowstorm while hiking. They dug into the snow, and like Inuits in an igloo, they sheltered there. Maybe the snow could insulate the car from the freezing temperatures outside, protecting her from hypothermia and frostbite—for a little while, anyway.

Breanna hit the ignition button to restart the engine and blast the heat for a few minutes. Not for too long. She hadn't thought to check to see if the exhaust pipe was clear, and she wasn't about to trade comfort for carbon monoxide poisoning.

Click, click, click.

She hit the start button again.

Nothing.

Squeezing her eyelids closed, her head fell back against the seat. What the fuck was she going to do now? She had a throw blanket in the backseat, the duffel bag she packed for the trip, a few bottles of water, and half a Styrofoam cup of cold, rancid coffee from the gas station on 395.

"Flashlight."

Breanna reached into the glove compartment. The last time she was home, her stepdad got her one of those heavy-duty Maglites, the same kind cops carry, and put it in there. Being he was LAPD, Nathan Benjamin was always doing things like that.

"Just in case," he said. "Makes an excellent weapon too, should you ever need one."

She laughed it off at the time. "Really, Dad?"

"Yes, really. Lots of nut jobs out there," he said, closing the glove compartment. "We worry about you, okay?"

She wasn't laughing now. Holding the flashlight in her hands, unbidden tears came to her eyes. Blinking them back, Breanna switched it on. She placed it on the dashboard, aiming the beam out the passenger side window, then reaching behind her, she covered herself with the blanket from the back seat.

And she waited.

Thump, thump, thump.

Scrape.

What the fuck was that? Startled, her eyes flew open. She didn't remember closing them.

"Hey, you in there?" The man's voice sounded muffled.

Thump, thump, thump.

A gloved fist pounded on the window.

"Yes, yes, I'm in here," Breanna screamed as loudly as she could.

Another scrape and the passenger door opened.

A scarf covered his face, but she recognized the coat. Suede lined with sheepskin.

He folded his large frame into the seat beside her, closing the door to the fury outside. Eyes, the color of whiskey, seared into her own, the corner of his mouth curling into a smirk. "Just had to go and slide into the mountain, now didn't you?"

"Better than sliding off it, I guess."

"Heh." His teeth rolled over his lip. "Yeah, I reckon so."

Chapter Three

Whiskey eyes slowly scanned her from across the center console of his big-ass, he-man truck. Snow stuck to his brows. It melted from his lashes. Without taking his gaze off her face, the man removed his gloves, holding large hands in front of the warm air coming out of the vents.

Despite it, Breanna still shivered. Her breath sawed in and out, chest heaving with exertion from lugging her duffel bag on her shoulder a mere ten feet against the blinding winter storm that pummeled them. She'd held onto her savior, gripping the belt loop of his jeans, until they reached the truck door, and he lifted her off her feet, slinging her inside.

Teeth chattering, Breanna asked him, "What about my car?"

"What about it?" Swiping his tongue across his bottom lip, he lowered his hands to his thighs.

"I can't just leave it like that."

"Well, it's not going anywhere." With a shake of his head, he snickered, releasing the parking brake. "There's a garage down in the village. You can call when you get to Dalton House. They're used to towing girly cars off the mountain."

Rolling her eyes, she abruptly angled her head. "Wait, how'd you know that's where I was going?"

"Lucky guess, Miss Dalton." He winked. "Overheard you and Hank."

"Oh." She pursed her lips to one side. "I don't even know your name."

Except for the fact he was hella gorgeous, and he thought little of her car, Breanna didn't know one damn thing about this man. She could just hear Kayleigh in her head.

Stranger danger, girl! He could be a serial killer or something.

Maybe. But at the moment, he was her only salvation. It's not like she had any other choice.

"Sinjin."

She coughed, choking down a fit of giggles that threatened to burst from her throat. "Sinjin? What the hell kind of name is that?"

"Old English." The corner of his mouth ticked up. "It's a family name."

"Oh." Breanna pressed her lips together.

Stepping on the clutch, Sinjin put the truck in gear. "Let's go. Storm's only going to get worse."

"Yeah," she agreed, tugging at the cuff of her jacket. Looking through the windshield, there was nothing to see but swirling white. "Think we'll make it okay?"

With a click of his tongue, he winked. "Sure as hell gonna try."

"Try?" Feigning a smile, Breanna expelled the air from her lungs. "Well, that's reassuring."

"Nothing to fret about, princess." Easing the Raptor around her stranded Miata, Sinjin chuckled. "Hang on. Enjoy the ride."

A handle protruded from the interior beside her for exactly that purpose. Holding onto it with both hands, she side-eyed him. He appeared unruffled, but the precariousness of their predicament was palpable, at least to her.

Breanna wanted to ask him just how in the fuck he could see where he was going. She didn't dare break his focus.

Sitting tall in his seat, Sinjin commanded the vehicle. The road she couldn't discern. Maybe it was familiarity with the mountain or the surround-view camera images on the screen that guided him, but after ten minutes that felt like ten hours, with the storm intensifying, he turned left off the pass.

Under the cover of the pine, visibility improved a little. Breanna could make out shapes, anyway. Sinjin chanced a glance at her. "You only missed it by a hundred feet."

"No fucking way. *This* is where I was supposed to turn?"

"And the princess has a potty mouth."

She didn't believe for a second that he was offended and didn't give a damn if he was. "It's a versatile word."

He snorted.

"How much farther?" Breanna inquired.

"We've got a ways yet."

It had taken them ten minutes to go a measly hundred feet. She didn't know how far *"a ways"* meant—one mile? Two? Hell, at this rate, it could be hours before they got there.

Sinjin picked up the pace somewhat, but the grade was steep, and their progress slow. She could make out tall, menacing formations on either side. *Trees, Breanna. They're just trees.* But bending back and forth, branches looked like arms, eerily waving, as if beckoning them.

"Fuck."

"Guess I'm not the only one with a potty mouth," she said, turning her face from the window to look at him. The truck came to a halt. Sinjin engaged the parking brake. "What's wrong? Why'd you stop?"

"We've got a problem."

Breanna followed his gaze to a fallen pine blocking their way. "This cannot be happening. Can we get around it?"

"On foot." He glanced down at her duffel. "You got a warmer jacket in there?"

"Why?"

"You're gonna need it."

"Are you out of your fucking mind? You said we had *a ways* to go yet." Emphatically shaking her head, Breanna snapped, "We'll die out there!"

"Would you rather die in here?" Reaching into the seat behind him, Sinjin tossed her a blanket. "Wrap this around you."

"You can't be serious."

But apparently, he was. Throwing the truck in reverse, he made a three-point turn. Backtracking for a while, he suddenly veered off to the right, maneuvering the truck through the swaying pines. Until he couldn't. Sinjin shut off the engine. He turned toward her then, head cocked, his commanding expression silencing any further dissent.

Looking away from him, Breanna bundled herself in a beanie of knitted wool, scarf, and gloves. Reaching down to the floorboard, she pulled her duffel bag onto her lap.

"Leave it."

"But I need my stuff."

"Listen, you don't need no books, or ballgowns, or whatever the fuck you've got in there, where we're going. It's gonna be hard enough just walking in this shit." He placed the blanket around her shoulders. Tying the ends together tight, his features softened. "Leave it."

With a nod, she licked her lips. "Okay."

"There's a cabin, maybe a couple hundred yards from here," Sinjin informed her, rifling through the contents of the truck's console. He pulled out a bungee cord. "This'll have to do."

Breanna swallowed. "What's that for?"

"So I don't lose you, princess." And with a deep chuckle, he winked. "Just don't fall into the stream, okay? Think you can manage that?"

Steeling herself to brave the brutal elements outside, she couldn't come up with a response—not that he waited for one. Sinjin opened his door, snow rushing in, before the force of the wind pushed it closed again. Dropping the duffel bag back onto the floor, Breanna watched him feel his way around the front of the truck to the passenger side.

His gloved hand skimmed beneath her jacket. Hooking one end of the cord to the belt loop of her jeans, Sinjin tethered her body to his. He rubbed the tender bump on her forehead. "Trees will give us some cover. Cabin's not too far. You can do this."

Emotion stinging the tip of her nose, Breanna pressed her lips together, offering him a brief nod, and he lifted her out of the truck, setting her on her feet beside him. Her boots sank into the heavy, wet snow, already calf-deep. Biting wind whirred in her ears. It whipped through her long hair, slapping her in the face.

Sinjin pulled her scarf up over her nose, and grabbing her by the hand led her away from the truck.

And with nothing more than blind faith, she let him.

Tilting her head down to keep frozen particles from blasting her eyes, Breanna set her sights on his big, black boots, making a path through the snow ahead of her.

They slowly made their way, moving from tree to tree along the mountain stream. A dull achiness set into her bones. Her lungs burned fire with every inhalation of frigid air. Snot dripped from her nose, grossly saturating the thin, knit wool that covered it. She couldn't be certain how far they'd already gone or how much farther they still had to go, but the trek was arduous and she was exhausted.

To make matters worse, cute UGG boots were not meant for hiking through a blizzard. Even though Breanna wore an over-the-knee pair, snow found its way inside them, packing her feet in slush. She could barely feel them anymore. Her foot struck a rock hidden beneath her, and she stumbled.

Sinjin stopped and pulled her up from the snow. Breanna leaned on him for a moment, his arms steadying her, wiping at the snot running from her nose with the heel of her gloved hand.

"C'mon." He gave her a quick squeeze and hunched over, patting himself on the back to show he wanted her to climb onto him.

Her arms cinched around his neck, legs locked at his waist, Sinjin straightened as if she didn't weigh a thing. "Don't let go."

As if she would.

"We should be almost there."

Breanna laid her head on his broad shoulder, face buried against the crook of his neck. She could smell the masculine scent of him. His woodsy, sensual musk infused her, blocking the frozen ozone and wintry pine. Dragging it greedily into her lungs, she closed her eyes, thinking of warm, pleasant things as he carried her on his back through the storm.

Venice Beach.

A rose honey latte topped with cardamom.

Disneyland.

Cozying up to a fire with a good book.

Fuzzy socks.

Taking another whiff of him, she opened her eyes. *Hot, delicious sex.*

Sinjin put her down on the porch of a small wood cabin. As November raged white all around them, Breanna stood there, shivering from the loss of her body melded to his, and watched him shove his shoulder against the door.

He swooped her up in his arms, carrying her across the threshold. "Your castle in the storm, princess."

"I do have a name, you know, and it's not princess."

In the dark, his whiskey eyes looked feral. His lip curled. "It's Breanna."

Chapter Four

It wasn't much warmer inside the cabin, but at least it was dry. Leaving her to stand there, snow caked to her boots, Sinjin skirted over to her left. Breanna couldn't see what he was doing, but she recognized the sound, and the smell of sulfur as a match was struck.

Down on his haunches in front of the hearth, flames illuminated his face. As if he felt her gaze on him, he rose, his eyes flicking up to meet hers. "Come over here and get warm."

Shakily removing her outer layers, she hung the wet items on pegs in the wall, leaving her boots at the door. Now that she could see, Breanna scanned the single room. Simple, but thankfully, it appeared to be clean. There was a rudimentary kitchen area to the right with a wood stove and a small table, an iron bed on the far wall in front of her, a couple of chairs, and a door—she prayed it went to a bathroom. She had to go, and just the thought of having to do her business in an outhouse caused a violent shudder to shoot through her.

Breanna pointed at it. "Please tell me that's a bathroom in there."

"Yeah." Sinjin sniggered from the stove, his back to her. "Can't handle roughing it, princess?"

"Sorry, I'm just not a squat-in-the-woods kind of girl."

"Guess I won't be taking you camping then."

As if.

He turned around to face her. "This place is pretty much only used for hunting and fishing. We're off-grid here." Taking a step closer, Sinjin angled his head and reached for a strand of her wet hair. He rubbed it between his fingers. "But you're safe now."

Her breath caught in her throat. *Am I?*

"I'm going to bring some more wood in." He let her hair go. "Can't let that fire die out."

The bathroom was small. A frosted window its only source of light. With most of the space taken up by an old cast-iron tub, there was barely enough room to turn around. Breanna peeled her wet jeans down her thighs, the flesh beneath the denim cold and clammy. She loathed pulling them back up again. At the sink, water ran from the faucet. She washed her hands in liquid ice, wishing for a toothbrush. A tube of Crest sat beside a bottle of soap. She used her finger.

Sinjin was stacking wood beside the hearth when Breanna came out of the bathroom, the wood floor rough beneath her bare feet. She sat on a rocking chair in front of the fire, fingers combing through her tangled hair to dry it.

"I checked the cabinets," he said, without looking at her. "We've got canned soup, oatmeal, coffee, powdered creamer, and sugar."

"No fava beans and a nice chianti to go with it?"

He turned around, his brow raised.

"*Silence of the Lambs,*" she explained. "Never mind."

"Sorry, no."

"Well, that's good." Breanna snorted out a laugh. "I don't have to worry about being eaten for dinner."

Flames reflected in his whiskey eyes, his lips rising to a smirk. He winked. "There's always dessert."

Turning back to the fire, Sinjin unbuttoned his shirt and tossed it on a chair. The Henley he wore beneath it followed. His skin was golden in the flickering light, each chiseled muscle defined.

The distinct sound of a buckle unlatching interrupted her ogling. The button popped on his jeans. "What are you doing?"

Lowering his zipper, Sinjin turned around. "Getting out of these wet clothes," he replied. Then, stripping off his pants, he kicked them over to the chair. "And I suggest you do the same before you catch pneumonia."

Working a tangle from her hair, Breanna looked away, but not before she stole a glimpse of *that* part of him. Good God, she'd never been so wrong. "That's *not* how you get pneumonia."

Comfortable in his nudity, he continued to stand there. And with a body like that, why wouldn't he be? Staring into the fire, she could feel his eyes on her.

"You're shivering." His voice came closer. "Jesus, if you don't take those fucking clothes off, I'll have no choice but to do it for you."

And he was bold enough to mean it. Breanna knew Sinjin was right, though. She'd never feel warm in these clothes, soaked to her skin. Keeping her back to him, she slowly got up from the rocking chair, and trembling, she removed the sodden garments.

He came up to her from behind. Wrapping her naked body in a blanket, his fingers lingered at her breasts, sweeping over her nipples. Breanna sucked in a breath. Electricity sparking at the back of her neck, goosebumps sheeted her skin, and not because she was cold.

Holy fucking hell.

"Get in bed," he ordered, leaving her standing there to go to the kitchen. "I'm going to make us some of that soup."

Compelled to comply, Breanna turned back the thick goose-down comforter and burrowed into the soft mattress. She watched him at the stove. Ass high and taut, he stood with his legs slightly apart, enough to see his balls and that more than impressive appendage hanging in the space between them.

I sure wouldn't have to ask him to go deeper with that thing.
"Chicken noodle or beef barley?"

"Beef." *Most definitely.* Biting her lip, she giggled to herself. "How long do you think we'll be stuck in here?"

"Hard to say." He glanced back at her. "A few days, maybe."

How in the world would she survive being trapped in here with this man for that long?

With the soup heating on the wood stove, Sinjin gathered their discarded clothing, setting them on a rack to dry near the fire. "Don't worry. I'm sure you'll be up at Dalton House in time for the big Thanksgiving spread."

Breanna shrugged. "Wasn't planning on staying that long."

"No? What'd you come for then?"

"Grandmama summoned me." Holding the blanket closed, she sat up in the bed. "Well, it was her lawyer, actually."

Was she worried about her? Valerie Dalton had to know she was due to arrive today. Would she call the police? Send Derek St. John out looking for her? Probably not.

"Sounds like you don't like her very much."

"Couldn't say." Breanna snickered. "I don't even know her."

"I bet you like her money, though, don't you?" Twirling her panties around his finger, he winked. "And she's got lots of it."

"I wouldn't know."

"Right. And how'd you get that pretty princess car of yours, hmm?"

Presumptuous asshole.

"I bought it with my own money, thank you very much," she informed him, nostrils flaring. Pausing briefly, her lips pursed to the side with a shrug. "Well, mostly mine. My parents helped some."

"Okay, okay." Chuckling, Sinjin put her underwear on the rack with her clothes. "Where do you live, Breanna?"

She liked the way it sounded when he said her name. "I'm going to school in Portland, but home is LA."

"You drove here from Portland?"

"Yeah."

His brows cinched together briefly before cocking his head. "For an old woman, you don't know?"

"Yeah."

"Why?"

Hadn't she been asking herself the very same thing?

"I'm not sure. Maybe because she wants to see me." Licking her lip, Breanna picked at a pulled thread on the blanket. "Could be she's just curious, and that's okay. I am too."

With a brief nod, a look of sympathy seemed to wash over Sinjin's face. Pressing his lips together, he took the soup off the stove.

"Eat." Placing a warm mug in her hands, he sat beside her on the bed. "You like Portland?"

"Yeah, I do," she said, blowing on a spoonful of the hot soup. "It's a pretty cool place. Eclectic, you know?"

"Hmm. Yeah, but there's plenty of really good colleges closer to LA, so what made you go there?"

Not bothering to use his spoon, Sinjin intently gazed at her, seeming to drink her in, along with the contents of his mug. Breanna couldn't help but stare, mesmerized by the muscle sliding up and down his throat as he swallowed.

"Uh…well, because I got a partial scholarship, so I could afford the tuition." She clinked her mug with his. "And it *wasn't* close to home."

He leaned back against the iron headboard, stretching his arm out behind her. "You don't like LA?"

"I like it well enough. It's home." Breanna leaned forward to accommodate the arm that rested on her shoulders. "Just wanted to experience something different for a while."

"What are you studying?"

"English."

"So you can teach?" he asked, setting his mug down on the nightstand.

"God, no, I would suck at that." Laughing, Breanna turned her neck to look at him. "I want to be an editor. I'm hoping to get an internship at a publishing house."

His finger slowly moved up and down her arm. "You got family? A boyfriend?"

"You ask a lot of questions."

"I'm interested."

In what? Her? Did he actually expect her to believe that? She was naked, in bed with a man who was essentially a stranger, and who also happened to be naked. That Sinjin affected her was disconcerting enough. He likely knew it, too. For once, Breanna didn't need Kayleigh to tell her what he was really after. She began tingling all over at the thought.

Tilting her head, she answered, "Of course, I have a family."

"Brothers? Sisters?"

"A little brother. He's ten."

"And a boyfriend?" Tipping his chin down, his brows climbed.

"Nope, don't have one of those." Shaking her head, she coyly smiled. "How about you?"

"I don't have a boyfriend either." Sinjin chuckled, then exhaling the amusement left his face.

Looking deep into her eyes, Sinjin fingered her damp hair, tucking it behind her ear. The wind still howled outside the windows, snow pelting against the glass. Yet it wasn't the storm that alarmed her.

"Be careful."

"What?"

"When you get to Dalton House." He got up, taking the empty mug from her hand. "Just be careful."

Of what? An old lady?

He sounded so serious, though. Ominous, even. Unsure what to make of it, Breanna smoothed the comforter over her lap, watching Sinjin bring their dirty dishes to the sink. He strolled over to the hearth, his features strained, and put another log on the fire. Then he turned around wearing a smirk, the tension gone from his face as if she had only imagined it.

Sliding under the covers, he yanked away the blanket he'd wrapped her in.

"Hey, what do you think you're doing?"

"Body heat." He laid the blanket on top of the comforter and spooned her from behind. "We'll be warmer skin to skin."

"But…we're naked."

"Isn't that convenient?"

Coiling his arm around her middle, Sinjin dragged her back to his chest and tucked her head beneath his chin. With his fingertips lightly stroking her stomach, Breanna felt his cock grow hard nestled against her bottom.

"We can fuck if you want."

"I do not want."

Pressing himself against her, he chuckled. "We'll see about that."

Chapter Five

Silky-soft skin was right there beneath his fingers. He squeezed the girl's hip, strumming back and forth over the flesh of her belly. The faint scent of oranges clung to her hair. Sinjin inhaled, opening his eyes to hues of cappuccino and buttermilk, married into long, flowing locks.

With his cock happy in its new home, snug between the globes of her shapely ass, he was loath to leave the bed. More so, he was reluctant to leave *her*—the warmth of her body. Breanna was anything but the entitled, simpering little princess he expected. Smart and sassy, this girl with a potty mouth intrigued him.

Allowing his fingers to roam closer to her bare pussy, Sinjin pressed his hardness against her soft curves. What would she do if he woke her, stuffing that hole full with his fat dick? He had the feeling she'd welcome it, that she could be a match for him—in bed and out. With the storm still raging out the window, they were trapped in here together for the time being—for days, probably. Days and nights that could be spent rutting. Fucking his cum into her. Filling her up with it. Was there a better way to keep warm and pass the hours? He didn't think so.

Wood snapped in the hearth, his gaze following the sound. The fire was almost out, and while the girl was a blast furnace beside him, the air in the cabin had grown cold. Grudgingly, he forced himself out of the bed, tucking the comforter around her.

Sinjin peered out the window on his way to the bathroom. The snow was already as high as the top of the porch steps and still coming down heavily. Rubbing his hands together, he glanced back at Breanna. "Yeah, baby, we're gonna be here a while."

There was just enough light coming through the frosted glass to see inside the medicine cabinet. Luckily, he'd left a toothbrush and some other toiletries behind the last time he was here. When was that? Mid-October, maybe. Brushing his teeth in frigid water reminded him to turn on the propane heater so his little princess could have a bath. She'd like that.

"Heh." *I'd like that.*

Throwing more wood on the fire, he built it up again. Their clothes were nowhere close to being dry, but the cabin would be toasty in no time. They weren't necessary anyway, and besides, he wanted to keep her naked.

His stomach grumbled. That soup last night didn't do shit to satisfy his hunger. Sinjin put some water on the stove to boil and looked through the cabinets once more, now that there was some light, faint though it was, coming through the windows. A dusty bottle of bourbon sat hidden in the corner. He added it and a sleeve of saltine crackers to their meager stash of provisions.

She'd pushed the covers off, exposing herself to the waist. Leaning back against the rough-hewn counter, Sinjin gazed upon her small, pink-tipped breasts. Nipples stiff peaks in the chilly air. They pleased him. A handful was enough. He'd never been a fan of big, jiggly tits—especially fake ones. Those hardened points, just begging to be sucked on, made his dick hard.

Fate was most definitely on his side. Running into Breanna at Hank's. Finding her on the mountain.

She was his for the taking.

And take her, I will.

Maybe he could figure out a way to keep her.

But for now, he'd wake her up with a cup of coffee. Feed her some oatmeal for breakfast. Give her a good, hard fucking.

Sinjin opened the tin, the aromatic grounds making his mouth water. Nothing beats making coffee the old-fashioned way, over a campfire or on a stove. Figuring she'd like hers sweet, he added plenty of sugar and powdered creamer to one mug.

Breanna was shivering by the time he made it over to the bed with their coffee. Setting it on the nightstand, Sinjin climbed in beside her and pulled the blankets back up to her chin. Rubbing her arm, goosebumps prickled the flesh beneath his fingers, her skin hot to the touch.

Mindful of the bump on her forehead, he checked her temperature using the back of his hand and attempted to rouse her. "Breanna."

She mumbled incoherently, but did not wake.

Returning to the bathroom, Sinjin rifled through the medicine cabinet. He found a packet of BC Powder. Great for a hangover. It was aspirin and caffeine, so it should work to reduce a fever too.

Positioning her on his lap, he cradled her in one arm and poured the powder into her mouth where it would dissolve on her tongue. She sputtered and grimaced. Nasty stuff. It was a bitter taste Sinjin knew all too well.

"Drink." He held a glass of water to her lips. "You're burning up, princess."

She managed to get a few sips down before sinking back against his chest.

He held her. Combing his fingers through her messy, damp hair, tracing them over her skin, Sinjin waited for the medicine to take effect. He watched her breathe through parted lips, the rise and fall of her chest. Her pink-hued nipples.

His thumbs swept over them. They beaded at his touch.

He touched her there again. Lightly rubbing with the pads of his fingers. Up. Down. Up. Down. Her jaw going slack, soft whimpers eked out of her throat.

"Very nice." He pinched them and she mewled. "That's better."

Holding her little tits, he squeezed the swells of supple flesh. He watched the pink buds blossom and swell. Pinching, rolling, and flicking them until he succumbed to his desire and leaned over to suck one into his mouth.

One small bite.

Hips thrashing on his lap, Breanna pressed her ass into his achy dick. Hot sweetness dripped from her pussy to his skin. "Want me to fuck that fever right out of you?"

He pressed a finger between her bare lips. She was soaked. "Fuck, yeah, I know you do."

She belonged to *him*. He got to her first. He saved her, didn't he? Slipping a finger inside her hot hole, Sinjin groaned. "You're gonna give me this pretty, little cunt to ruin, aren't you, princess?" His finger sawing in and out, he added a second.

Her legs fell open, offering her pussy to him.

With just a thrust of his hips, he could slide his dick inside.

"What a good girl you are already," he crooned, finger-fucking her hard. Smashing into her clit. "This tight little pussy already knows who it belongs to, and as soon as you're with me, baby, so will you."

Awake, yet not, Breanna panted out these sweet-sounding cries, her hips rising to meet his merciless fingers, plunging deep inside her. "More, princess?" He scissored them, and spearing in a third, that sweet sound turned guttural. "Better get used to it. Gonna stretch you way more than that with my dick."

With it rubbing between the cheeks of her ass, Sinjin

fingered her harder. Faster. Her pussy squelched with each penetration. Sweetness ran down his forearm, it dripped from his wrist. Letting her head loll on his chest, his other hand dropped between her legs to rub her clit.

Breanna arched her back, the sweet sound ceasing, then relaxed against him.

He licked her from his fingers and watched her breathing slow.

Grazing his knuckles along her cheek, he whispered, "Wake up now, princess."

I want in.

Chapter Six

Breanna gazed down into the ballroom from the top of the staircase. Like a scene from some wicked fairytale or the pages of a Gothic novel, couples whirled around the dance floor, ethereal beneath a candlelit chandelier. Gathering the skirts of her gown, she descended.

He stepped out from the shadows with that almost imperceptible smirk on his face. His presence commanding in an elegant black suit, Sinjin stood waiting for her at the bottom of the stairs. Extending a gloved hand, his deep voice amber honey, he spoke, "Breanna."

She took it, the name euphonious to her coming from his mouth.

Appraising her with an unwavering stare, his eyes flashed feral. Sinjin picked up a glass and held it to her lips. "Drink."

Its contents bitter, Breanna only managed a few sips. Choking, leather-encased fingers trailed down her throat to slip inside the low-cut bodice of her gown. He rubbed her nipple. A delicious sensation pooled low in her belly, and she whimpered.

"Very nice," Sinjin crooned, pinching the sensitive flesh.

Holy hell.

A cat-like sound came from somewhere deep inside her.

"That's better."

His arm encircling her waist, Sinjin escorted her to the center of the floor. He led her in the dance, diaphanous silk swirling at her feet, faster and faster. The air was cold and dank but embraced in his arms, whiskey eyes locked on hers, tiny beads of sweat erupted on her skin. As the room revolved around her, faces blurred. Abruptly, he stopped, and the blood drained from her head to her limbs, making them heavy.

Sinjin thrust his hands inside her gown, squeezing her breasts. "You're gonna give me this pretty, little cunt to ruin, aren't you, princess?"

Yes.

Do it.

Do it.

Please. Do it.

Fingers clutching the edge of her bodice, Sinjin tore the gown from her body, and naked, pushed her down to the floor. He penetrated her pussy, filling it. His thrusts were merciless. Her weighted limbs wide open.

"What a good girl you are already."

The room kept spinning around her. And though the band played on, the featureless couples stopped their whirling to watch them. As they stood, trance-like, witnessing the hedonistic display, one by one, their heads detached from their bodies. Severed by an invisible blade, ribbons of crimson spewing from their necks, they rolled across the floor.

Unaffected by the macabre scene unfolding around them, thrusting in time to the frenzied melody, Sinjin continued his fucking. "Better get used to it."

She writhed with him in the bloody mess, her whole body seizing. A dark figure, whose face she couldn't see, emerged from the recesses of the hall.

She screamed, but it made no sound.

"Wake up now, princess."

Cold.

Wet.

Breanna blinked her eyes open to Sinjin sponging her face with a washcloth. A sheet draped over them, he held her on his lap, worry evident in the lines of his forehead. She glanced around the dimly lit cabin. Flames danced in the hearth, casting shadows on the walls, but no menacing figure appeared. No music played. The only sounds were the crackling of wood, the howling of the wind, and the rapid beat of her heart.

A nightmare then.

But it hadn't started that way. It was strange, yes, as dreams often are, but still oddly exhilarating. Parts of it had felt so real. Too real.

"That's *not* how you get pneumonia, huh?" Sinjin teased, repeating her words from last night.

"Shut up. I don't have pneumonia." Breanna brought her fingers to her temples. Her head hurt and her body ached. "But I feel like shit."

"You'll feel better after a nice, warm bath. Water should be good and hot by now." He scooted her off his lap and got up from the bed. "I'll get it ready. Then we'll get some food in your stomach."

"Yeah, okay," she said. Missing the warmth of his body, Breanna pulled the covers up to her chin. "Thanks."

He wasn't naked anymore, and eyeing the rack by the fireplace with their clothing, she wondered how that was. Sinjin wore a pair of long johns that left little to the imagination. Not that Breanna needed to use it, considering she'd already gotten an eyeful and then some. She watched him put a pot on the stove.

"What's for breakfast?" she sniggered, knowing full well that oatmeal was all they had.

"You slept through it." He glanced back over his shoulder. "You've been out of it most of the day, in fact."

"Damn." She rubbed at her forehead. "I was having the craziest dreams."

"Oh, yeah?" Sinjin turned around. Leaning back against the counter, he folded his arms over his chest. "What about?"

"Ballgowns. Blood." *Fucking.* Heat infusing her cheeks, Breanna cleared her throat. "You were there."

"Fever dreams," he responded, his mouth quirking up on one side.

You have no idea.

"I'll just go and run that bath."

With the comforting sounds of crackling wood and running water harmonizing with the wailing wind, Breanna curled into the thick, soft comforter. She turned her head on the pillow to see the snow blowing past the window. Minutes passed, her vision blurring at the stark white bleakness, until his tall, muscular form appeared, and she blinked.

He scooped her up from the fluffy nest of down. "C'mon, princess."

Although she was perfectly capable of walking, Sinjin carried her into the bathroom. Steam rose from the tub. He set her on her feet but didn't leave.

She glared at him. "If you don't mind, I have to pee."

"Not stopping you." Presenting her with his backside, he pushed the long underwear down his legs.

"What the fuck are you doing?"

"What's it look like?" Sinjin turned around, naked as the day he was born, and, of course, her eyes went right *there*. He smirked. "I'm getting in with you. That tank only holds so many gallons of water. We have to share."

"Oh, for fuck's sake," Breanna muttered under her breath, relieving herself as he settled back in the tub.

He chuckled. "Potty mouth."

"Shut up." She held onto his hand and got in, making room between his thighs. "I think you like it."

"Yeah." Strong fingers circled her arms. "Maybe I do."

Despite the distraction of having a two-hundred-pound man in the bath with her, or perhaps because of it, the water felt heavenly. Sinjin pulled her back to his chest, and with her head upon his shoulder, heat seeped into her body. Closing her eyes, Breanna released a sigh.

She felt his cock grow thick and hard beneath her. Snug up against her flesh. Impossible to ignore. Lifting her bottom in a futile attempt to put a modicum of space between them, Sinjin's fingers skimmed down her arms to trail back up her middle. Thumbs caressed her nipples and a zapping jolt of awareness coursed through her body.

Eyes flashing open, Breanna gasped. "I wasn't dreaming, was I?"

His movement stopped.

She could feel him smirking behind her. "You *were* touching me."

Warm breath fanned her neck, his lips ghosting over her sensitive skin as he resumed thrumming her nipples. "And you liked it." Teeth pressing into her flesh, Sinjin pinched them hard.

"Fuck," she moaned.

"You still do."

He was wrong.

Breanna didn't like the way he was touching her.

She loved it.

His hands on her. The feeling of his rock-hard cock pressed against the split of her ass. His lips on her skin.

Hell, she hadn't been fucked since that party on Venice Beach last summer—and that was only because Kayleigh wasn't there to stop her. She wasn't here to stop her now, either. Breanna was stranded here, in this remote mountain cabin, with a beautiful, sinful stranger. She might as well enjoy it, right?

It's not like she'd ever see him again once they got out of here, anyway. No one would ever know. She could let herself go. Take her pleasure. Be brazen and bold and…

Sweet fuck.

Fingers parting the lips of her pussy, he rubbed circles on her clit. "Hook your legs over the tub."

She complied. Opening herself up to him, Breanna reached behind her to grasp his broad shoulders.

Sinjin sucked her bottom lip into his mouth. Teeth nipping, he kissed her while two fingers pushed their way inside. This man was no fumbling college boy. He knew what he was doing. Stroking her walls, he massaged her clit.

"God, what are you doing to me?"

"Mmm, warming up this sweet cunt."

His cock pulsed like a heart beneath her. Thick and heavy and slow. With the tips of her breasts rising out of the steaming water, Breanna pressed down on top of him.

He penetrated her, over and over again, fucking her with his fingers.

Feels so good.

She lifted her hips for more.

"Want my dick, don't you, princess?"

He stopped.

Eyes burning black with desire bored into hers. Grasping her nape, Sinjin pulled on her hair and sealed her lips with his, tongue fucking her mouth like his fingers had her pussy.

"Answer me." He growled, pinching her nipple.

"Fuck," Breanna cried out, her nails sinking into his thigh.

I do.

I do.

I do.

"Yes, I do."

She brought his mouth back to hers.

"I want you."

Chapter Seven

Sinjin toweled off her skin.

Standing before the fire, he knelt in front of her, thoroughly drying every inch, inspecting every dimple, crevice, and crease. Then, dropping the towel, he turned Breanna around. Squeezing her hips, he kissed the plush globes of her ass, sinking his teeth into her flesh like he wanted to eat her.

"Spread your legs," Sinjin ordered, penetrating her to the third knuckle. "You're not a virgin, are you?"

"No."

"Good." And he plunged three fingers in deep.

They twisted inside her, and she screamed.

"Yeah, that's it, princess. Scream for me." Withdrawing his fingers from her dripping pussy, Sinjin shoved them in her mouth. "Makes my dick hard."

He swooped her into his arms and tossed her onto the bed. "I'm going to obliterate the memory of every worthless piece of shit who's been inside this pretty cunt by the time we're through."

"You make it sound like there's been a lot."

"Doesn't matter if it was one or one hundred." Thick, muscular thighs caged her in. "You're with me now," he rasped, his fingers going back inside her. "And this tight little pussy is mine."

Only while the snow falls.

Breanna knew what this was. She knew what it wasn't.

And right now, she didn't care. Because his mouth was on hers. Kissing. Nipping. Plundering. His fingers worked her pussy, knuckles banging into her swollen lips with every penetration.

Drawing her legs up, Breanna grabbed onto the soles of her feet, to spread herself open as much as she could for him. Seeming to like that, Sinjin growled into her mouth. Sucking on her neck, licking her skin on the way to her breast. He bit into her nipple, soothing the delicious sting with his tongue.

Jutting her chest out, Breanna bit her lip with a whimper. Sinjin latched onto the other nipple. Stretching it with his teeth, he mashed his thumb hard into her clit at the same time. She screamed.

"Yeah, keep doing that." He trailed his tongue down to her belly button. "You want to be my dirty girl, don't you, princess?"

She did. Holding back, pretending to be the good girl, grew tiresome. Just once, Breanna wanted to be like the girls in the porn videos she watched, alone in her room at night, when she got herself off. They seemed so free. It had to be liberating to be given so much pleasure. So, yeah, she wanted to be his dirty girl. To choke on that big, fat dick. To feel him fuck her starving cunt. And maybe, if she was brave enough, even her ass.

"Yes."

"Course, you do. I knew it the second I laid eyes on you." Flipping her over, Sinjin pushed her legs up. Her ass in the air, face pressed against the pillow, he suckled on her clit. "Gonna fill all these holes up."

She heard him spit. Warm saliva dripping down the crack of her ass, he pushed a finger inside it. *Oh, fuck.* It burned. It burned. Oh, God, it burned, but she loved it.

Slowly, he sawed his finger in and out. "My princess needs her ass fucked, doesn't she?"

Whimpering, Breanna clenched her cheeks together.

"Keep them open." Sinjin smacked her ass with his open palm. "Have you ever?"

"No."

"Ohh, princess, I'm going to love making you my fucking good, dirty girl."

With a finger in her ass and two fucking her pussy, Sinjin tongued her clit. He suckled it, licked and laved it, whispering wicked promises to her pussy with his mouth.

She was so close to coming. "Fuck."

He flipped her over again and his hands squeezed her breasts, teeth sinking into them. "Love seeing big, swollen nipples on these little titties." Pushing the mounds of flesh up on her chest, he asked, "Can you reach? I want to see you lick them."

Stretching her tongue, Breanna sought her nipple. He pushed higher, and she flicked at it. Pushing higher still, she could finally do as he asked.

Sinjin let go of her tits. Hand delving between her legs, he filled both holes with his fingers. "Play with those nipples for me."

Rolling them between her fingers, Breanna stared into his eyes. He fucked her slow and easy, groaning at the sound his fingers made inside her wet pussy.

"Look at all of this." Sinjin pulled them out, showing her the wetness dripping down his forearm. "Gonna squirt for me?"

"Gonna make me?"

"Fuck, yeah."

Filling both holes once more, he hooked two fingers inside her pussy. Sinjin massaged her G-spot, pressing up hard on her wall. With his other hand, he rubbed her clit from side to side. Fast. Fervent. Stopping briefly to slap it before beginning the relentless assault all over again.

She held onto her nipples. "Oh, my God. Oh, fuck. Fuck, fuck, fuck, fuck…"

Fuck.

With her body exploding, the air was sucked out of her lungs. Breanna tried to suck it back in, but suspended in this cataclysm of sensations, she let it go.

"Yes, that's my good girl." His fingers rubbed in the mess on her stomach. He scooped a handful from between her legs, feeding it to her, then licked his palm.

Sinjin pulled her up to sit. Gripping his cock in his hand, he tugged on her hair with the other. "Suck me."

Still shaking from her orgasm, Breanna leaned over, her tongue darting out to lick the salty precum oozing from his little slit. Moaning at the taste of him, Sinjin gathered her hair, holding it out of the way. She glanced up at him, fire blazing in his eyes, and pushed him backward onto the mattress.

Sputtering, eyes watering, Breanna proudly got every inch of him down her throat. Just like the girls in the videos. Her lips touched the hair at his groin. She could kiss him there if they weren't already stretched thin, filled with his cock. Pulling back slowly, she gently used her teeth, just enough to remind him she had the power. Sinjin was at her mercy now.

"Go ahead, baby." Holding her head to his dick, he yanked on her hair. "Take a bite. Let me feel those teeth. I like it."

Breanna pressed in harder, scraping her teeth up and down his shaft. Sucking him. Squeezing and jerking the base. She couldn't say what made her do it. Maybe it was the deep, guttural noises coming out of his throat. Her finger, wet with saliva, found its way into his ass.

"Fuck." Sinjin thrust into her throat. "Now you're asking for it."

She gagged.

Fisting her hair in his hand, he pulled her off his dick. "Milk me all you want while I'm fucking you."

And before she could blink, he had her on her back. Pressing one leg against her shoulder, that thick, curved cock poised at her entrance, Sinjin thrust home.

So big.

She swore she could feel it pulsing inside her.

Fingers circled her throat, his lips covered hers, their mouths mating in a frenzied, wet dance. Then, squeezing her neck tighter, he pounded into her, again and again and again.

"Harder," she squeaked, her voice whisper-thin.

"So perfect." He let go of her throat and pinched her nipples. "That's the only way I know how."

And putting her on her hands and knees, Sinjin gave Breanna exactly what she asked for.

She wasn't sure how many times he made her come. Too many to count. Kissing the side of her face, still half on top of her, he caressed her well-fucked pussy, fingers strumming through her swollen lips, sticky with his cum.

"You didn't use a condom." She rolled out from under him.

He snickered. "Nope."

"I could get pregnant, you asshole."

"Can you?" Sinjin turned to his side. "You're not on the Pill or anything?"

"No."

And he smirked, pushing the cum that dripped from her pussy back inside her.

Chapter Eight

Breanna woke to snow softly falling outside the window. What day was it now, anyway? Monday? Tuesday? She'd lost all sense of time here.

Handing her a mug of coffee, Sinjin got under the covers. He laced their fingers together, and bringing her knuckles to his lips, he kissed them. "What shall we do today, princess?"

"I have a name, you know." She sniggered, blowing on the piping hot brew.

Not that she'd ever tell him, but she liked being his princess. And she loved being his dirty girl.

"So you've said, Miss Dalton." He nuzzled up the side of her neck, whispering into her ear. "Breanna."

She giggled, his breath tickling her skin. "You know, I've told you a lot about me, but the only thing I know about you is your first name."

"Oh, I'm pretty sure that's not true." Fingertips skimming along her jaw, he asked, "What would you like to know?"

"How old are you?"

"Old." Sinjin dropped his hand, sinking back against the pillow. "Thirty. Too old for you."

"Is not."

He turned onto his side, bringing Breanna to his chest. "No?"

"I don't think so." Dragging her teeth over her bottom lip, she smiled. "What is it you do? For a living, I mean."

"This and that."

Whatever that meant. 'This and that' must be quite lucrative, considering he drove a truck that cost more than most people earn in an entire year.

"Do you live up here on the mountain?"

"Not far." Fingers moved up and down her spine.

"So, I could run into you after we leave here?"

"You could." The movement on her back ceased, Sinjin's ever-present smirk widening into a grin. "Would you like that?"

Yes.

"Maybe."

"I'd like that." Cupping her bottom, he pressed her body into his. "Even though I shouldn't."

"Why shouldn't you?" She froze. "Are you married or something?"

"I'm not married." With an amused chuckle, his hand slid off her ass to squeeze the flesh between her legs. "Or something."

"You swear?"

"I swear." He kissed the tip of her nose. "So, Breanna, what shall we do today?"

She glanced outside the window. "More of what we did yesterday."

"God, you weren't supposed to be this perfect." Threading his fingers in her hair, Sinjin held her face and kissed her. Gently. Tender-like. It almost felt sweet, which in the short time she'd known him, she learned wasn't his way. "Will you do something for me?"

"What?"

"I want you to make yourself come, and I want to watch you while you do it," he said, his fingers combing through her hair.

Her pulse skittered. "Why?"

"So I can always remember how beautiful you were." A

flash of vulnerability on his face, he cupped her cheek, stroking it with his thumb. "With those fairytale blue eyes of yours looking right at me."

At a loss as to how to even begin, Breanna sat up. Placing a pillow behind her, she leaned against the iron spindles. Of course, she'd done this by herself countless times, but no one had ever watched her before—not that she knew of, anyway. Maybe it was silly, considering they'd been fucking like rabbits, but she'd be lying not to admit the thought of it made her a little nervous.

Sinjin positioned himself in front of her. His eyes on hers, he urged her to proceed. Tipping his chin, the movement was subtle.

He didn't look at her breasts as she toyed with her nipples. He didn't follow the trail of fingertips sweeping down her belly toward the place that pulsed between her thighs. Those heated brown eyes of his stayed right on hers.

Penetrating herself, Breanna's lips parted. Liquid silk coating her fingers, she sucked them into her mouth. His tongue swept over his bottom lip, nevertheless, his gaze did not waver.

And gazing right back, blue locked on whiskey, she stroked her clit. Barely there circles. Slowly, up and down. Swiftly, side to side.

What did he see looking at her?

A girl in lust? Surely.

A girl falling in love? She hoped not.

But she was afraid that perhaps she could be.

And with the thought of loving this man in her mind, Breanna rubbed herself until she came.

Sinjin held her after. Kissing her as the tremors subsided, he stroked her skin and whispered, "I'm sorry."

Sorry? What for?

Glancing at the window, he got out of bed and began

putting on his clothes. "The snow is letting up a little." He went over to the door, grabbing his coat from the peg on the wall. "Gonna see how much shit there is to shovel. Try to clear the porch steps, anyway."

"Oh, okay." Covering herself with the blanket, she drew her knees up under her chin.

"Think you can manage our lunch, princess?"

She nodded. "Chicken noodle?"

"Yeah." He came back. Sitting on the edge of the mattress, Sinjin tucked her hair behind her ear. "You've got to be sore. Have a nice, long soak while I'm gone."

Their time together was almost up. The snow would stop soon. She knew it, and so did he. Breanna laid back in the hot water and closed her eyes. She should be glad to be getting out of here. She had to get to Dalton House and a drugstore for the morning-after pill. Never mind, she'd just finished her period—better to be safe than sorry. And then there was her car. God, how much was that going to cost, and how long would it take them to fix it? Didn't matter. She had to get back to Portland. Her life was there, so why did the thought of leaving here make her feel so out of sorts?

Sinjin. Duh.

She must be thinking with her vagina. Good orgasms can do that. She'd seen it happen to her friends at school time and time again. It's like a guy who shows skills with a clit is some precious commodity or something. Apparently, that can make a girl do stupid things.

She was so *not* catching feelings for him.

Yes, you are.

Yeah, okay, she was. But Breanna was too smart to do anything stupid.

"Looks good on you." He smiled at her.

Sinjin stood just inside the door, removing his gloves and

knocking snow from his boots. With his skin reddened, watery eyes, and lips chapped from the cold air, he hung up his coat, and, leaving a trail of footprints on the wooden floor, padded barefoot over to the kitchen.

"Hope you don't mind." She'd thrown on his soft flannel button-up after her bath.

"I like seeing you in my clothes." Leaning over her shoulder, he kissed the skin beneath her ear. "I think you'll be seeing the sun tomorrow."

Grabbing it from the back of his neck, Sinjin pulled off his Henley. He shucked off his jeans at the bathroom door, and gloriously naked, stepped inside.

The door left ajar, Breanna could hear him at the sink. Bath water running. She picked up his discarded clothing, placed them on the rack by the fire, and took the pot off the stove.

They sat at the table, eating soup and saltine crackers, without talking.

He stayed quiet, sipping bourbon all afternoon.

When evening came, Sinjin pulled her down to his lap. He just held her. Snuggled together in a chair for hours, he kissed her hair, stroking her skin in front of the fire.

And the snow stopped falling.

"C'mon, princess. Let's go to bed."

He knelt beside her on the goose-down comforter. Feathering kisses along her face, her neck, her pulse bounding beneath his lips. His fingertips traced across her collarbone, then downward to release the buttons of her shirt. The soft flannel gave way, and pushing the sleeves off her shoulders, he lowered his body onto hers until their mouths met.

Sinjin kissed her soft and deep and slow. Lips lingering on her skin, he trailed exquisite kisses down her neck. He took his time as if he wanted this to last. Fingers tangled in his hair, and softly sighing, Breanna held onto him.

His hands slid over her skin to squeeze her breasts in his palms. Breanna sucked in a breath and his lips left her neck to suckle a nipple. Breathy sighs became soft moans.

Her fingertips skated down his back, memorizing the smooth, firm feel of his flesh as she held him there. God, what was he doing to her? Tender and sweet, Sinjin kissed his way down her body to bury his head between her thighs.

Lavishing her pussy with languid sweeps of his tongue, he pushed his fingers inside her. *Fuck, yes.* That always sent her flying. Breanna waited for the fervent finger-fucking that was sure to follow, but it never came. With long, purposeful, drawn-out strokes, suckling on her clit, Sinjin coaxed the mind-numbing orgasm out of her.

Pushing her leg back to her shoulder, he kissed her then. Frenzied and urgent, their mouths collided. Clutching at his hair, Breanna tasted herself on his tongue and smelled herself on his beard. Sinjin devoured her until he ran out of air.

And then he filled her.

Holding her tightly to his chest, he gazed into her eyes, and never let go.

They lay together after, stroking each other's skin. Breanna was trying so hard to stay awake, because what if tonight was the last night she had with him? But it was so warm beneath the goose-down comforter, lying in the circle of Sinjin's arms, with the crackle of wood and the flickering flames lulling her to sleep.

"I swear to Christ, Breanna…I'd keep you if I could."

She felt his lips on her forehead.

Fingers stroked her hair.

A whisper.

"Forgive me."

Chapter Nine

It was the light that woke her.

The morning sun, so bright it hurt her eyes, poured in through panes of glass. She blinked several times, turning away from the window to an empty pillow beside her. And her eyes flew open.

"Sinjin?"

Breanna sat up, glancing around the one-room cabin. His clothes were gone from the rack, but a fire was roaring in the hearth, so he had to have just tended to it. Figuring Sinjin went back outside to shovel, she set a pot of water on the stove, then bathed and got dressed for the day.

She fixed herself a cup of coffee and peered out the window. Pine trees soared into a cloudless blue sky beneath a blanket of pristine white, but there was no sign of him.

Oatmeal congealed into a glob of wet cement.

Her coffee grew cold.

"He went for help," she told herself.

Sinjin would never leave her here all alone.

Hours passed, the sun was high in the sky. Fearing something had happened to him, Breanna stepped out to the porch and screamed his name.

The silence that followed mocked her.

He left me.

Wrapped in a blanket, her head on her knees, she sat staring at the flames through her tears when she heard the knock on the cabin door. Not believing it at first, Breanna ignored the sound. Then it came again.

"Hello?" And again. "Hello?"

He's back…Sinjin!

Still wrapped in the blanket, she jumped up from the chair and ran to the door.

It wasn't Sinjin.

A portly man wearing some kind of uniform—a sheriff or maybe a ranger—and a cowboy hat on his head, stood on the porch. "Breanna Dalton?"

"Yes, that's me," she answered, somewhat baffled by how he knew her name.

Sinjin told him. Duh.

"Thank God." He stepped inside. "We've been searching for you. You all right?"

"Yeah." She smiled, the tension draining from her shoulders. "I'm fine."

"Got a nasty-looking bump on your head there."

Her fingers felt along her forehead. She'd forgotten all about it.

"C'mon, I'll get you up to Dalton House."

"Okay." Taking her coat from the wall, she stepped into her boots. "Where's Sinjin?"

"Ma'am?"

The man looked at her like she was speaking a foreign language.

"Sinjin. He brought me here."

"Don't rightly know." He shrugged.

"Then we have to find him."

Extending his hand, the man nodded, but Breanna could tell he was just placating her. He helped her into a big pickup truck with a plow fixed to the front. "It's a miracle you found this place in the storm. When we found your car and you weren't in it..."

"But I already told you, Sinjin brought me here. He was taking me to Dalton House, but there was a tree blocking the road and...I had a fever. He took care of me."

"What does this Sinjin look like?"

"Tall—over six feet, dark hair, beard." Sitting across from her, he lifted his brow. "Wait, he drives a black Ford Raptor. We'll pass it. My things are inside."

Reaching into the seat behind him, he held up her duffel bag. "This?"

The fuck?

He pulled her phone from his pocket and handed it to her. "Where'd you get that?"

"From your car before they towed it."

"I don't understand." Breanna slowly shook her head. "How did you know where to find me, then?"

"I didn't. Saw smoke coming from the chimney and took a chance it was you." He reached across the seat and squeezed her hand. "Look, honey, you hit your head pretty hard, and you said so yourself, you had a fever."

"*You were there.*"

"*Fever dreams.*"

"I'm sure he seemed very real."

"He was real." Tears welling, she bit her lip. "I met him at Hank's—that place right off the highway. He was making fun of my girly car. Said I'd slide right off the mountain in it."

"You almost did." The portly sheriff chuckled. "You've seen *The Wizard of Oz*, haven't you?"

"Of course."

"You know how Dorothy wakes up at the end and recognizes her friends were the scarecrow, the tin man, and the lion?"

"You think that's what happened to me?"

He patted her shoulder. "Makes sense, don't it?"

No.

"Yeah, I guess so."

Static came over the two-way radio. Pushing a button, he spoke into it, "Yeah, I got her. Heading there now." He turned his head toward her and gently smiled. "He's been so concerned about you. Ready?"

Breanna nodded, and the truck pulled away from the little cabin.

A tear slid down her cheek.

You were real.

She wiped it away.

Hidden from view in a thicket of trees about thirty yards from the cabin, Ian watched her get into Jordy's truck. The husky sat sniffing at his feet.

I'll be looking out for you, princess.

"C'mon, girl. Let's go."

He turned around, the dog faithfully following him up the mountain.

Chapter Ten

Snow crunched under the truck tires beneath her. A thick, heavy layer of vanilla frosting, it clung to boughs of pine. Gazing out the window, Breanna swiped at her cheek and looked for some kind of sign she hadn't lost her mind. But there were none.

No footprints.

Nothing.

Except for the path the sheriff made plowing his way in, the surrounding snowscape appeared undisturbed.

With her thumb to her temple, Breanna rubbed at the tender bump on her forehead. Could she have dreamt it all? She squeezed her eyes closed. Maybe her scrambled brain *had* conjured up the bold stranger from Hank's to see her through her ordeal, to keep her safe in the storm.

The sheriff drove across a small bridge, a stream cascaded over icy rocks below.

"So I don't lose you, princess. Just don't fall into the stream, okay? Think you can manage that?"

I think I must be going crazy, Sinjin.

Because there's no way she could have imagined all that. Every minute detail. His woodsy masculine smell. Eyes the color of whiskey. The warmth of his skin. The feeling of that thick, curved cock filling her.

Peeling her gaze from the window, Breanna turned to the portly fellow. "What day is it?"

"Tuesday."

Yeah, a chance encounter with a stranger hadn't put the past three days in her head, and no one could convince her otherwise. Sinjin was real, and he was out there somewhere. She'd better keep those thoughts to herself, though, or else Grandmama might have her committed.

"How much further to Dalton House?"

"Not too far." He patted her knee. "Just a few miles. That cabin you were in is one of a dozen scattered on the property. Folks reserve 'em for hunting and fishing."

"Hold up." Her brows cinching together, Breanna asked, "This is Dalton land?"

"Yes, ma'am." He chuckled. "Darn near the whole mountain belongs to the Daltons."

"It does?"

Dalton Pass Road. Course, it does.

"Has for generations. Back to the pioneer days," he said with a bob of his head. "See, crossing the Sierra Nevada in covered wagons was tricky business, and the timing of it meant life or death. When George Dalton and his traveling party reached the pass, it was already October, so he had a tough choice to make. Build a shelter and stay here, or take the risk of getting caught in the snow and perishing."

"He had another month before winter. That wasn't enough time?"

"A wagon train could only travel about fifteen miles on a good day, dearie. It's a hundred miles across this range. Peaks twelve thousand feet high. Not to mention these mountains get more snow than most others. Massive snowdrifts from September onward."

"So, no, not enough time then," she absently said, her gaze following their winding path through the trees. "He stayed, I take it."

"He sure did." Turning toward her, the man clicked his

tongue. "Built the original house down there at the start of the pass. You might've seen it."

"I think so." Pursing her lips, she shrugged a shoulder. "Did everyone else stay too?"

"Some wagons did. The rest of 'em pushed ahead on their journey."

Breanna thought of the Donner Party tragedy then. Pioneers migrating to California from the Midwest in 1846, became snowbound here in the Sierra Nevada. When their food supply ran out, with no other alternative, they resorted to cannibalism—surviving off the bodies of those who had succumbed to starvation, sickness, or the elements. Only forty-eight of the eighty-seven people who were trapped in that early snowfall survived.

She shuddered. "What happened to them? Did they make it?"

"Don't rightly know."

Her father's family had quite a history, of which Breanna knew nothing, but then she didn't even know what her dad looked like. She'd never seen a photo of him. Her mother choked up every time she asked about him, so she quit asking a long time ago.

"How did George end up with an entire mountain?"

"No one else wanted it, I reckon," the sheriff said, shrugging his shoulder. "Living up here ain't for the weak, you know. That storm you were stuck in was just the first of many. Won't see the grass again until May. June, maybe."

"Why live here then?" Breanna wondered out loud.

With a lift of his brow, he grinned. "Well, I'd say you're about to find out."

The snow-covered road curved to the left, sharply inclined, and then went right, coming out of a forest of trees. And there in the clearing stood Dalton House. Grand, rustic elegance. The house—no, scratch that—the mansion appeared to be three levels. Stacked stone, timber, and glass. Blue sky and snow-capped peaks for a backdrop.

Holyyy…

Words escaped her. Breanna didn't know what she'd been expecting, but it sure wasn't this. She smirked. "Must have been for the lovely view."

"Well, they do say it's better from the top." With a soft chuckle, he stopped and threw the truck into park. "I'm glad you're all right, Miss Dalton."

"It's Breanna." She smiled.

"Jordy." He smiled back with a dip of his chin. Coming around with her duffel bag, Jordy opened her door and gave her a hand out of the truck. "Watch your step now. It can get slippery."

The large stained wood door, inset with squares of beveled glass, opened as they approached. A woman stood just inside the threshold. Hair more salt than pepper, cut in a shoulder-length bob. Black horn-rimmed glasses accentuated her perfectly arched brows. Dark red lipstick. Her makeup was impeccable.

Grandmama?

Immediately, she dismissed the thought. This woman, while older, appeared to be far too young to have a son who would've been forty-three if he were still living. With fillers, Botox, and whatnot, it was hard to tell these days, but Breanna guessed the woman to be in her mid-fifties—sixty at most.

Clutching her sweater tight around her middle, she waved, hastening them inside. "Thank God, we've been so worried."

"She's all right, 'cept for that goose egg on her noggin. Must've knocked it pretty hard." Jordy closed the door behind them. "Found her down in one of the hunting cabins—the one by the stream."

"Goodness, it's a miracle you found the place. You surely have a guardian angel looking out for you," the woman said, inspecting the bump on her forehead.

Sinjin.

Though she'd hardly describe her dark savior as an angel.

"We'll have to get Randall up here to take a look at her."

"I'll call him." Nodding, Jordy looked at Breanna. "He's the chief paramedic down in the village. Darn good one, too. Closest doctor is in Sacramento, and that's a couple of hours from here."

"I'm fine." She forced a smile. "Really."

"Better safe than sorry." Her arm circled Breanna's shoulders, and she took her bag from Jordy with the other. "Mr. St. John asked me to extend his thanks. He's on a Zoom call with a client, or he'd have told you so himself. Let me know when we can expect Randall."

"Will do, Francie."

"You'll be here for Thanksgiving dinner, won't you?"

"As long as the weather holds." He winked. "Wouldn't miss it."

Breanna's gaze flitted around the grand foyer, though it was much too large to call it that. The space was bigger than her and Kayleigh's entire apartment. Stacked stone and textured walls. Exposed wood beams in the ceiling, a massive chandelier of black antlers suspended from three floors above.

"You take care now, Miss Breanna." The sheriff tipped his hat. "You're in excellent hands with Francie here. I'll be seeing you."

"Thank you, Jordy."

He just smiled, and with that, he was gone.

"How about I take you up to your room?" The woman Jordy called Francie led her toward the right side of an imperial staircase. "We can get you settled while Mr. St. John concludes his business."

"Derek St. John or the other one?"

"Yes, Derek." She lowered her gaze. "There's only one, dear."

"Oh." *St. John, Maynard & St. John.* "There were two on the letter."

"Raymond St. John started the firm—Derek's father. He passed away several years ago. It's just he and Mr. Maynard now."

"I see."

At the landing, behind a sitting area, a central staircase went up another level. Francie steered her to the right, away from it. Each recess in the hallway housed a double door, sconces on either side.

She stopped at the third one on the left and opened it. "Here we are."

Following her inside, Breanna contained a gasp. *Jesus.* This wasn't merely a room, it was a suite of them. A fire burned in the living area with a flat-screen TV mounted above it. A bedroom lay beyond an open set of double doors. But it was the floor-to-ceiling glass, the majestic mountainscape on the other side of it, that took her breath away.

"Oh, wow..."

"Beautiful, isn't it?"

"I'll say." But the word didn't do it justice.

"You never tire of it, because you won't ever see it the same way twice." Clasping her shoulder, Francie tipped her chin toward the expansive covered deck, complete with an outdoor seating area, fireplace, and a fancy schmancy hot tub. "I have a feeling you'll be out there a lot."

Breanna followed her into the bedroom. Francie sat her

duffel bag on a chair. It looked woefully out of place in its sumptuous surroundings. "Do you live here?"

"Not here in the main house," she said. Opening the drapes, she pointed out the window. "My husband and I live in the caretaker's house just over there. A breezeway attaches it."

"I see it."

"I'm always here should you need anything." Tilting her head, Francie smiled, her gray eyes kind. "I'll let you unpack, and I'm sure you're dying for a nice, warm shower. Bathroom's through there. You've got plenty of towels. Mr. St. John or myself will come and get you for dinner."

"Does he live here too?"

"Oh, no." She snickered. "His office is in Sacramento, but he'll be staying with us through the holiday. He only came here for you."

What about Grandmama, his client? Speaking of…

"I'd like to see my grandmother. She's who I came all this way for."

Not some stuffy old lawyer.

"Wait for Mr. St. John." Biting her lip, Francie's hand fell to her forearm. She squeezed. "I have to get to work on dinner. Hope you like duck."

"I don't know. I've never had it," Breanna admitted.

"You're going to love it," she assured her. "Trust me."

As much as she wanted to flop down on the plush-looking king-sized bed and take a nap, Breanna figured unpacking, showering, and making herself presentable for Valerie Dalton was a much wiser decision. Not that she wanted to impress the old lady—okay, maybe she did a little—but for her mom, truth be told. To win the approval she never got.

Rifling through the travel bag she once thought cute, Breanna removed her laptop and set it on the bed. The iPhone

Jordy rescued from her Miata was dead. "Where's my charger, dammit?"

In the car, of course. Duh.

Cursing her dumb luck, she hefted her stuff into a bathroom that was at least the size of the bedroom and shrieked at what she saw in the mirror. "Oh God, this is hideous."

The swollen lump over her right eye, a lovely shade of purple, broken skin in the center of it scabbed, was impossible to miss. "Ugh, some impression you're going to make, Bree. How am I supposed to cover this?"

After a decadently long, hot shower, she carefully applied her makeup. Patting foundation and concealer over the spot did little, so she opted for a simple eye and went bold with her lip. Parting her hair on the side, Breanna swooped it over the bump.

"Best I can do." She wrinkled her nose at herself.

It's not like she had a plethora of clothing options with her, but Breanna had chosen what she brought with her grandmother in mind. She opted for a chunky, cream-colored half-turtleneck sweater that reached a bit past mid-thigh. Together with leggings and a pair of suede booties, she deemed it suitable enough. The outfit would have looked better with her cute over-the-knee boots, but she ruined them during her trek through the storm.

As ready as she was going to be for dinner with Grandmama and her stodgy, old lawyer, Breanna returned to the living room, taking a seat in front of the fire. Darkness veiled the mountains, yet the snow-capped peaks seemed to glow beneath a moon she couldn't see.

It was out there somewhere, though.

And so was Sinjin.

Of that, she was sure.

A knock sounded upon her door. She got up, and when she opened it, her eyes went wide.

The man standing there wasn't stuffy or stodgy, and he sure wasn't old.

"Miss Dalton." He extended his hand.

Stunned, Breanna shook it.

"Derek St. John."

Chapter Eleven

H is hair was dark, a rich milk chocolate with some lighter strands and glints of red from time spent outdoors—judging by his suntanned skin. It wasn't long, but it wasn't short either, the ends barely touching his collar. Full and thick, it was probably wavy too, except she could tell he used plenty of products to tame it.

Brown eyes that were *not* the color of whiskey.

Short beard, neatly trimmed.

A pair of smart, plaid chinos, leather loafers—Prada or Gucci, no doubt—and a cashmere crewneck sweater that probably cost more than her monthly car payment. Derek St. John could be considered handsome, Breanna supposed, though not typically so.

Her palm sweating, she let go. "Breanna. Nice to meet you, Mr. St. John."

"Breanna then." He swept the hair back from her forehead. "Ouch. We've got someone coming to take a look at that."

"Randall."

"Yes, he'll be by this evening." The corner of his mouth lifted. "And we don't have to be so formal, do we? Call me Derek."

Okayyy.

"How did you ever make it to that cabin?"

"Blind faith." *And a dark savior.* "Francie thinks I must have a guardian angel looking out for me."

"I'm inclined to agree with her," Derek said, rubbing a lock of her hair between his fingers. Taking a step back, he let it go. "Do you feel all right? Have everything you need?"

"Yeah, I'm fine." And with a nod, she smiled. "Except the charger for my phone is in my car. I don't suppose there's an extra one around here?"

"iPhone?"

"Yes."

"I can get you one."

"Thank you." With a sigh of relief, Breanna fiddled with the cuff of her sweater. "Kayleigh, my roommate, will worry if she can't get a hold of me, and I'm going to have to call my mom to tell her about my car."

And that was not going to go over very well.

"She doesn't even know I'm here."

"No?" His brow lifted, and he smirked. "Why not?"

"Because I didn't want to upset her."

"Oh, I see." The lawyer stepped inside and sat on the overstuffed sofa, patting the space beside him. "Just know cell service is unreliable up here. It comes and goes depending on the weather, even with a signal booster. Wi-Fi works most of the time, though."

Great.

"She's gonna kill me."

"For wrecking the car?"

Breanna shot him a look. *For starters.*

Derek's hand came down on her leg, patting her knee. "We can fix the car. I think she'll be relieved you're okay, so don't worry."

"How bad is it?" Biting her lip, Breanna turned in her seat, and his hand moved away.

"It's going to be in the shop for a few weeks, but it'll be as good as new," he assured her.

A few weeks? Jesus, with school, she couldn't possibly stay

here that long. Well, technically she could. She did bring her Mac with her, but she only brought enough clothes for a few days, not a few weeks.

"Did they say how much it's going to be to fix it?"

"You don't have to worry about that, Breanna." His hands gently settled on her shoulders.

"Yes, I do," she insisted. "My credit card has a limit, you know, and it's only five grand."

Of which she'd already used a thousand, give or take, so make that four.

"You're a Dalton." He winked. "I already took care of it, so no, you don't."

Grandmama's money.

"*She's got lots of it.*"

Still, this man seemed so very kind, and for that she was grateful.

Nervously, Breanna licked her lips. "I don't know what to call her."

"Who?"

"Valerie…my grandmother." A snigger escaped. "I mean, yes, she's my father's mother, but I don't know her at all."

"Who do you think of her as?"

Just a name.

"I call her Grandmama in my head," Breanna admitted with a soft giggle. "Can't say why."

"She'd probably like that."

"Don't know if I can call her that to her face. It might feel weird." She shrugged. "I guess we'll find out at dinner."

Rubbing his lips together, Derek looked down at his lap. "Your grandmother won't be joining us."

Brows pulling together, Breanna shook her head. Isn't that why Derek summoned her here? Isn't that why she drove almost six hundred goddamn miles? Because after twenty-one years, Valerie Dalton wanted to see her son's only child. She didn't get it. Did the old lady change her mind and not want to see her, after all?

"Oh." Fighting the sting building in the back of her eyes, Breanna looked at the lawyer. "Why not?"

Taking her hands in his, Derek lifted his gaze. He opened his mouth to speak, then pursed his lips as if gathering his thoughts for a moment, and taking a breath he found his voice, "Because she can't. Your grandmother passed away two months ago. That's why I contacted you."

"But why didn't you just tell me then?"

"I couldn't tell you in a letter, and as her only living relative…well, it's left to you to settle her estate."

"And here, after all this time, I thought she wanted to see me." A lone tear made a trail down her face. Swiping it away, Breanna got up and stood in front of the floor-to-ceiling glass. She snickered. "Silly me. Guess not."

Derek came to stand behind her. He massaged her shoulders, his front pressing into the small of her back. "I'm sorry."

"It's okay." Though he was only trying to comfort her, he was too close, too familiar, and it made her uncomfortable. Breanna turned around.

Looking down at her, he offered up a sympathetic smile. "Hungry?"

"Starving." Literally. She hadn't had an actual meal in days.

"Shall we then?" Derek gave her his arm. She took it. "Francie's duck is out of this world."

He didn't lie.

Roasted to perfection and paired with a blackberry-orange sauce, the duck was surprisingly delicious. Ready and waiting for them when they got to the family dining room, they served it with a medley of roasted root vegetables and arugula salad. Heavenly fresh-baked bread and butter. It was like being in an exclusive restaurant instead of dinner at home, then again, this was no ordinary house.

"Do you always eat like this?"

"Francie loves to cook," he said with a chuckle, pouring burgundy wine into her glass. "She wanted you to feel welcome, same as I do."

"You've both been so kind." Breanna sipped on her Pinot Noir, glancing out the window.

"If you're feeling up to it, I can show you around the house after dinner."

"That'd be great." Her eyes flicked back to him. "What did you mean, it's left to me to settle my grandmother's estate?"

"Just formalities. Documents that require your signature." Derek smirked and cut into his duck. "We can go over everything tomorrow."

"Oh, okay."

Using his fork, he pointed to her plate. "What are you doing?"

"Picking out the beets."

Carrots, parsnips, and fingerling potatoes, she could do—even rutabagas. But not beets.

Gross.

"Why?"

"They've always tasted like dirt to me."

"They're good for you." He speared one from her plate, popping it into his mouth. "And delicious."

"You can have them." She placed her napkin on the table. "I'm stuffed."

"No room for dessert?" His napkin joined hers. "Chocolate mousse. Francie adds a touch of Grand Marnier—exquisite."

"That sounds good."

"Tell you what, let me show you around." Derek stood.

Extending his hand, he assisted Breanna up from her chair. "And afterward, we can have our dessert."

Escorting her from the dining room, his arm came around her waist. She didn't want it there, but didn't particularly mind it either. Besides, it would come across as rude if she shrugged him off, wouldn't it? His touch didn't thrill her as Sinjin's had. No sparks. Her pulse didn't race. Her breath didn't catch. Though surely that wasn't his intention, anyway.

Or was it?

Derek St. John, with his posh GQ clothes and suave politesse, seemed to be the type of man who'd go for a sophisticated woman. Someone who could play hostess at his dinner parties and make him look good. Breanna envisioned a trophy wife in his future, but then perhaps he already had one.

Beyond the three-story foyer that really couldn't be called a foyer, he led her through a media room, game room, library, and study. That's what Derek called it anyway, but it looked like a home office to her. A sunroom, he referred to as the solarium. *Fancy schmancy.* An outdoor fireplace and kitchen on the terrace.

"Oh cool, a pool table," she exclaimed, coming to yet another room.

He snickered. "Billiards."

"Whatever."

"Do you play?" Leaving her at the door, Derek walked toward a wall-mounted cue rack.

She sauntered up behind him. "I never miss a Thursday night at The Cheerful Tortoise."

"The what?" he asked, turning around.

"Cheerful Tortoise. It's a bar on campus."

"I see." Smirking, he gathered a lock of her hair between his fingers. "And what's so special about Thursday?"

"Dollar beer night."

He was kind of cute when he laughed, brown eyes crinkling at the corners.

"What? It's two-dollar wing night too." Cocking her head, Breanna grinned. "And I'm always down for a game of eightball."

His eyes locked onto hers, and taking a step closer, Derek lowered his lips to her ear. "Are you any good?"

She took a step back, putting some space between them. "Maybe."

"There you are."

Francie stood in the open doorway, a man alongside her. Breanna presumed he was the paramedic who they summoned to check her head.

"I was just about to challenge Miss Dalton to a game," Derek explained, a smug look on his face. He tipped his chin. "Randall."

"Breanna." She extended her hand to the somewhat bemused stranger.

"I think we'll be more comfortable in the sitting room, yes?" Derek said, steering them toward the hall.

On the other side of the kitchen, which was also bigger than her entire apartment, pantry, and morning room—translation, breakfast room—and past the stairway that went down to the wine cellar, Breanna followed him into an inviting, cozy space.

Jesus Christ, this place is massive.

A fire burned in the hearth, photographs displayed on its mantel. Faux fur rugs on gleaming wood floors. She sat down on a cloud-soft sofa, styled with mounds of pillows and sumptuous throws, Derek close beside her.

"May I?"

Hunched in front of her, Randall pushed the hair from her brow, gently palpating the tender bump she fruitlessly tried to conceal. He shined a penlight in one eye, and then the other. "Did you blackout after the accident?"

"I'm not sure. Maybe for a moment."

"You hit your head pretty hard, I'd say. Split the skin. That's gonna leave you with a nice trophy."

Huh? She shot him a puzzled look.

He smiled. "A little scar."

Lovely.

"Any headaches?"

Slowly, Breanna shook her head. "At first, but none lately."

"Nausea, vomiting, ringing in the ears, sensitivity to light?" Randall inquired, setting the hair he had disturbed back into place.

"No. I had a fever, though."

"How did you ever find the cabin in that storm?"

Derek and Francie, their gazes homed in on her, looked at Breanna expectantly. She couldn't tell them the truth, though, could she? "I don't know."

"Don't you remember?" Randall appeared concerned.

"No."

"Don't worry. Memory loss, disorientation, and confusion are common after a head injury." Patting her shoulder, he got up off his haunches. "What do you remember?"

"I went to Hank's," she recalled, gazing up at the medic. "They stopped me at the checkpoint and said I had to have chains on my tires. He put them on for me."

"He's been asking after you," Randall said with a smile.

Hank could assure her Sinjin was real, now, couldn't he? Tell her who he was, where she might find him. Breanna hadn't dreamt him up. Unless she really was out of her mind.

She smiled back. "His wife makes the best banana cream pie."

"That she does." Randall chuckled. "He'll be glad to know you're okay."

"Am I?" she wondered out loud.

Derek threw his arm around her shoulders, pulling her even closer against his side.

"I think you're going to be just fine, but you have symptoms of a mild concussion, so you need to take it easy. If you get a headache that gets worse or won't go away, experience any weakness, numbness, vomiting—things like that—we're going to have to get you to the hospital over in Sacramento, okay?"

"Okay."

The medic glanced over at Francie, then addressed Derek, "Call me right away if she seems confused or you can't rouse her. Any unusual behavior."

"We'll be sure to keep a close eye on her. Thank you, Randall."

"Would you like some coffee, honey?" Francie asked, holding onto his forearm.

"I'd love some, but my wife's holding supper for me." He patted her hand. "Another time."

"I'll see you out then." Turning to leave with Randall, she glanced back at Derek. "Do you want your dessert in here?"

"Please."

His arm remained around her shoulders even after they had gone. Shaking her foot, Breanna's gaze shifted around the room, falling to the pictures on the mantel. She stood and went over to them. "Who are all these people?"

"Your family." Derek came to stand at her side. He nodded toward an older photo of a striking couple. "Lawrence and Valerie Dalton."

And the name had a face.

Her father's parents.

She studied the image, looking for some resemblance

to her own. It was hard to tell from the black-and-white photograph.

His fingertips brushed over the frame of a picture of two gentlemen in a boat, one of them proudly holding a prized catch. "My father, Raymond St. John, and your grandfather…I remember that day. They took me fishing with them." His voice seemed strained. "Both of them are gone now."

"I'm so sorry." Her hand brushed over his forearm. "You're related to the Daltons then."

"Not exactly, no, but our families have been connected, so to speak, from the very beginning. It's a long story. I wouldn't want to bore you." Returning the photo to the mantel, Derek turned to look at her. "My father was their attorney. His firm handled everything until he passed."

"And now it's up to you."

"Yes, Mr. Maynard and myself."

St. John, Maynard & St. John. Of course.

Derek walked over to the other end of the mantel and handed Breanna a photograph. The man in it was young, around her age maybe. Handsome. Dark hair brushed his shoulders. Familiar blue eyes. He was smiling at the camera.

A feeling tugged at her chest. It looked like he was smiling right at her. Silly thought. Her eyes filling, she glanced at Derek.

His arm coming around her, he nodded. "Your dad. The last photo ever taken of him."

A tear slid down her cheek. Breanna didn't understand why she was crying for a man she never got to know, but then, maybe that was the very reason. She was robbed of the chance.

"Did you know him?"

"I did, though I was just eleven when Shane died."

She nodded, doing the math in her head. That would make Derek around thirty-two.

Francie returned with the mousse and once Breanna swallowed the last bit, she rested the spoon on her plate, covering a yawn with her hand. "I'm sorry, it's been a day."

"You need your rest." His fingertips grazed across her forehead. "Let's get you back to your room."

"Thanks. This house is a labyrinth, but I think I can manage."

"Regardless, I'm taking you." Derek rose, pulling her to stand with him. "What if you became dizzy on the stairs or something? I did say I'd keep a close eye on you, didn't I?"

Good grief.

"You did."

Breanna paused when they reached the second-floor landing. "I think I've got it from here."

With a lift of his lips, his thumb hitched to the left. "I'm at the end of the hall should you need me."

I won't, but thanks.

She nodded. "See you in the morning."

"I'll come get you for breakfast." Winding a blonde tendril around his finger, he murmured, "You intrigue me, Miss Dalton."

Her head tilted to the side.

Derek leaned in closer.

"*Danger, Will Robinson!*" Kayleigh's warning rang in her head.

Breanna stiffened.

Smoothing her hair over her shoulder, warm lips touched her cheek. "Sleep well. Goodnight."

And he turned away, going left down the hall.

Goodnight.

Chapter Twelve

Breanna pulled a pillow to her chest and held it there. As exhausted as she'd been when she got under the covers, sleep evaded her. She tossed and turned, every moment of the last few days replaying in her head. Only twenty-four hours ago, she slept in the shelter of Sinjin's arms.

Then poof, he was gone.

Not a crumb left behind as evidence he'd ever been there. *Face it, girl. He left you. If he was even real at all.*

Okay, Breanna did *not* believe Sinjin was simply a figment of her vivid imagination, but the fact she woke up all alone remained. And what did that tell her?

It was just sex.

A wild, delicious tryst with a stranger in the storm. And when the snow stopped falling, it was over. She knew it would be. But Breanna never thought the fucker would just leave her to fend for herself—with a concussion, no less—stranded in a cabin in the woods.

It was obvious, wasn't it? Rather than suffer through an awkward parting of ways, Sinjin slinked out of their haven at the first sign of sunlight. *Without a second thought or a backward glance, I bet.* Breanna supposed she should be grateful he put her bag back in her car before they towed it off the mountain. He must've, right? How else could Jordy have gotten it?

She punched the pillow.

Because the more she thought about it, Breanna wasn't grateful.

She was pissed.

At herself, mostly.

For thinking with her vagina.

The black void outside the window beginning to lighten, Breanna gave up. She switched the bedside lamp on. Her Mac rested there on the night table beside her. *Six a.m.* Seeing she had a gazillion messages from Kayleigh, she typed one back. A nanosecond later, the FaceTime app flashed on the screen.

"About damn time. I thought you were dead…abducted by aliens…or…" Her friend stared at her like that's exactly what she was. "Jesus Christ, you look like shit. What the hell happened?"

"Gee, thanks." She made a face, fingering the hideous bump on her forehead.

After filling Kayleigh in on everything that had transpired since her last text on Saturday, albeit a sanitized version, Breanna asked for a favor, "Since I'm stuck here until my car is fixed, can you send me some more clothes? I only packed for a weekend."

"Sure, I'm leaving for my mom's this afternoon. I can stop at FedEx on the way." With a smirk, Kayleigh pursed her lips to the side. "What do you need, exactly?"

"God, everything. Pants, sweaters, undies…" She shrugged. "Throw in that bra that makes my boobs pop—the teal one with the thong that matches."

"Trying to impress the lawyer guy?"

"God, no, but you should see this place." Breanna flipped her Mac around, offering Kayleigh a panoramic view. "And that's just my bedroom."

"Damn."

"Yeah."

"I got you, babe," Kayleigh assured her.

"I'll Cash App you to cover it."

"No problem." She worried her lip. "Have you, uh, told your mom?"

Do I really have to?

"Not yet."

"Ohhh, good luck with that."

Yeah, she was going to need it.

Following a long, indulgent shower, with her makeup on and a fresh blowout, Breanna sat criss-cross applesauce in her underwear, rifling through her duffel. She'd have to make do with the clothes she brought until Friday, at least. Opting to save the sweater dress for the Thanksgiving bash she hadn't planned on being here for, she only had a pair of ripped-up skinny jeans or leggings to choose from.

Gah, I wore leggings yesterday.

Tossing the jeans, along with a low scoop-neck Henley, on the bed beside her, she sighed. "Thank fuck for Kayleigh."

"Miss Dalton." Looking rather amused, Derek leaned against the doorway to the bedroom. He snickered. "You're much too pretty to be using such foul language."

"And the princess has a potty mouth."

"Formal now, are we? Does it offend you?"

A smirk on his face, he stepped into the room. "No, but your grandmother would've been mortified."

"How'd you get in here?"

"I've been knocking," Derek explained, coming to stand beside the bed. "I became concerned when you didn't answer, so I let myself in."

Odd, I heard nothing. Wait a minute...

"The door was locked."

"I have the master code for all the keypads." He pursed his lips with a shrug.

Rolling her eyes, she deadpanned, "That's reassuring."

"I'd ask if you're ready to go down to breakfast, but I can see that you're not."

His eyes fixated on her breasts encased in lace of the palest blue, Breanna stood. Not embarrassed in the slightest, she watched him swallow, his Adam's apple bobbing in his throat, as she pulled tight, faded denim up her thighs. Leaning over the bed, she reached for her shirt.

Strong fingers tightened around her wrist. Dark eyes bored into her own. "What do you think you're doing, Breanna?"

Tugging her hand from his grasp, Breanna pulled the Henley down over her head and fluffed out her hair. "Now, I'm ready."

She turned to leave the room.

His fingers catching hers from behind, Derek pulled her back to him. "Not so fast."

"What?"

He wet his lips, the corner of his mouth slowly ticking up, and tucked a piece of hair behind her ear. "You're barefoot."

God forbid.

"Oh." She glanced down at her pink-painted toes. "I'll, uh, just put some shoes on."

Breakfast was served in the family dining room, where they had dinner the night before. Eggs Benedict. Roasted asparagus. Savory potatoes.

Francie set a carafe of fresh-squeezed orange juice on the table. "I'll be back with coffee in a minute."

"You really didn't have to go to all this trouble. I'm more than good with a bowl of cereal—honest—but thank you." Sleep outranking sustenance, Breanna skipped breakfast most days, unless a granola bar counted.

"It's no trouble." Francie waved off her concern. "Besides, you're both on your own for lunch—dinner, too. I have to get started on Thanksgiving, but there's plenty of sandwich fixings in the fridge. Just help yourself."

"Do you need any help?" Breanna offered. "I'd be happy to."

"Do you know your way around a kitchen?"

Not really, but how hard could it be? She'd watched her mom cook the turkey a bunch of times. "I know how to make a mean bowl of ramen."

"You're a doll to offer, but I've got it." Patting her shoulder, Francie chuckled. "And Mr. Keeler will help me out this afternoon."

"Oh, and does he know his way around the kitchen?"

"He sure does," she replied with a wink.

Diving into her eggs, Breanna licked hollandaise sauce from her lip. Maybe sleeping in was overrated because she definitely could get used to this. She glanced up at Derek. "Who's Mr. Keeler?"

"Francie's husband, Ted." He went on to explain, "He's the caretaker here."

"Oh." And she wondered what they did, who Francie cooked for, in this mountain mansion all alone. "You don't live here, right?"

"I have a place near my office in Sacramento. Why?" His brows pulling together, he raised a glass of juice to his lips.

Breanna shrugged. "They must be lonely here, without my grandmother."

"My partner keeps them company," Derek said with a snicker.

"Mr. Maynard?"

"Yes, he's been managing Valerie's property for several years, though he's in Sacramento at the moment. He's supposed to return tomorrow. You'll meet him then."

Can't wait.

She popped some asparagus in her mouth and smiled. "Will there be a lot of people here tomorrow?"

"That depends on the weather, but I imagine so." Studying her, he wiped his mouth and set the napkin on the table. "Business associates…hell, the entire village has an open invitation."

"*Do you live up here on the mountain?*"

"*Not far.*"

Her eyes went big. If Sinjin lived nearby somewhere, then it's possible he would come.

"It's a Dalton House tradition—always has been." Reaching across the table, Derek patted her hand. "We all agreed your grandmother would want us to carry on."

"Of course."

"Oh, I almost forgot." He grinned and pulled a phone charger from the pocket of his Ralph Lauren slim-fit pants. "Got you one."

"You're a lifesaver." Well, the phone *was* her lifeline, wasn't it? "Thanks, I appreciate it."

"Don't mention it."

Francie quietly set a tray with coffee on the table, and just as quietly slipped away. Pouring them both a cup, Derek glanced at the Movado on his wrist. "I've got some business to attend to—conference calls with clients. I'm afraid I'm going to be tied up for a while."

"That's all right. I think I can keep myself occupied." Breanna welcomed the reprieve, to be honest. She could use some downtime to reset and explore on her own a little, maybe.

"Tell you what." Smiling, he took her hands in his and squeezed. "Come by the study at two. We can get those documents I need you to sign out of the way and go for a walk around the grounds."

I've done enough prancing through the snow, thank you very much.

"Yeah, sure."

This whole thing was weird. Everything about it. Breanna got off that exit on 395 and drove straight into the fucking *Twilight Zone.* After kicking off her shoes, she connected her phone to the charger and sank into the cushy, down-filled sofa. Fingertips skimming across the soft linen fabric, she closed her heavy eyelids. Even the fact that she was lounging on a fifteen-thousand dollar couch was weird—especially that. "This can't be a dupe. It feels too much like heaven."

She should get up, call her mother, and get it over with, but between the lack of sleep and a food coma calling her name, Breanna sighed, dozing off instead.

Warm breath, the scent of rich, black coffee, tickled her nose and fanned her skin, while fingertips trailed through her hair. Down her chest. Across her breast. Recognizing the familiar feeling his touch provoked, she heaved a sigh.

"I'm right here, princess."

Fabric rustled. Cool air. Kisses on her skin. Wet lips suctioned her nipple.

"Sinjin."

I'm dreaming.

Dreaming.

Dreaming.

Dreaming.

"Shhh. Rest now."

Okay.

Blinking her eyes open, Breanna glanced down at her chest. Nothing looked out of place. A furry blanket covered her.

Did I put that there?

Reasoning, she pulled it off the back of the couch in her sleep, Breanna put her feet on the floor and gazed out through the floor-to-ceiling glass. In the distance, an animal—a wolf, if she were to guess—ran across the snow-covered terrain.

She wrapped the fur throw tightly around her, and opening the glass door, stepped out onto the deck to peer over the railing. Taking in the unspoiled splendor all around her, Breanna thought she understood what drew George Dalton to stake his claim here all those years ago.

Picking up her bare foot, she rubbed it on the leg of her jeans. "It's fucking cold, though."

Turning to go back inside, Breanna surveyed the cozy patio nook outside her room, with its outdoor sofas, fur blankets, fireplace, and hot tub. She could see herself curled up, reading a book out here—or editing one—watching the snow gently fall.

"It's a shame," she murmured to herself.

This big house, filled with expensive, beautiful things, was sadly empty. Its rooms unoccupied. No one really lived here.

At five minutes of two, Breanna left her room. She paused at the landing, quickly glancing at the stairs that led up to the third floor, then made her way down to see Derek.

The door to the study was cracked open about an inch. She was about to knock when she heard his voice. Lowering her hand, she stood away from the opening and waited for him to finish.

"Yes, I should have everything wrapped up here shortly." Snicker. "It won't be an issue…it's too bad, she *is* quite lovely." The clink of ice cubes swirling in a glass. "See you tomorrow then."

Silence.

She waited a moment, then knocked.

"Breanna." He opened the door. "Come in."

His laptop was open on the desk, a glass of whiskey sat beside it. Picking up a thick file folder, Derek steered her over to a leather sofa. "Would you like a drink?"

"Uh, no, thank you," she said, taking a seat.

Their thighs touching, he sat down close beside her. "This won't take long. I point. You sign."

"What am I signing?"

"Probate documents. They're formalities, as I said." He handed her a pen. "As Executor of your grandmother's estate, you're acting on her behalf and carrying out her wishes."

"But I don't know what they are."

"That's why you have me." Derek squeezed her knee. "I know."

"Isn't there a will or something?"

There should be, right? That's how it went in the movies, anyway.

"Of course," he asserted, taking a sip of whiskey. "And since you're Valerie's only blood relative, she named you Executor and sole beneficiary—less the estate debt and asset distribution, of course."

"I don't know what that means."

"Taxes. Sorry, the government gets its share." Turning toward her in his seat, Derek rested his hands on her shoulders. "Look, when all is said and done, you're going to have a million bucks to put in your bank account. That's a delightful addition to the trust fund your father set up for you, isn't it?"

Trust fund?

Breanna pulled away from him. "What?"

"I assumed you knew." He pressed his lips together, then audibly expelled a breath. "When Shane died…well, all of his assets became yours."

"I know nothing of this." Stunned, she slowly shook her head. "And what assets? He was only twenty-two."

"It was a substantial amount. Valerie and your mother jointly controlled it on your behalf."

Her jaw dropped. Literally. This was just too much to process.

"I'm sorry." Stroking her hair, Derek tipped his chin. "Let's get this done and go for that walk, shall we?"

Durable Power of Attorney. IRS forms. Letter of Testamentary. Distribution of assets. Transfer documents.

Yikes.

Breanna put the pen down. "I'd like to read these first. Have someone look them over."

"Who?"

"My stepdad. A lawyer."

"I am a lawyer," he reminded her.

"Right." Biting her lip, she nodded. "Yes, I know, but you're my grandmother's lawyer."

"And now I'm yours," he said, his hand on her cheek. "Don't you trust me?"

"Be careful. When you get to Dalton House. Just be careful."

Yes. No. I don't know.

"It's not that. I'd just like to read them." Breanna placed her hand on top of his. "And I want to see my grandmother's will. I need to know I'm doing everything right. Like she wanted."

"Of course you do, sweetheart." His thumb moved over her skin. "There's no need to rush. These are only the signature pages. The full documents are back in my office, along with Valerie's will. I'll email everything to you on Friday. You can read them, and Mr. Maynard will be here, should you have any questions."

"Okay." She nodded.

"Now, how about we take that walk?"

In her room that evening, her mind spinning, Breanna stared into the crackling fire. She had no good reason not to trust Derek. Her grandmother must have, and he'd been nothing but kind to her, so why did she have this nagging feeling something wasn't right?

"*Be careful.*"

In the black void outside her window, a wolf howled its warning.

"I will be," she whispered to the flames. "I will."

Chapter Thirteen

The guests wouldn't start to arrive for another few hours. Then, all afternoon, the doors to Dalton House would be open for people to come and go as they wished. An array of food. Plenty of liquor. Some people stayed the entire four hours, while some stopped by on their way to other holiday obligations. After the emigrants made it through that first year, George Dalton gathered everyone together to give thanks and the annual tradition continued to this day.

"It's all about fellowship and community," Derek had explained on their walk yesterday.

There was no more talk of estate matters, for which Breanna was grateful. Instead, linking his arm with hers, he told her the story of how the Daltons ended up here. She'd already heard it from Jordy, of course, but she listened as if she were hearing it for the very first time.

Breanna picked up a warm croissant from the tray Francie had sent up to her. "To tide you over," she said.

Slathering it with butter and raspberry jam, Breanna gazed outside the glass. The sky unfettered, crystal flakes sporadically fluttered in the air. Not falling to the ground, they simply danced along with the wind. Briefly, she wondered if another storm was on the way. Not that it mattered.

It's not like I'm going anywhere.

She had to get ready, though. Breanna wasn't sure why she cared, because she didn't know these people, and she'd likely never encounter them again, but she was Shane Dalton's daughter, wasn't she? She wanted to do him proud.

Washing the croissant down with some coffee, a scratch sounded on the glass. Breanna turned her head and shrieked. The wolf she'd spotted yesterday, only it wasn't a wolf at all, pawed at her door, as if asking to come in. White with black markings and ice-blue eyes, the dog wagged its tail, seeing it had her attention.

"Oh, my goodness." Putting her cup down, Breanna got up and moved to the door. She opened it, wintry air and the dog pushing past her. "And who do you belong to?"

The Siberian Husky, at least she presumed that's what breed it was, nudged her hand with its nose, looking for a pat. Petting the dog's thick, well-groomed coat, there was no doubt in her mind someone cared for him—or was it her?

With a soft giggle, Breanna checked. He was definitely a she. "Sorry, girl."

What am I supposed to do with you?

"C'mon." She patted her thigh for the dog to follow her. "I guess you can hang out with me for a while."

Her sweater dress was a dusty, pale pink, and as soft as the finest cashmere, though it wasn't. Modest from the front, the V-back dipped almost to her waist, with crisscrossed straps that kept the garment from falling down her shoulders. To show it off, Breanna pulled her hair up, twisting it into a loose knot at her nape, while leaving some strands free to frame her face.

Five days old now, the mark on her forehead had faded some, but it was still noticeable—at least to her. Concealing it as best she could, Breanna carefully applied her makeup, her new furry friend lying at her feet. "There. How do I look?"

"Beautiful."

She whipped her head around.

Silhouetted in the doorframe, his arms folded across his chest, Derek leaned against it as if he had every right to be there.

"Do you have a habit of sneaking into people's rooms?"

"No, actually, I don't." Smirking, he pushed off the jamb and moved toward her. "And I didn't sneak. You were just too preoccupied to notice."

With a glance down at the pup, she turned back to the mirror. "Some watchdog you are."

"She knows me." Chuckling, Derek's hands came to rest on her shoulders. "Besides, Hera wouldn't hurt a fly."

"Hera?"

"That's her name." His fingers swept along her collarbone. "Goddess of women, marriage, and birth, she was married to—"

"Zeus." Breanna dabbed a bit of gloss on her lips and turned around.

His hands falling to the marble vanity, Derek caged her in. He leaned forward, his hard form pressing into her soft one. Head dipping to her neck, he murmured in her ear, "It's a deadly combo."

"What is?"

"Smart and beautiful." He pulled away, a devilish smirk on his face. "Come now, the guests are going to arrive soon."

Thankful she had the sweater dress to keep her somewhat warm, Breanna took her place in the grand foyer, meeting and greeting every guest as they arrived.

"It's your duty," Derek said.

He stood with her, his hand at her waist like they were the new power couple or something. *As if.* Folks from the village and business associates alike welcomed her warmly, each offering their condolences on her grandmother's passing.

"The last Dalton," the old lady lamented with a shake of her head. Breanna had forgotten who she was already. "Such a shame the name will die with you."

Morbid.

Clasping the woman's hands between hers, she feigned a little smile. "Why would you say that?"

"This is *Dalton* House, and so it should stay." Her beady eyes glared up at Derek. "Let me tell you—"

"It's all right, Mrs. Fellows," he interrupted her.

Jeanine. That's it. Jeanine Fellows.

"We can take comfort Miss Dalton is here for now, can't we?" Derek patted the old lady's hand, steering her away. Once she was gone, his arm came around her again, squeezing Breanna to his side. "Pay Jeanine no mind. She's just missing the old days, grieving your grandmother."

"I see that." The massive door opened yet again, making her shiver.

His fingertips skimming over her bare back, goosebumps prickled her flesh. Derek leaned into her. "You're cold."

Duh.

Standing six feet from the door, who wouldn't be? Not that he'd know in the genuine cashmere crewneck he wore beneath his tailored blazer. Well-fitted trousers in that subtle plaid he seemed to favor. Sleek leather loafers. *Ralph would be so proud.* Okay, maybe he looked hella fine, but that wasn't the point.

"A little."

"Forgive my thoughtlessness." His arm remaining around her, Derek situated them away from the door, closer to the foyer's welcoming fireplace. "Better?"

"Much. Thank you."

From this vantage point, she could see into other areas of the house. People walked about, holding drinks and little china plates piled with hors d'oeuvres. Starving, Breanna licked her lips. That croissant she had earlier stopped tiding her over ages ago.

And, of course, Derek noticed. "Hungry?"

"Famished."

"Me too." He chuckled, lacing his fingers with hers. "Tell you what, we can join the party in a little while. Have some drinks. Get a little something in your stomach, okay?"

"Okay."

"But don't go overboard." Glancing down at her, the smile nearly reached his eyes. "We'll have our Thanksgiving dinner in private once the guests are gone."

Ready to tell him she could stuff herself full with canapés and still make room for turkey and all the trimmings, Breanna pursed her lips. But then the sheriff came through the door carrying a white bakery box tied with string, and the retort flew from her head.

"Jordy." She hugged him like an old friend, and considering he was the first person she met on this mountain, he was.

Balancing the box in his hand as they swayed, the portly man patted her back. "How're you gettin' on, Miss Breanna?"

"I'm good," she said, pulling away from him. "Everything's good."

"Well, you're as pretty as a picture now that you're all cleaned up."

Derek scowled. Whether because of her lack of decorum or the sheriff's compliment, she couldn't say.

Jordy cleared his throat. "Hank and his wife asked me to bring this for you."

Breanna all but squealed. "Is this what I think it is?"

"Could be." He grinned. "If you're thinkin' banana cream

pie. Hank's been beatin' himself up over lettin' you go out in that storm."

"He couldn't have known," she said, hugging him again. "And I'm all right. Please thank him and his wife for me. I'm going to savor every delicious bite—it's the best banana cream pie on the planet."

"She was downright flattered that you thought so," Jordy said, tipping the brim of his hat. "I'm gonna mosey on over to the kitchen, see what Francie's up to. I'll just, uh, tuck this away in the fridge for you."

"Thank you, Jordy." Breanna kissed his ruddy cheek. "For everything."

Dammit. She was hoping Hank would be here, then she'd have the chance to ask him about Sinjin. Now, the only hope she had left was for the man himself to appear. And with every minute that passed, it seemed more and more unlikely.

Fuck him. He left you, remember?

How could she forget?

Derek's hand slipped from her waist to her hip. He squeezed. "We've done our duty long enough, I'd say. The arrivals are winding down, so let's go get ourselves a drink, hm?"

Thank fuck.

"Sounds good."

God, she needed this. The bubbly alcohol-infused concoction, whatever it was, slid so easily down her throat. Full of fall flavors, Breanna tasted pear and apple and cinnamon—never mind the vodka she knew was in there. Garnished with a pear slice, cinnamon stick, and star anise, it was darn pretty too.

"That was good." She smiled at the bartender hired just for the occasion. "I'll have another, please."

Derek approached with two small plates of hors d'oeuvres. Pulling her close, he lifted a canapé to her mouth. "Here, try the salmon. It's delicious."

"Mm." Breanna nodded as she chewed.

The bartender returned with her drink, and Derek ordered one for himself. "Whiskey ginger, my man—go easy on the ginger." He winked. "And one for the lovely lady."

"I already have one, Derek." She held up her glass. "Are you trying to get me drunk?"

"This coming from the girl who never misses dollar beer night at The Cheerful Tortoise." His brow lifted, creasing his forehead, and he smirked, while his palm came to rest on her ass. "Do I need to?"

What the hell?

Breanna pushed his hand off her bottom. "Are you hitting on me?"

"Hardly. I know you're only used to boys, Miss Dalton, but I can assure you grown men don't do that. We do, however, pursue what we want, and I think I've made what I want quite clear."

Don't fall for it, Bree. He's just a fuckboy in a suit.

Shut up, Kayleigh.

The bartender placed their drinks in front of them. Pulling her against him, Derek's arms came around her. He dropped his forehead to hers and exhaled. "Look, Breanna, I like you… I'm attracted to you, and I'm hoping we can still see each other after the estate is settled."

Oh boy.

Thumb skimming her cheek, he lifted his head. She'd bet a million dollars he was going to kiss her. Right here. In front of God knows who.

"There you are, dear." Kissing Derek's cheek, a woman with jet-black hair inserted herself between them. "I should've known I'd find you at the bar."

Stunningly beautiful, the woman reminded her of Priscilla Presley when she was younger, before she fucked up her face.

DYAN LAYNE

Sophisticated. Rich, judging by her impeccable clothes. Just his type, albeit much older than she would've thought he'd go for.

"Pamela, this is Shane's daughter, Breanna." Derek pulled her back to his side. "Breanna, may I introduce Pamela Maynard?"

Ohh. Must be his partner's wife.

She held out her hand. "It's nice to meet you, Mrs. Maynard."

"I've been dying to meet you, and it's Pamela." The woman hugged her, then stepping back, she appraised her, tucking a loose tendril behind Breanna's ear. "Shane, what a wonderful young man your father was. I can see him in you. He'd be so proud."

"Thank you," she choked.

Just hearing those words from someone who knew him brought tears to her eyes. She blinked them back, though.

"Where's Ian? He should've been here long before now." Downing his drink, Derek signaled the bartender for another. "Most of the guests have come and gone already."

Breanna glanced around the sitting room they were in. He was right. Only a few stragglers remained. She waved to Randall, here with his wife and kids, chatting up Jordy by the window.

"Relax, will you? I left him at the buffet with Francie maybe ten minutes ago."

Randall came over, his family and Jordy in tow. He addressed Derek, "It looks like snow, so we're going to get going, but I wanted to thank you and see how Miss Dalton's feeling."

"But I don't wanna go yet, Daddy." A little girl tugged at his arm. "It's only a few snowflakes."

Breanna closed her eyes. *"And every storm starts with just one."*

"I'm fine, Randall." She smiled. "Really."

108

"No headaches?" He raised his brow.

"No headaches."

"All right then." Randall turned to Jordy. "You heading out?"

"In a few." He patted his belly. "Need to digest a bit."

And then they were the only ones left in the room. Breanna drained her watered-down drink and began sipping the one Derek had ordered for her. A wet nose nudged at her hand.

"Hera." She giggled, petting the dog. "That tickles."

She glanced up and, holding a plate in his hand, there he was.

Shorn at the sides, his wild locks were gone. Beard now short and neatly trimmed. A cream crewneck and black Armani replaced plaid flannel and jeans. But the whiskey eyes locked on hers were the same.

"It's about time. Ian, get over here and say hello to Miss Dalton." Derek wrapped his arm tightly around her shoulders. "Breanna, this is my partner, Ian Maynard."

"Pleasure." He tipped his chin. Then, as if she was of no consequence to him, began speaking with Pamela.

What the fuck?

Tears rushed to fill her eyes. She couldn't breathe. Breanna glanced at Jordy beside her. "That's—"

With a subtle shake of his head, the sheriff squeezed her hand so hard it hurt.

That's Sinjin.

Chapter Fourteen

Ian's gaze locked on hers.

Sorry, princess.

He had to appear indifferent. To keep his fist from connecting with Derek's jaw. To stop himself from bending Breanna over that bar, slipping her little silk panties to the side, and slamming his cock home. It took every ounce of self-control he possessed.

With a brief kiss on Pamela's cheek, he leaned past her, waving the bartender over. "Bourbon, please. Neat."

"Yes, sir."

"And don't give me the cheap shit." Nothing against Jim Beam. Normally he didn't mind it, but not today. "Make it Van Winkle."

"You got it," the bartender said with an easy nod.

While Ian needed to keep his mind sharp, fortification was required to make it through this sham of a family dinner. He picked up the crystal Glencairn placed in front of him, and swirling the whiskey around the bowl, he sniffed it before raising the glass to his lips. Smooth and rich, he welcomed its nuanced flavor.

From the corner of his eye, he chanced a glance at Derek, stroking Breanna's skin. Oblivious to his touch, her bewildered blue eyes turned to Jordy.

"You know what, my friend? Leave the bottle."

Pamela's eyes widened.

Fingers plowing through his fresh haircut, he snickered. "Give her a citron and tonic, will you?"

"Someone's on edge."

"I'm fine."

The bartender returned with the Van Winkle and Pamela's drink. "Oh, and that's why you're setting out to drink a thousand-dollar bottle of bourbon?"

"Exactly," Ian said and tossed back the contents of his glass, only to pour himself another.

"You best keep your wits about you, darling." And with a knowing smirk, Pamela took a sip of the lemony vodka. "Derek isn't stupid. The girl isn't, either."

"What do you know about her?"

"I know I like her," she answered with a shrug.

"I like her, too."

He almost wished he didn't. It'd make things easier. But no, Fate had to go and throw Breanna in his path, and now it was too late. The one girl he shouldn't feel anything for, except loathing, perhaps, captivated him. *How in the fuck did she do that?* Ian Maynard had more than his fair share of women through the years, yet somehow he'd managed to remain immune to their vain attempts to claim him.

Francie poked her head out from the formal dining room. "Are we ready?"

"God, yes," Pamela piped up. She dipped her head to his ear and lowered her voice. "Good. Don't fuck it up, then, dear."

Right.

Glass in hand, Ian walked over to Jordy. "Staying for dinner, my friend?"

Her fairytale blues glaring, Breanna looked at the sheriff before turning them on him.

"You know, as much as I'd love to stick around for this…" He pressed his lips together. "…I, uh, think I should be going."

Snickering under his breath as Jordy made his farewells, Ian took his place at Breanna's side. "Enjoying yourself?"

Hera sat at her feet.

Breanna sipped on her drink, declining to answer him.

Derek absently trailed his fingers up and down her arm.

"Try the salmon, princess." Ian picked up a morsel from his plate, and holding it to her perfect mouth, he winked. "I hear it's delicious."

The six of them sat at the long table that could easily accommodate twenty. *Ridiculous.* The family dining room would have been much cozier, but Francie did things as Valerie had always insisted upon, and Thanksgiving dinner, with George Dalton's oil-painted eyes staring at them, had always been held in here.

Across the table from Ian, Breanna pretended to eat her food, moving it around on her plate and taking the occasional bite, while pretending his presence didn't affect her. She acted as if she'd never seen him before. Never felt him inside her. That's how he wanted it. Even so, it stung.

Because he craved more of her. From her. With her. Right now, more than anything, he wished they were back inside that cabin in the storm. Without Ted and Francie hovering. Without Pamela's whispers in his ear. Without Derek's lecherous glances her way.

Don't look at him, baby.

He wanted her eyes on him.

Ian toed his shoe off beneath the table. Dare he? Why yes, he certainly did. Chuckling to himself, he reached for her with his foot while sipping on his bourbon. Making contact, his toes rubbed up along her shin, then down and up again.

No reaction whatsoever.

Nothing.

A fork poised at her mouth, Breanna swallowed, her gaze flitting over to the avaricious motherfucker sitting there beside her.

Dipping beneath the hem of her dress, he went higher. With the feeling of her delicate skin and the enticing taste of that sweet cunt fresh in his memory, Ian's foot slid over her tights, toes pressing, up the inside of her thigh.

Her blue eyes going round, Breanna's pupils flared.

Got your attention, now, don't I, princess?

He winked and, inching to that place between her legs, Ian pushed forward. The thin, stretchy tights an ineffective barrier, he prodded, stroking her pussy as deftly as he would with his fingers.

The fork slipped from her grasp, falling to her plate.

Without missing a beat, Derek picked it up and handed it back to her.

"Thanks," Breanna sputtered. Face strained, she bit her lip.

His partner none the wiser, Ian continued his deviant game of footsie. How wet was she? Knowing his dirty girl, those tights she wore were more than damp. Ian bet he could push his toes halfway in her hole if he tried. Should he make her come right here?

Might be fun with Derek right next to her.

Nah.

As much as he wanted to, he enjoyed toying with her. He'd rather keep her needy and wanting until after Derek left. Once the nuisance was gone, he would be more than happy to remind her just who this pussy belonged to.

He pressed into her clit. *Me.*

"No more." Breanna kicked his shin.

Turning their heads, everyone looked at her.

"Food," she added, raising her napkin to her mouth. "I couldn't eat another bite. I'm so stuffed."

Not yet. Ian snickered under his breath, teeth raking over his lip.

"Me, too," Pamela said, patting her toned belly. "I could use some coffee."

"I've got it ready and waiting for us." Francie got up from the table, her husband going over to her.

"Dessert, too?"

"Yes, Pam." With a soft chuckle, the eyes behind her horn-rimmed frames rolled.

"Come on, dearest." With a smirk, Ian glanced at Breanna while assisting Pamela from her chair. "You're the only woman I know who can claim to be full and ask for sweets all in the same breath."

Much better.

Coffee service laid out on a square low-set table, Ian made himself comfortable on the sectional in front of the fire. Derek stood over at the bar, pouring brandy into snifters. Pamela took a seat beside him, while Breanna sat down on the other end, as far away from them as she could be.

"Come on over here, sweetheart." Fixing herself a cup of coffee, Pamela fixed her gaze on Breanna. "We can't carry on a conversation if you're all the way over there, can we?"

"I suppose not."

With a somewhat apprehensive smile on her face, which Ian already knew wasn't like her, she moved to sit directly across from him on the big U-shaped sofa. Hera jumped up beside her, the dog settling her head on Breanna's lap.

He grinned at that. *Traitor.*

"Coffee, dear."

"Yes, please."

"Ian?"

"No, thanks." He tipped his chin at the bottle of Van Winkle. "I'm good."

"Uh-huh." And returning her attention to Breanna, she asked, "How do you take it, dear?"

"Sweet," Ian answered with a wink, bringing the glass of bourbon to his lips.

Breanna shot him a look. "Just cream, thanks."

"So," Pamela said, handing her a cup. "My son tells me you're going to college in Portland—which school?"

"Son? You're his mother?"

Ian had to stop himself from laughing because the slack-jawed expression on Breanna's face was truly comical.

"Course, dear." She graciously smiled and took a sip of her coffee. "What did you think?"

"You look far too young to be…" Her cheeks turning pink, Breanna shrugged.

"Thank you," Pamela said, waving off the compliment. "Botox is my friend. I was already thirty-three when Ian was born. So then, which school?"

"Portland State."

"Lovely campus. Beautiful city." She nodded. "And you're an English major?"

"Yes," Breanna answered, glancing at him. "I graduate in May."

"And then what?" His mother went on with her disguised interrogation. Ian knew how she rolled. "What are your plans after that?"

"I applied for an editorial internship with Penguin Random House." Her voice becoming animated, Breanna's face lit up. "It's only twenty hours a week, but it's a paid position. Gets my foot in the door, you know?"

"You'll be moving to New York, then?"

"No, it's remote. That's the best part. I can work from anywhere."

How convenient.

"Fingers crossed you get it," Pamela said to her, doing exactly that. "Your father was a writer, you know. Well, that's what he aspired to be."

"No, I didn't, but then I don't know much about him."

"Why is that, dear?"

"It makes my mom sad to talk about him." Petting Hera on her lap, she shrugged. "So, we don't."

"Oh, sweetie, we have to fix that." Pamela reached across the table and took Breanna's hand. "You should know everything you possibly can about your daddy. And your family. They're such a big part of who you are."

Annoyed, Derek put a tray of brandy down on the table. "And just who is she, Pamela?"

"A Dalton, that's who." Looking smug, she picked up a glass from the tray. "Now, where is my pie?"

"Get her some pie, Ian." Shooing the dog off the sofa, Derek claimed his place beside Breanna.

His lip curling, Ian stood. "Can I get some for you, too, Miss Dalton?"

"Um, yeah, sure."

"What kind would you like? Pumpkin?" He winked. "The banana cream from Hank?"

Yeah, baby, I know all about that.

"Uhh…" She bit her lip. "…both?"

"Why not?" Chuckling, Ian noticed Derek lifting his brow. "What's that face for, Derek? Miss Dalton can have two pieces of pie if she wants to."

"Of course she can." Throwing his arm around her shoulders, he hugged Breanna to his side. "That's too much for her, though."

Jesus Christ.

What are you, now? The motherfucking food police?

He needed Derek to go back home to Sacramento, where he belonged. Ian never cared to get involved in this goddam mess. But Fate handed him Breanna for a reason, right? She was no match against the devil on her own.

Returning with the pie, Ian found Breanna rubbing at her temple, trying to put some space between herself and Derek. "Here we are. Pecan for you…" Handing his mom her pie, Francie and Ted sat down with plates of their own. Then, turning to his princess, he winked. "And pumpkin, with a side of banana cream for you. I put extra whipped cream on it. Thought you'd like that."

"Thanks," she deadpanned.

"Randall was right," Francie noted, looking through the glass. "It's snowing."

"Just a dusting," Ted said with a squeeze to his wife's knee. "Six inches, they say. Another big one's supposed to hit come Monday, though."

"Jesus, is that all it ever does here?" Attacking the pie with her fork, Breanna licked the cream from her lip.

His dick twitched. Course, it didn't take a lot for that to happen when he was around her.

"Feels like it sometimes. Last season was insane. Started in December and didn't let up until April. We got what? Seven hundred inches, wasn't it?" Ted asked his wife.

Francie nodded. "Seven hundred and twenty-two, dear."

"Pure bedlam. We were snowed in here for a good long while with the pass closed." Shoveling pie into his mouth, Ted shrugged. "Makes for good skiing over in Tahoe, I suppose."

"Holy sh—" But Breanna stopped herself and muttered, "Sorry."

"Do you ski?"

Of course, Derek would ask her that. Diamond Peak. Sugar Bowl. Palisades. He'd been addicted to the thrill of the slopes from the time they were kids.

"Oh, no." Breanna put her plate down with a shake of her head. "Tried it once and nearly killed myself. I have no desire to ever do it again."

"Shame." Derek looked from Breanna to Francie and Ted. "I should probably head back to Sacramento tonight—just in case."

Yes, you definitely should.

Ian caught Breanna pressing her fingers to her temple again. "Are you all right?"

"Yeah, just a little headache."

Derek and Francie turned where they sat to scrutinize her.

"It's the alcohol, I think," she said and narrowed her eyes at him. "I probably shouldn't be drinking with a concussion."

"Why don't you go lie down, hm? Get some rest." Hugging her to his side, Derek kissed the top of her head.

Fucking bastard. Ian poured himself another shot. So much for staying sober.

Breanna's fingers fidgeted on her lap. "Yeah, I think I'll do that."

"I'll take you up."

"No, it's okay, you don't have to." She stood, smoothing the pink dress down her thighs. "I know my way."

"I'll come see you before I go."

If Breanna responded to that, Ian couldn't hear it. She wished them all a good evening, and with a brief parting glance, went upstairs.

Ian slammed his glass down on the table, his finger pointing at Derek's face. "What in the fuck do you think you're doing?"

"What?" With a shrug of his shoulders, he smirked.

"Don't give me *what*," Ian seethed. "I saw you—we all did. Keep your grubby paws off of her."

"Why should I?"

"Well, from what I could see, dear, she doesn't want them on her." Smirking, Pam swallowed a healthy dose of brandy.

Ignoring her, Derek sniggered. "Plan B—if we can't get Breanna to sign, I'll convince her to marry me instead."

We?

"Are you out of your ever-loving mind?"

He had to be, not that Ian would ever allow it. And besides, Derek was practically married already. He and Miranda had been a thing since he got out of law school, so he couldn't be serious, could he?

"No. Rightfully, all of this should be ours, and if I have to walk her down the aisle to get it, then I will. I have to marry and make a few little St. Johns soon, anyway, don't I? Having Breanna for a wife wouldn't be that much of a hardship."

"What about Miranda?" Ian shouted. Head cocked, he stared at Derek in disbelief, daring him to cast aside the girl who, it seemed, had wasted the last seven years of her life with him.

The man didn't even blink. "What about her?"

"I think she might have something to say about that."

"So Miranda won't get to change her last name." He shrugged as if it was of no consequence to him. "We can still be together when I'm in Sacramento."

Francie gasped. "Derek…"

"You're a pig," Pamela spat.

A laugh, dark and deep, rumbled from his throat. "Come on now, Auntie, I'm willing to take one for the team."

"*And* you're delusional." Her disgust clear, his mother

slammed the empty brandy glass on the table. "Just like your father was."

"No, he wasn't, and neither am I." Leaning forward, he smirked, then said with all seriousness, "The Daltons owe this family."

"All the money in the world can't change the past, Derek," Pamela beseeched him. "And that poor girl had nothing to do with it."

"She's hardly that. Would've been better for all of us if she'd never made it out of that storm."

Without another word, Derek stood, and turning from the room, left the four of them reeling, silent in his wake.

"Our boy's been nipping too much Hennessy, I reckon." Ted broke the silence, taking the last glass of brandy from the tray. "He's blowing smoke out his ass. He didn't mean it."

"Francesca." His mother turned toward her sister. "Did you know Derek was up to this?"

"No, of course not." Glancing at Ian, Francie shook her head and grabbed onto her husband's hand. "I thought he was genuinely concerned about the girl—that's all."

Nodding, Pamela worried her lip. "Well, it's a long drive back to the city. Ian, walk me out to my car, will you?"

Out on the drive, glittery frozen stars tumbled softly from the night sky. Derek's Jag was missing from its spot underneath the porte-cochère, and presuming he'd already left for Sacramento, his mother spoke openly, "I don't like this, son."

"I don't either."

He didn't. Not one bit.

"You can't let him—"

"I won't."

Her fingers brushed snowflakes from his beard. "You need to tell Breanna."

"You know I can't."

Not yet.

Ian kissed her cheek. "She wouldn't believe me, anyway."

"You're not giving the girl enough credit." Pamela opened her car door. "I have a feeling she's going to surprise you."

"Heh. Maybe so." Of that, he had no doubt.

"It's up to you to look out for her."

"I am." And he had, from the moment he saw Breanna at Hank's. Holding her by the hand, he assisted his mother into her car.

"I raised you right, Sinjin."

"Love you, Mom." He kissed her again. "Text me when you get home. Drive safe."

By the time he went upstairs, the room next door to his was dark. Ian took his dog and his half-empty bottle of bourbon out onto the deck and tossed a log into the fire. How the fuck was he going to pull off this shit?

He kicked a shot back straight from the bottle.

The faint scent of oranges mingled with crisp, wintry air and burning wood. Ian sensed her presence even before she made herself known.

"You sonofabitch."

"Don't say that about my mother, princess." And turning around to look at her, he smirked. "She likes you."

But Breanna didn't appear to be amused.

"You left me."

Chapter Fifteen

Once she'd cleared the stairs and was out of sight, Breanna tore down the hallway, escaping inside her room. She'd never been so grateful to get away from someone in her entire life.

Which someone?

All of them.

Derek refusing to give her even an inch of space. Treating her like a child one minute and hitting on her the next. Pamela and all her questions. Breanna made such an ass of herself thinking the woman was his wife. *God, how could I be so stupid?* Even now, her cheeks burned hot at the thought.

And Sinjin? Ian?

"Whatever the fuck he's calling himself today," talking to herself, she pulled the tie from her hair and the pink sweater dress over her head.

At least you know you're not crazy, Bree.

The dude might not have a shrimp dick, but his brain must be the size of a pea if he thought for one minute a haircut and expensive clothes would keep her from knowing he was who he was.

A fucking liar.

Jordy, too. With his *Wizard of Oz* bullshit.

Lying was the one thing Breanna couldn't tolerate in a person—especially one she considered a friend.

One day, many years from now, she might look back on all this and laugh, but ripping the ruined tights from her legs, Breanna was fuming. The audacity of that sonofabitch. If Sinjin thought he was getting into her pants ever again, he was sadly mistaken.

Sadly enough for her, too, considering he'd given her the most amazing orgasms of her life. A taste of what she wanted—no, what she needed—from a man.

Didn't I tell you, Bree? Quit wasting your time with fumbly-bumbly, idiot fuckboys.

Yeah, Kayleigh, you did. You sure did.

Sinjin wasn't fumbly-bumbly, though, dammit.

After taking a quick shower to wash off the dried-up havoc the asshole wreaked between her thighs, Breanna got dressed in the last clean pair of pajama pants she had. Praying the predicted dusting wouldn't delay her expected delivery from FedEx, she figured becoming acquainted with the laundry room would be wise in the event it did.

Breanna left the ensuite, slipping a bralette over her head. Pushing her arms through, she slid the ultra-fine Merino over her breasts and looked up. "Jesus, Derek, you really need to stop doing that."

"Doing what?" He grinned, stalking his way toward her.

She turned around to adjust her breasts. "Sneaking in here."

"I told you I was coming up to see you." Wrapping his arms around her from behind, smooth fingertips brushed across her middle.

"Well, most people knock," she said. Admonishing him, Breanna pushed at his hands. "It's disturbing, quite frankly. I was naked and…"

"And I didn't mind." Derek turned her around.

"Oh, I just bet you didn't."

"I don't think you did, either." Holding onto her hips,

his head dipped to her ear. "I'm not afraid to admit I liked what I saw, and I'd love to see more."

"Derek, please, I…"

"And I'm not afraid to tell you, I want you, Breanna." Lips skating along her neck, he whispered, "In my bed. We'd be so good together."

Somehow, I don't think so.

"You're a little bit wicked, aren't you?" Walking her backward, fingertips sinking into her ass, his plain brown eyes turned black. "I think you must be, because I can't get you out of my head. You keep me up at night, Breanna. I think about you all the time, and I want you to think of me while I'm gone."

Caged between his body and the wall, he smashed against her, the buckle of his belt digging into her skin. She shifted but pressed against the wall she couldn't get away from it.

That fucking hurts. Get. Off. Me.

"Don't resist, now, sweetheart." His hand went to her throat. "Let me kiss you goodbye. If that storm hits Monday, I won't be able to come back until the pass gets cleared."

And closing her eyes, Breanna prayed for snow.

"I…" Trying to get a word in, her lips parted to speak.

But before she could, her face in his hands, Breanna felt Derek's lips on hers.

…don't want to kiss you.

His hand falling to her breast, he plundered his way inside her mouth with his tongue. Derek squeezed the small mound of flesh, rubbing her nipple with his thumb. With a mind of its own, her clit zinged awake, ready and waiting for his fingers to make their way between her legs. *Noooo. Fuck.* Why was her body betraying her like this? She didn't want him. Her heart wasn't on board, anyway, but it seemed like her vagina might have other ideas.

He pressed the erection trapped inside his plaid pants into her belly. *Nope, this is so not going to happen.* Her lungs ready to explode, gasping for air, Breanna turned her head to break off the kiss.

"I'm of a mind to fuck you here and now, but I'm not going to," Derek rasped, easing himself off her. "Because I am a gentleman, unlike some. You'd do well to remember that."

"What are you talking about?" She panted.

"Most men look at a girl like you with one thing in mind—fucking."

"But not you?"

"No."

Could've fooled me.

"It takes a while for some of us to quit thinking with just our dicks—usually after college, Ian being the exception, it seems. The guy is thirty and getting laid is still the only thing he's after." With a soft chuckle, his arms went around her. "But see, Breanna, I want more than that."

"Yeah?"

"Yes." Raising her chin, Derek touched his lips to the bump on her head. "I hate that I have to go, but I'll be back as soon as I can. In the meantime, Francie and Ted will see to anything you need." He took a step back. "I'll email you in the morning. My cousin will be here, should you have questions."

Sinjin's your cousin? The fuck?

After Derek left, hoping to shake off her headache, Breanna took some ibuprofen and got into bed. Why couldn't she have fallen for him instead? At least he wasn't a big, fat liar like Sinjin. "To hell with him."

Unable to sleep, she padded into the living room and flipped a light on. Wrapping herself in a furry throw, Breanna plopped down on the sofa, intent on watching a movie. Anything to get her mind off the crazy shit going on here.

Reaching for the remote, she glanced at the snow falling on the other side of the glass. And that's when she spotted him. Sinjin sat out on the deck—*her* deck, goddammit—a bottle hanging from his fingers, in front of the fire.

"You sonofabitch."

"Don't say that about my mother, princess." He turned around and looked up at her, the corner of his mouth quirking up in that irresistible way it always did. "She likes you."

Breanna wanted to smack that smirk right off his face. "You left me."

"I didn't leave you." His gaze returning to the fire, Sinjin lifted the bottle to his lips. "Sent Jordy to get you. Watched you get into his truck."

"*You* are a liar."

"I haven't lied to you, Breanna. Not once."

"Yeah, right, *Sinjin*." She snatched the bourbon out of his hand. "Oh, wait, it's Ian now, isn't it? Or is that a lie, too?"

"Neither one is a lie. It's the name my mama gave me, princess. Ask her if you don't believe me."

"I don't."

"My mother's maiden name is St. John." He stood, and grabbing her by the wrist, pried the bottle from her fingers. "That's Sinjin in Old English."

"Oh."

"Anything else?"

Where do I even begin?

"Keeping things from me is still lying," Breanna reasoned. "And why are you here?"

"I live here, princess—most of the time, anyway." There was that damn smirk again. "And maybe you didn't ask the right questions."

Sounds like something a lawyer would say.

"I knew that." Meeting his whiskey gaze, she adjusted the furry blanket slipping from her shoulder. "I meant here outside my room."

Sinjin hitched his thumb to the left.

Her jaw dropped. "Your room is next to mine?"

His brows waggled. "Isn't that convenient?"

Maybe that's what you think, asshole, but I don't.

"Fuck you!"

"There she is." Throwing his arm around her, Sinjin held her to his chest. "Mmm, say it again, baby. You know it gets my dick hard."

"I don't want anything to do with you, Ian," she said, wriggling in his hold.

That's a lie.

"Sinjin. And I don't think you mean that," he crooned, his hand slipping under the blanket.

Fingertips skated over her bare midriff, beneath the bralette of fine Merino wool, to palm her breast. He wasn't gentle pinching her nipple, but then he rarely was. Breanna whimpered, Sinjin groaning at the sound. Funny, isn't it? As much as she loathed Derek's touch, she craved more of his.

He reached inside the drawstring waistband, hand skimming down her belly, the blanket fell to the floor. His fingers swept between her lips. Beyond the covered deck, snow continued to fall, and even though she shivered, she couldn't feel the cold.

"Feel how wet you are for me, princess?"

"No." Breanna shook her head, but fuck, she felt it. "Please. Don't do this to me."

"Do what?"

Then his mouth was on hers. He kissed her, the taste of bourbon on his tongue, citrus, and honey, and grain, reminding her of their time together in the little cabin. And right then, she knew.

No other kiss would feel as perfect as this one.

No other touch.

No other man.

Her thighs parted all on their own. Sinjin pushed two fingers up inside and, with his thumb pressing into her clit, he fucked her without mercy. *More.* It was his beautiful cock she longed for, but as if he knew what she needed, he shoved another finger in, filling her with three. Breanna sank into his chest, jagged lightning erupting from the place deep inside her that only he could reach.

That. Don't do that. God, I'm fucked.

"This pretty little pussy is mine. *You* are mine." Pulling on her bottom lip with his teeth, he took his fingers out of her pussy.

"I don't belong to anyone." *Liar, liar, liar.* "You have no claim on me."

"I claimed you the moment I saw you, princess." His head tipped to the side, he grinned, licking up her cum from his fingers.

"You're drunk."

"Maybe. Heh, probably." Leaning in, Sinjin traced her lips with his thumb. "Doesn't change the fact. Every part of you, from the hair on your pretty head, all the way down to your polished toes, is mine."

She pushed his hand off her mouth.

"I filled you up with my cum, Breanna, and I do *not* share. My baby could very well be in your belly, so you best let Derek know to keep his filthy, fucking hands off of you."

"It's not like that." *As far as I'm concerned, anyway.* "He's been nothing but kind to me."

"I warned you to be careful, didn't I?" Sinjin's hand went to her throat, fingers stroking the tender skin.

Nodding, she swallowed.

"Because, baby, you have no idea what my cousin's capable of."

Chapter Sixteen

The sun wasn't shining, but at least it stopped snowing. If six inches was considered a dusting, Ted was right, but when she surveyed the scenery outside, it looked like more than a dusting to her. Sipping on her coffee, Breanna glanced across the deck patio to Sinjin's room next door. Was he awake yet? *Doubtful.* Especially considering the amount of bourbon he'd consumed the day before. And that had to account for all the nonsense that came out of his mouth last night, too.

Maybe Breanna hadn't always been the best judge of people, but as far as she could tell, Derek wasn't someone to be all that concerned about. So why the cryptic warning? Yeah, he'd been a little bit handsy, and a whole lot flirty, but she was a big girl—she could take care of herself. There was no need for Sinjin to go all caveman on her.

He's jealous. That's what it is.

Sure seemed so, anyway. Not that Sinjin had a right to be, despite his insistence she was his. Was she? *I wish.* It was just sex. So what if it was the mind-blowing kind Breanna only saw in movies or read in romance novels, right? Surely, it meant nothing.

Besides, he was drunk. Sinjin probably wouldn't remember a word of what he said when he woke up this morning. And even if he did, he still had a helluva lot of explaining to do.

Dressed in the only clean outfit she had left, Breanna took her coffee cup and her duffel bag of dirty clothes downstairs to the laundry room. "What in the hell kind of fancy-schmancy washing machine is this?"

The control panel had more buttons than the cockpit of an airplane, for chrissakes. Two doors. Breanna wasn't sure if she should load the laundry on top or in the front until she realized the machine could wash two separate loads at the same time.

Isn't that convenient? She giggled to herself. *Get out of my head, Sinjin. Ian. Whatever your name is.*

Francie stood flipping pancakes at the stove as Breanna made her way into the kitchen for a refill. "Good morning, dear. How's the headache?"

"Good morning," she said, heading toward the coffeemaker. "Couple of Motrin and a good night's sleep…" *That I never got.* "…I'm totally fine."

"Hmm." Francie peeked over her shoulder like she didn't quite believe her. "There's fresh coffee and breakfast in the morning room."

"After all that cooking you did yesterday?" Breanna hugged the woman. "You shouldn't have, but thank you."

"It's what I do." With a nod, she placed a platter of pancakes in her hands. "And I enjoy doing it. Go on and eat, now."

Yes, ma'am. You don't have to tell me twice.

After picking at her food yesterday, too flustered to eat, her angry belly was screaming to be fed.

Chair pushed back, one leg casually crossed over the other, his ankle resting on his thigh, he sat at the table reading something on his phone, a coffee mug poised at those luscious lips. For a brief moment, Breanna saw the bold stranger she met at Hank's, the man she shared a bed with during the storm. Dressed in a gray crewneck sweater that molded to his muscled body and a smart-looking pair of matching slacks, it was difficult to imagine Ian Maynard ever wearing faded jeans and plaid flannel.

"And she's awake," he murmured without glancing up from his phone. "Five more minutes and I was going back to get you."

"What are you doing here?"

"Told you, princess," he answered with a throaty chuckle and took a sip of his coffee. "I live here."

"I didn't think you'd be up already is what I meant." Putting the platter on the table, she took a seat. "Francie made pancakes."

"Better than oatmeal, eh?" He winked at her, spearing some onto his plate. "There's scrambled eggs and bacon, too. Dig in."

She did.

Eating in silence, Sinjin sent messages on his phone in between bites of bacon. Then he scrolled and tapped away some more, as if she weren't sitting there right across the table from him.

Rude. Especially considering he had his fingers in her lady bits not eight hours ago.

"Breanna." Francie entered the room carrying an extremely large box. "A package came for you, honey."

"I got it, Auntie." Sinjin jumped up, taking it from her as he kissed her cheek. "Thanks for making me pancakes."

"Of course, dear." Glancing at Breanna, she kissed him back. "You two should go outside today. Play in the snow, and show her the mountain. Get some fresh air while the weather's still good."

"You heard Miss Dalton." He appeared uninterested. "She prefers the beach."

Pretending not to care, Breanna cut into her pancake.

Sinjin snickered under his breath.

And with a shake of her salt-and-pepper bob, Francie went out the door.

Wait a gosh darn minute… "Francie's your aunt?"

"She's my mother's younger sister," he answered, going back to his phone. "What's in the box?"

None of your fucking business. "Stuff."

A boom crashed from outside. It sounded like an avalanche. Not that she'd ever heard one before. "What the hell was that?"

"Snow."

"But it's not snowing." Confused by his answer, Breanna cocked her head, her brows pulling together.

"From the roof," he explained. "It's copper—standing metal. That way, the snow slides off."

"Oh, I see." *Not really.*

"Now, what's in the box?"

"Nothing that concerns you."

"When it comes to you, princess…" Taking her package, Sinjin strolled toward the door. "…everything concerns me."

"Hey, that's mine," she called out, chasing after him up the stairs. "Stop being a dick."

Ignoring her, he punched the code into her door and went inside.

Asshole.

Sinjin stood in the middle of her living room, balancing the package on his shoulder. "You want it? Come get it."

"Give me." Breanna swatted at the box, her efforts fruitless.

Amused, he swiped his tongue across his lip and grinned. "So, I'm a dick, huh?"

"Yup, sure are."

"Yeah, well, you would know." Tossing the box to the sofa, his arm curled around her waist, and dragging her to his chest, he slammed his mouth into hers.

Shivers—the good kind—tickled their way up her spine. Pancakes and coffee and warm maple syrup. With just one taste of his wicked skillful tongue, Breanna forgot she was mad at him. Fingers threaded in her hair, Sinjin held her lips to his, cradling her head in his hands. Consuming and possessive, the intensity of his kiss addled her brain. She couldn't think, and with all reason gone, she gave in.

Hands skimmed down her back, his electrifying touch leaving a trail of tingles on her skin. Softly groaning, he sucked at her bottom lip, pulling it with his teeth, while pressing his hardness against her belly.

Yesss. A whimper of sound escaped her.

Would he fuck her now? Tear the clothes from her body and consumed with want, lay her down right here on the floor? *God, please.* Because she was dying. Breanna couldn't breathe, and she ached, her need for this man burning her alive.

But he didn't.

With a brush of his lips, Sinjin pulled away. Whiskey eyes gazing into hers, he combed his fingers through her hair.

Breanna shook her head and sighed. Rubbing her lips together, she went to the sofa, her fingertips tracing the mailing label on Kayleigh's package.

Sinjin planted his hands on her shoulders. "What's in the box?"

"I told you." She shrugged him off. "Stuff."

"What exactly?"

"Books and ballgowns." With a snicker, Breanna whipped around and let him have it. "Clothes, all right? I left Portland thinking I was finally going to meet my grandmother, and instead, I met you. Wrecked my car on this godforsaken mountain, only to find out she's dead and I'm stuck here with *you* for three fucking miserable weeks."

He looked at her like she'd gone and lost her mind.

"I only packed for a weekend."

"You seem…angry," Sinjin said, tucking a loose strand of hair behind her ear. "Who sent it?"

"Kayleigh, my roommate."

Nodding, he asked, "Have you spoken to your mom? Does anyone else know where you are?"

Her eyes flicked up. What an odd question. And what difference did it make?

"I texted her yesterday to wish her a happy Thanksgiving. She assumed I was having dinner with Kayleigh's family…and I…I let her think it. She doesn't have a clue that I'm here. No one does. Why?"

Sinjin sat on the sofa, pulling her with him to sit on his lap. Framing her face in his hands, he kissed her forehead. "We're going to have to let her know you're here, and that you're safe."

"We?"

"Yes, we. I'll speak to her—as your attorney. Put her mind at ease." Fingertips trailed up and down her spine. "What about school?"

"What about it?"

He smirked. "Well, princess, you won't be sitting in class come Monday."

"Yes, I will," Breanna smugly replied. "I've got my Mac with me."

"Isn't that convenient?"

Of course, he'd say that. And what was up with all these questions?

"Why do you ask?"

Sinjin shrugged, but his grin was deliberate. "Your car might be fixed in a few weeks, but that doesn't mean you'll be leaving Dalton House."

"And why not?"

"We could have ten feet of snow by then, sweetheart. Maybe more." His hand slipped beneath her sweater, fingers strumming her skin. "Imagine it, being stuck here with *me* the entire fucking miserable winter."

Fuck. Just the thought. But even if Breanna wanted to, she couldn't.

"No."

"No? You wouldn't like that?" He squeezed her breast. "I'd like that."

"I don't get it." She swatted at his hand. "First, Jordy has me half-convinced I dreamt you up, and then you come strolling in, acting like you've never seen me before. But as soon as no one's around, you're on me like flies on shit. Like, what the fuck?"

Raising his brow, Sinjin didn't utter a word.

"You knew who I was and what I was coming for all along, didn't you?" *God, I'm so stupid.* "Don't answer that. Of course, you did. You summoned me here."

"It was Derek who did that."

"Your cousin." Breanna scrambled off his lap. "And Francie's your aunt. Are you all fucking related? I find it really strange no one thought to mention it."

"Did you sign anything?" Dragging her back, Sinjin sat her on his lap so she straddled him.

"What?" she panted.

Face to face, eyes level, whiskey bored into blue. "Derek told me he went through the documents with you, and that you had questions." Stroking her hair, he implored, "I need to know. It's important. Did you sign any of them?"

"No." Breanna shook her head emphatically. "And I won't until I see the will and know what it is I'm signing. He's supposed to email the documents today."

"Good," he said, the tension draining from his face.

"What's going on here, Sinjin?"

"Listen to me." His tone brooking no argument, Sinjin

tugged on her hair, fisting it in his hand. "For now, it's best Derek and Francie believe we never met before yesterday. Jordy, Hank, and my mother know differently, of course, but I know they can be trusted."

"With what?"

He opened his mouth, then closed it, his eyes shifting from side to side. "Aunt Francie is a people-pleaser, a doer. She likes to make people happy. Not that it's an altogether negative trait, but it makes her easy to manipulate, so I'm on the fence with her. Ted, too."

"What the fuck are you talking about?" Exasperated, Breanna shouted, shaking him by the shoulders.

"Protecting you." His knuckles grazed her cheek. "Making sure you're safe."

She didn't understand. "From what?"

"I can't tell you." He looked down to where Breanna sat on his lap.

She raised his chin with her finger. "Why not?"

"Because I'm not sure I can trust you yet, either."

Chapter Seventeen

He probably shouldn't have said it like that.

It's not that Ian didn't trust *her*, per se, more so how she'd react once she learned the whole truth. Breanna was fiery—her heart ruled her head, and while he loved that about her, he needed her to play it cool. He feared that could be a tall order. What if she went running to Derek and fell right into his trap?

No way was he going to let that happen.

I should've stopped him before it ever got this far.

He should have. But back then, Ian didn't give a fuck. He was so angry for Valerie, even though in life the woman rarely was. Breanna had to be a heartless, spoiled brat who only cared about her grandmother's money. She'd already gotten way more than she deserved—at least, he thought so at the time.

And I was wrong.

Even if he hadn't been, what his cousin was trying to pull wasn't right. While he took no part in it, and would take no gain from it, wasn't he just as culpable for looking the other way? *I am, dammit.* What he needed to do was set things right—thwart Derek's underhanded scheme, and somehow, hold on to Breanna.

Hera looked up at him, her tail thumping on the wood floor. "You want out, do you?"

The pup responded with a bark that he took as a 'yes', and putting his iPad aside, Ian got up from the couch. As he opened the door, he glanced across the deck. Breanna sat in her living room with her laptop, gazing intently at the screen. "Go on, girl."

She looked up then.

He tipped his chin and went to slide the door closed when she motioned for him to come over.

She'd left her door unlocked. With the cold glass at his back, he casually leaned against it, folding his arms across his chest.

"Can you explain to me what it is I'm looking at?"

"Let's see what you've got there." Ian crossed the room, and sitting down beside her on the sofa, Breanna placed her laptop in his hands. Derek must've emailed her the documents. She had at least eight tabs open on the screen.

Holding in a snicker, he gave his head a shake. "Can you make us some coffee? This could take a while."

"Yeah." She got up and popped in a pod to brew, glancing back over her shoulder. "It would make it a helluva lot easier for us non-lawyer people if it was written in English."

"This *is* English," he said, not bothering to hold the snicker in this time. "Well, mostly."

Breanna set down a mug on the coffee table in front of him, then opened the door for Hera. "You've got snow stuck to your paws. Poor baby, you must be freezing."

"She's a Husky, Breanna."

"And?" She disappeared into her bedroom, returning with a towel.

While maybe he should've taken the opportunity to do a quick scan of the documents his cousin sent, he didn't. Ignoring the screen on his lap, Ian watched her, almost spellbound, as Breanna sat on the floor wiping snow from the dog's coat in front of the fire. Flames reflecting in her shining blue eyes, the sleeve of her oversized top slipped down her shoulder, giving him a perfect glimpse of the rose-tipped breast he once possessed.

I want back in, princess.

He swallowed, and peels of musical laughter rang out, making him blink. Licking her face, his dog rewarded Breanna for her efforts. With her arms wrapped tight around Hera's neck, she hugged the pup, stroking her damp fur.

Ian cleared his throat.

Glancing over at him, she stood. "Give me a sec, will you? I'm coming."

Oh, I'll be making sure of that. He snorted to himself.

"What's so funny?" she asked, taking a seat beside him with a cup of her own.

"Nothing."

"Yeah, okay." With a roll of her eyes, Breanna took a sip. "Start explaining then, so I can sign the papers and be done with it."

"This is a document petitioning the court for a Letter of Testamentary."

"What's that?" She leaned in a little closer to look at the screen.

"It gives you, as the Executor, the legal authority needed to handle all financial and formal duties necessary to close out your grandmother's estate."

"Say that again in English, please."

"It's a formality that allows you to access Valerie's accounts, so you can pay off any debts and taxes. Distribute assets. Virtually everything," he explained. "The petition gets filed with your grandmother's Will and death certificate, along with documents verifying your identity. Once the court reviews everything, the letter will be issued and you can move forward."

Breanna rubbed her lips together and nodded. "I think I understand."

"Of course, anything held in Trust is exempt from all this. It's already yours."

"I'm a trust fund baby and I didn't even know it." Setting her cup down on the table, she sighed. "Derek told me my father had one set up for me."

Valerie had done the same. Ian was almost sure of it. They shouldn't be in this mess.

"This is an accounting of the estate assets as of the date of her death—Dalton House, the land, other properties, stocks, bank accounts—things like that. And debts, such as taxes. A listing of assets to be distributed under the terms of the Will…"

"What is Dalton Trust Development Opco LLC?" She pointed to the line in the document.

Christ, Derek. You're more cunning than I gave you credit for. "That would be who."

"Well, it says Dalton House, and the mountain it's sitting on, it looks like, goes to them. You just said anything in Trust is exempt, so I'm confused."

"Don't let the name fool you," Ian said, fingers gripping into her thigh. "That's not a Trust. It's a corporation—an operating company."

"Who are they?"

"We'll have to find out." But then, he figured he already knew. A dummy corporation for Derek to hide behind, no doubt, named in such a way so Breanna wouldn't question it. Hell, he'd probably try to convince her *she* was Dalton Trust Development.

Her brows pulling together, Breanna angled her head to look up at him. "You're my grandmother's attorney. You don't know?"

"Listen up, princess—"

"Breanna," she insisted, almost sounding angry. "Why do you keep calling me that?"

Because that's who you are to me, baby.

"Listen," Ian said, softening his voice. *I need you to put the pieces together yourself.* "Valerie would've planned her estate a long, long time ago—likely soon after your grandfather died, and I wasn't old enough to grow a beard yet, then. My uncle, Raymond, would've been the one to draw up her Will."

"Derek's father, right?"

"Yes."

She opened another tab on the screen. "Well, there it is. A trust fund for me with the rest of the estate going to Dalton Trust Development Opco LLC, which is more than generous when you consider she never even wanted to meet me."

"This isn't right." A cursory glance was all it took, not that Breanna would know it. Dated just last year, Raymond St. John and Francesca Keeler witnessed Valerie's signature.

"That's what it says." She took his hand, rubbing her fingers over the back of it. "It's okay, Sinjin. A million dollars is a heck of a lot of money."

"A million ain't shit, baby." Not to Valerie, anyway. "This house alone is worth at least twenty times that amount."

Letting his hand go, Breanna shrugged. "It's a house. Okay, so it's a massive house, and it's beautiful, but I didn't grow up here, my father did. I have no ties to it."

"You're a Dalton, and this house is *your* legacy. Valerie would have never let it go to anyone else." Turning her chin toward the screen, he pointed. "Look at the date."

"Yeah, so?"

Here we go. "The document's been altered."

"How do you know?"

"That's Raymond's signature all right, but my uncle keeled over from a heart attack three years ago."

"What the fuck is going on here, Sinjin?"

"You want answers?" Taking Breanna by the hand, he led her down the hallway. "You're going to have to trust me."

"You don't trust me." She stopped dead in her tracks. "Why should I trust you?"

"You shouldn't." His thumb brushed across her cheek, and he smirked. "But listen to your gut. It won't lie."

At the landing, Breanna followed him up to the third floor. She held onto his arm, her fingers digging into the muscle, as he fit a key into the lock of the double door that guarded it. "What's up here?"

"Your grandmother's name was Kimball before she married Lawrence Dalton," Ian informed her, opening the door to a long hallway, half the length of the house. "Does it ring a bell?"

"No. Should it?"

"As in the hotel chain." He shrugged. "Maybe you're too young to remember—Kimball sold off all their properties by the early 2000s. Think Hilton or Marriott or Hyatt. See, Valerie came from money, she didn't marry into it, and once, she had plans to turn Dalton House into a bed-and-breakfast—a mountain retreat, of sorts, that never came to be. Anyway, the family's private apartments are here on this floor."

"So, the second floor…"

"Was supposed to be for guests," Ian said, nodding. "She wanted to add cottages, too, after your grandfather had the hunting cabins built."

"Why didn't she?"

"Shane died." With an exhale, he gnawed at his lip. "And everything changed after that."

For all of us.

He punched the code into the keypad. "These are her rooms."

"We shouldn't be up here," she whispered with a shake of her pretty head.

"If we want to find answers, Breanna…" Taking her hand, Ian laced their fingers together and squeezed. "…this is where we start looking."

Her eyes swept around the room and she gasped. He didn't have to follow her gaze to know what she was looking at.

Breanna went over to the mantel and picked up the photo of herself that rested there. "How did my grandmother get this?"

"She never told me. Your mom must've sent it to her, I guess." He walked up behind her. "Sometimes I'd come in here and find her holding that picture of you, crying."

And I hated you for it.

"I don't understand." Her fingers trembling, Breanna put the photo back and turned around. "Why?"

"You really want to know? I can show you." Grabbing her by the hand, Ian took her to the other end of the hall and unlocked the door. "Your father's apartment."

She took an apprehensive step inside and upon seeing the photo of her mom, and the dad she never knew, holding her as a newborn, she held her fingers to her lips, a tear trickling down her face. "I've never seen this picture before."

"Everything is just as Shane left it. His room is through there." Ian tipped his chin to the door on the left. "But I want you to see this one. Open it."

Glancing back at him, Breanna turned the doorknob.

The room, fit for a little princess, was done in a soft, pale pink, a hand-painted garden of flowers covering the walls. The ornate white crib with soft muslin bedding had never been slept in. The rocking horse hadn't been ridden. The dollhouse remained untouched.

Breanna picked up a plush pink teddy bear, holding it to her chest.

"She did all of this for you." Softly, Ian swiped at the tears falling from her eyes. "See? Your grandmother loved you, Breanna…but you never came home."

And even now, he had to ask himself why.

Chapter Eighteen

Ian paced the living room, waiting for signs of life from Breanna's suite next door. Well past nine, and it didn't appear she was awake yet. Subdued throughout their dinner of Thanksgiving leftovers last night, she excused herself during dessert, pushing aside a half-eaten piece of banana cream pie.

Maybe he should have gone after her, but thought it best to let her be. He'd laid a lot on her yesterday. Breanna needed some time to herself to sort through it, process it, and come to her own conclusions.

From her spot by the hearth, Hera lifted her head. Ears pointed up, tail thumping, ice-blue eyes tracked his path back and forth. She barked at him, though it sounded more as if she were speaking without words.

"Time to wake up our princess. Is that what you're thinking, girl?"

Her pink tongue hanging out, the dog got up on all fours.

"Yeah, I am too." With a pat on his thigh, Ian signaled Hera to follow him. "Let's go."

She'd left the glass door to the deck unlocked again. *Tsk, tsk.* He made a mental note to speak to her about it. Breanna shouldn't be so careless with her safety.

Dying embers littered the firebox. Ian added some wood and lit the kindling, so the room would be warm, a fire burning, when he woke her. Then he made them some coffee, got water from the mini-fridge, and quietly slipped inside her room.

He set the coffee down on the nightstand and watched

her sleep, all alone in the middle of the king-size bed. Hair a mess. Arms stretched over her head, elbows bent. With the covers jumbled at her waist, Ian fixed his gaze on the gentle rise and fall of Breanna's chest and the taut, little breast that peeked out from the loose nightshirt she wore.

Jesus.

She looked so beautiful like that. Reminded of the first morning he woke up beside her, Ian was of the mind to crawl into that bed and rouse her with his cock in her cunt and that nipple between his teeth. His dick more than twitched at the thought.

He eased himself down onto the bed, carefully, so as not to wake her just yet. The sweet scent of fresh oranges drifted from her hair. He buried his face in it. Ian inhaled, infusing his lungs with her, and slowly, softly, he trailed his fingertips over the delicate, silky fabric. He cupped her breast, her warm breath fanning his ear, his thumb circling her nipple.

With a puff of air blowing past her lips, Breanna squeaked.

"Wake up now, princess."

She moved. Soft hands settling on his back, her sleepy voice whispered, "Sinjin?"

"Good morning."

Dark lashes fluttered. Fingertips grazing his cheek, Breanna looked at him with those fairytale eyes. "Good morning."

"Here." Reaching for the cup on the nightstand, Ian offered it to her and winked. "I made you coffee. Cream, no sugar. Just the way you like it."

"Thanks." Sitting back against the headboard with a yawn, she took it from him. "Is this a cousin thing?"

Huh? His brows cinching together, he cocked his head.

"Showing up in a girl's room uninvited."

"*You* left the door to the deck unlocked," he said with a shrug of his shoulders.

"Oh, my bad." She made a face, lifting the cup to her lips. "I didn't realize an unlocked door meant an open invitation."

"For some people, it does." Ian smirked, twisting her hair around his finger. "Unsavory characters…"

"Like you?"

"Exactly." He watched the silken strand unravel. "I hope you're not this reckless at school…and what do you mean, cousin thing?"

"Derek has a habit of sneaking in here, too."

The no-good sonofabitch.

Anger surged. His cousin's threats weren't empty then. He meant what he said. If Breanna didn't sign Derek's phony documents, and Ian would make sure she didn't, he'd get what he was after some other way.

Fisting the hair in his fingers, Ian brought her face closer to his. "Keep the fucking doors locked, Breanna."

"Yeah, okay," she said, snickering. "Except he knows the key code."

"I can change it," he gritted.

Blue eyes searching his, Breanna nodded. "All right."

"I don't want you alone with him. Ever." Loosening his grip, Ian's lips brushed over hers. "Am I clear?"

"Perfectly."

"Good girl." He let her go. "Now, I want you to take a shower and get dressed. I hope your roommate sent you something warmer than your leather jacket because we're going out after breakfast."

"We are? Where?" Setting her coffee down, Breanna didn't sound very thrilled with the idea. "I wanted to go back upstairs and…"

"Later." Ian captured her lips between his. "There's something I want you to see first."

She came down the stairs, floating like a cloud in a white puffer jacket, pulling a beanie on top of her head. Good thing he still had his wits about him, because if he didn't, he'd have taken her right back up those stairs and into his bed. That would come later, too, but right now, Ian needed her to realize just what Derek was trying to take from her.

Extending his hand as she neared the bottom, Breanna took it.

"Are you taking my advice, dear?" Francie asked, coming down the hall.

"Yes, Auntie." He laced their fingers together to stop himself from kissing her.

"It's lovely outside today," Francie said, giving each of them a hug. "So make good use of it. Last I heard, that storm may hit sooner than expected—as early as tomorrow."

Fine by him. It would buy them some time, and with any luck at all, Derek would keep his sorry ass in Sacramento.

Ian opened the front door, and taking Breanna by the hand, led her down the walkway, past the portico, to the service garage. He entered the code, and the panels lifted, her stunned gaze sweeping over an array of ATVs, snowplows, and power shovels.

She ignored his Mercedes-AMG GT, walking right over to the Raptor parked next to it. "I remember you." Running her fingers along the glossy black paint, Breanna glanced back at him. "Okay, let's go."

"We're not taking the truck." With a grin, he nodded toward the waiting Polaris. "Hop on, princess."

"I am so *not* getting on that thing," she said, her head tossing from side to side.

"Yes, you are." Ian lifted her onto the sled's passenger seat. "How else am I supposed to show you your mountain?"

"I've seen enough of it, thank you." Putting her gloves on, Breanna blew out a breath. "Besides, it isn't mine."

"Yes, it is." He sat down on the sled in front of her, placing her arms around his waist. "And, baby, you ain't seen nothin' yet."

It took but a moment for the rush of adrenalin to hit her. Taking a drink of brilliant sunshine, surrounded by the bluest winter sky and the purest white snow, Breanna held onto him tight, the sound of swooshing wind accompanying her gleeful laughter.

Ian took her up past the edge of the tree line. Stopping there, he sat her on his lap and pointed. "See that shimmer way out there on the horizon?"

"Yes, I see it."

"That's Tahoe." Watching her face, he rubbed her gloved hand with his.

She smiled. "We went there the summer my brother turned two."

So close. Why didn't her mom bring her to see Valerie?

Breanna would have been thirteen then, and Ian, twenty-two. He'd spent so many of his days—and wild nights with women he could no longer remember—at Tahoe that summer before law school. He could've walked right past his princess, not that he'd have noticed her then.

"You've got a lake here too." *Kind of.* "There's a waterfall that empties into a large pool, then makes its way down the mountain. We swam there as kids. I know your dad did, too." He chuckled at the memory. "The water's always fucking freezing. We never did seem to mind, though. C'mon, I'll show you."

And he did.

Ian took her to see the bighorn sheep. Told her all about the mountain lions who preyed on them, the black bears that would slumber until the return of spring, while pointing out redwood, and cedar, and pine. He wanted Breanna to fall in love with this place. Needed her to. She'd fight for it then. If she didn't, Derek would surely win.

Powder flying, he followed the stream on his path down the mountain. Then, reaching his destination, he skidded to a stop. After switching off the engine, he removed his gloves and lifted her from the sled. "You're tied to that house, this land, whether or not you want to be. It's in your blood, baby." Warming her cold, windburned cheeks in his hands, he touched his lips to the fading bruise on her forehead. "That's our cabin."

"*Your castle in the storm, princess.*"

She turned around. Knee-deep in snow, thirty feet from the back of it, Breanna gazed at the small frosted window and smiled. "I want to go in."

His arms came around her, holding her back to his chest. Seven days. Why did it seem like a lifetime ago? Ian brought her here, fed her soup, and fucked her bare—except it felt like a lot more than just fucking. He made love to her, didn't he? And that was something he'd never done with anyone before.

Nope, and I told myself I never would, so, how'd you get me to do it, princess?

"We can." Ian gripped her nape, and bringing her mouth to his, he nipped at her lips. "But I have a much better idea."

"Yeah, and what's that?"

"I'll show you." He kissed her. "Let's go home."

Chapter Nineteen

They cleaned the snow off their boots at the front door. Taking Breanna by the hand, Ian gestured for her to be quiet and led her toward the stairs. But the dog possessed supersonic hearing, apparently, and before they could make the furtive climb, Hera came running over to greet them.

"Hey, sweetie." Of course, the traitor went to Breanna for a rub between the ears first. "Did you miss me?"

It would appear so.

"Ian?" Francie's voice rang out from somewhere in the house. It sounded like it was coming from the kitchen. "Are you two back?"

"Yes, Auntie."

"We've been waiting on you. Food is about ready."

Well, there goes that idea.

"C'mon," he said with a sigh, squeezing Breanna's hand before letting it go. "Looks like we're having lunch first."

Uncle Ted sat at the kitchen island, hunched over a bowl of soup, while his aunt commanded the stove. The woman missed out on her calling. She should've been a chef, opened her own restaurant, or something, because when she wasn't fussing in the kitchen, Francie didn't know what to do with herself.

"Sit yourselves down right here," she said, not bothering to turn around. "Thought you'd like something to warm your insides, so I made fresh tomato soup."

"And grilled cheese sandwiches to go with it?"

"You know me better than that, dear."

He sure did.

Francie spread mayonnaise on thick slices of brioche bread she no doubt baked herself, topping them with paper-thin slices of ham and mounds of shredded mozzarella. After dipping the sandwiches in an egg batter, she fried them in butter. Real comfort food. Ian fondly remembered coming into the house to find those sandwiches waiting for him as a kid, after long hours spent outdoors building snow forts with Derek.

"Oh, wow." Topped with a swirl of heavy cream and fresh basil, Breanna inhaled the steaming bowl Francie put in front of her. "You even make tomato soup fancy."

"It sure ain't Campbell's," Ted said. Wiping his mouth on the back of his hand, he glanced over at his wife. "If you want to make it down to the village and back before dark, you best get to it, Francie."

"Last two. I made extras for my boys." She chuckled, sliding the sandwiches onto a plate. "I know how you like to gobble them up. Ian, honey, do you think you and Breanna can manage dinner on your own?"

"I'm sure we can rustle up something."

"Okay, good. I have a big grocery order to pick up and your uncle wants to stop by the hardware store." Passing a grilled cheese to Breanna, she explained, "We have to make sure we're all stocked up before the storm hits."

"We've got enough foodstuffs and toilet paper to last until May," Ted said with a chuckle. "But you know your aunt."

"After last season, I'm not willing to take any chances." Making herself a plate, Francie finally sat down. "Three months solid we were snowed in here with the pass closed. Thought we'd never see the end of it. We still had patches of snow on the ground come Fourth of July."

"That was a once-in-a-decade fluke." Ted reached for a

second sandwich. "Atmospheric rivers brought us twice the amount of precipitation we typically get."

"What's that?" Breanna asked Ted.

And his uncle's face lit up.

"Picture a river in the sky, stretching far across the Pacific. Strong winds carry moisture from someplace warm—like Hawaii—then that moisture gets dumped on us as heavy rain and snow. Lasts for days and days. We get hit with one, oh, four or five times a season. Last year seemed like it was one after the other."

"That doesn't sound good." Giving her head a little shake, Breanna pursed her lips.

Smirking, Ian discreetly squeezed her thigh and winked. "They're not so bad as long as you're ready for it."

"Where do you think the West Coast gets its water from, young lady?" Wiping his mouth with a napkin this time, Ted swallowed the last bite of his grilled cheese sandwich. "The snow melts in the spring, replenishing the lakes and rivers here."

"How much snow are we going to get this time?" Breanna wanted to know.

"They're predicting two to four feet over forty-eight hours, much the same as the storm you got caught in. And that's pretty common." Ted rose from his chair and turned toward him. "If we get more than that, be prepared to help me with the roof, Ian."

"Don't I always?"

"That you do." Bobbing his head, he went over to his wife. "We need to get going, Mrs. Keeler."

"All right, all right, Mr. Keeler." Francie got up, and her husband playfully swatted her bottom. "Just let me clean up."

"I can do it, Francie," Breanna offered with a smile. "Go on."

"You sure?"

"I'm sure." She nodded as she stood. "I might not be much of a cook, but I've had plenty of practice doing dishes."

"You're such a dear—thank you." Looking on as Breanna went about her task, Francie leaned into his ear, her anxious voice low, "Derek called while you were out."

"What'd he want?"

"She's a lot like her daddy." Glancing at Breanna, she shook her head. "I don't care how you do it, but you keep your cousin away from her."

Before he could even close the door, Breanna brought his mouth down to hers and kissed him. Hera jumping at their feet, she held his face in her hands and slipped her sweet tongue inside.

That's how she does it.

Addicted to her taste, he slipped his hands beneath her sweater. Ian squeezed her little tits, capturing the nipples between his fingers.

She whimpered, a sound he loved when it came from her. His dick wasn't just twitching. Hard and heavy and throbbing in his pants, he was ready to fuck. And, oh, how he wanted to. Needed to. God, she made him crazy. Primitive. Feral.

At this rate, they'd never make it to the bed.

"Your turn."

"My turn?" Breanna glanced up at him, her head tipped slightly to the side.

He let his fingers slip through her hair. "Show me."

"What?"

"You," Ian answered, lifting the sweater over her head. He removed her bra to gaze upon those luscious tits. "All of you."

"But you've seen me." Her gaze never leaving him, she

unzipped her pants and pushed them down her thighs. "You kept me naked for three days."

"Not like this."

Not with the bright winter sun pouring in through the glass. He looked his fill, taking in every dimple, angle, and curve. This girl, his princess with the fairytale eyes, was beautiful.

Standing in front of him, naked, vulnerable, and unashamed, Breanna watched as he stripped off his clothes.

Ian reached for her, fingertips caressing her breasts. "Love your big nipples. They're so perfect on these pretty little titties."

Her cheeks turning pink, she glanced down at her chest and shrugged. "Maybe they're still growing."

"Hope not." He kissed the tip of her nose. "I love them just as they are."

Toying with her nipples, his lips skated along the vein pulsing in her neck. Reaching her ear, Ian whispered, "Yeah, I think I'm going to fuck you right here."

He could feel the shiver go through her.

His hands swept down her sides. Sinking his fingers into her ass, Ian pressed her soft body to his aching dick. "Is that okay with you?"

Breanna answered with a kiss. "I've missed feeling you inside me."

Fuck, I've missed being there. Easing her down onto the fur rug, Ian hiked her leg high on his chest. "That's it," he praised, her arms coming around his neck. "Hold on to me."

Without looking, he grabbed a pillow from the couch and placed it beneath her head. He pinched her nipples, hard, both at the same time, twisting the pink, swollen buds in his fingers. Her nails scored down his back, and it stung. *Yeah, baby, make me bleed.* He wanted her marks on his skin, his blood on her sheets, and her cunt filled with his cum.

Ian deepened their kiss. Pulling on her nipples, he thrust

his tongue in, fucking her mouth with it, his aching dick grinding against her thigh. But then greedy, hungry for her, that ripe, delicious nipple was in his mouth.

"Sin…" Breanna sucked in a breath, pulling on his hair. "Please…put your fingers in me."

"You need that, don't you?" He thrust two into her sopping-wet hole. "Need to be fucked."

"God…yesss," Breanna moaned, spreading herself wider. "More…hard the way you always do…until I'm raw."

My princess and my dirty girl.

Made for him is what she was. Her appetite matched his own.

Ian added a third, wedging his fingers in as far as they could go. *So wet.* If Breanna wanted him to, he could work his fist inside her. "How's that feel, baby?"

"So good it hurts."

Fuck, yeah. Ian withdrew, only to plunge back inside her with four.

"I love…" Biting into her lip, she yelped.

Me? You better, because I think I might be in love with you, too.

"…this."

I'll make you love me, baby. You'll see. We're already halfway there.

Sinjin was right about one thing, he'd ruined her pussy for anyone else.

Breanna spread her legs as far apart as they would go. With four fingers fucking her, she wanted to open herself up for him as much as she could. Wet noises. His knuckles slammed against her pubic bone, smashing into her clit as he stretched her. It felt like his entire hand was in there.

Heavenly fucking torture.

She glanced down.

Not quite, but almost.

Perhaps someday she'd ask him to. Was she a freak to want such things? Maybe, but the way she felt right now, with every cell in her body firing, Breanna wanted this man to annihilate her.

Possess her.

Control her.

"Mm," he groaned. Fingers wedged inside her, Sinjin teasingly rubbed her clit with his thumb. "You like watching what I do to this pussy?"

She could only nod, her thighs shaking.

"Does my baby need to come?"

"Yes."

He pulled his fingers out and fed them to her. "Ask me to, princess."

"Please, Sin..." Greedily sucking her wetness from his fingers, Breanna touched herself. "...I want to come on your cock."

"And I want you to come all over my face." He flipped her on top of him and crooked his finger. "C'mere, baby. Feed me."

As much as his fingers were delicious torture, Sinjin's tongue inside her felt sublime. Breanna didn't know how he could breathe with her pussy smashed against his face. His fingers gripping her hips, he held her there, and, deeply groaning, he ate her alive. Slurping the juice out of her hole. Nibbling at her clit.

Breanna pulled on her nipples. "Oh, God."

His fingers probing her pussy and ass, Sinjin sucked on her clit, then he pushed them inside.

"Fuckkk." She came so hard.

He pulled her down to his chest. "Shall I?"

"Please."

His beard drenched in cum, Sinjin kissed her. "Ride this dick, baby, so I can fuck you."

Breanna held onto his hands and lowered herself onto that beautiful curved cock, watching it disappear inside her, inch by delicious inch until she was fully seated, her bare lips flush against the coarse hair at his groin. *Damn.* Tucking a loose strand behind her ear, Breanna grinned at the sight of it.

"Look, baby, I got all of you in me this time."

"I'm so proud of you, princess," he praised, slowly thrusting upward.

She was proud of herself, too.

"I knew you could take it." Groaning, he flicked at her swollen clit. "This dick was made to fuck this pussy."

"Ooooh, you feel so good." Breanna rode him, the head of his cock hitting a spot inside her that… "Fuck."

"I'm going to take this little virgin hole," Sinjin promised, sliding a finger into her ass. "You want me to fuck you here, don't you, baby?"

"I do." Breanna sucked the air in through her teeth. "So bad."

"I need you addicted to my dick."

Oh, God, I already am.

"Don't want anyone but you."

"Good girl." He made a fist, pressing it firmly into her belly, a handbreadth beneath her navel. "Because you're *my* princess and no one gets to touch you but me."

His finger fucked her ass and his cock fucked her pussy, while his fist touched something way down deep inside her.

"What are you doing to me?"

Collapsing on his chest, she exploded.

"Giving you what you asked for." And with a loud growl, he thrust once more. "You're coming on my cock."

Boneless on top of him, Breanna caught her breath, sweaty and naked on the faux-fur rug. "You didn't use a condom again."

"I didn't." Sinjin grinned, his fingers swirling in the cum dripping out of her. He cupped her pussy. "My babies are going to come out of here."

The fuck?

"You could already be pregnant." He seemed pleased with himself. "And if you aren't yet, you will be."

"You're crazy."

"Maybe." Smirking against her cheek, he kissed it. "But just the thought of putting a baby in you makes my dick hard."

"I don't want to have a baby," she said, rolling off of him.

Sinjin turned onto his side and gathered her to his chest. "No? Why not?"

"Because I'm only twenty-one, and there's a lot of things I want to do first." And that was the truth, not that she was altogether opposed to the idea. *Someday.* Breanna half-heartedly giggled. "Maybe when I'm thirty, you can put one in me, but not now."

"Fair enough," he said, fingering her hole. "We best get you on birth control then because I won't stop fucking you bare."

"Mm, yeah, okay." She moaned, succumbing to his fingers all over again.

"It's too late for that, anyway." Picking her up from the floor, Sinjin carried her into the bedroom. "I'm already there inside you."

Chapter Twenty

He slipped from her room in the early hours of the morning.

With a kiss to her brow, Sinjin tucked the blankets in around her, the scent of him lingering long after he'd gone. Lying awake in the still, heavy darkness, Breanna held his pillow to her chest. She should go back to sleep. Lord knows, after last night, she could use it.

Her well-used body thrumming in all the right places, Breanna's mind would not rest. Alone, pesky thoughts crept in to niggle at her brain. She tried to make sense of them, but she couldn't. It seemed as if everything she'd once surmised wasn't true at all.

An average middle-class upbringing, she saved up birthday and babysitting money and worked a part-time job for the down payment on her car. She studied hard to earn a scholarship so she could go to college, not knowing she had a gazillion dollars at her disposal.

But Mom knew all along, didn't she?

If her mother and grandmother managed the money her father left for her, they had to have kept in touch with each other, which explained her photograph in Valerie's room. Taken the summer before last on Venice Beach, Breanna had a strawberry ice cream cone in her hand. She made a dripping mess of that cone. A scorching hot day, the ice cream melted faster than she could eat it.

That Breanna never got to meet her grandmother no

longer made any sense, but then keeping memories of her dad from her didn't either.

Why, Mom?

And what else was Sarah Benjamin keeping from her?

Breanna started thinking about all the things she could've had, but didn't. Time. Painting flowers with her grandmother, building a snowman with her grandfather—how old had she been when he died? Maybe Francie would've taught her how to make something other than a bowl of cheap ramen noodles.

She could've known Sinjin, Derek, and all the St. Johns long before now. And that was weird to think of.

She could've known her family. And her dad through them.

She could've made her own memories in this house, on this mountain.

But her mom kept her away. Did she even know Valerie was dead? Or did she keep that from her, too?

And Sinjin? He wasn't telling her everything, either. Breanna felt it in her gut.

"Your gut won't lie."

Yeah, and hers was screaming.

Sinjin didn't come right out and say it, but then he didn't have to. She wasn't stupid. Despite her lack of fluency in legalese, it was quite clear. Derek was trying to get her to sign her family's legacy away. Don't attorneys take an oath or something? Because the falsification of documents was downright criminal.

There was a lot more going on here than she knew. Of that, Breanna was sure.

Secrets and lies.

The past could never be changed, but knowledge is power, right? As long as she was stuck here, she'd unearth every last one. And she knew exactly where to start.

Knowing sleep was futile, Breanna pushed the covers off and got out of bed. Still naked, she went over to the window, peering out into the predawn darkness. Beyond the mountain peaks, a moonless sky was just beginning to lighten, and the snow hadn't yet begun to fall.

She switched on the lights to the ensuite, the sudden brightness jarring. Standing before the full-length mirror, Breanna studied her reflection. She wasn't the girl she was before she came here. She didn't feel like the same girl either. It wasn't her swollen lips or her just-fucked hair that made her see herself differently.

Sinjin had irrefutably altered her perception of herself. In a good way. The best way. Unlike the rest of the world, he expected nothing of her, except to be her true self. And that was fucking life-changing.

After a long, luxurious shower and a fresh blowout, Breanna sat at the vanity crisscross applesauce, putting on her makeup. The bruising faded, the swelling above her eye was gone. She could conceal what remained easily, so at least she wouldn't resemble a hideous Gila monster.

With another storm coming today, she had no intentions of leaving this house. *Not like I could, anyway.* She snickered to herself. Her only plan was to go back up to the third floor and poke around a bit. Fill her belly with more of Francie's fancy food. Maybe later she'd curl up with a good book and watch the snow fall with Sinjin.

Thanks to Kayleigh and her Pinterest-worthy packing skills, she dressed herself in a loose, soft, surplice-wrap sweater, her favorite ripped-up jeans, and a cute pair of knit ankle booties. And by the time she made her way downstairs, the dark morning sky had turned into a shade of deep and dismal gray.

His cheeks reddened, wearing jeans and plaid flannel, Sinjin sat warming his hands on a mug of hot coffee when she came into the kitchen. Breanna couldn't help but smile at the sight of him looking like that.

Then, glancing up, he smiled back. "Good morning, princess. Thought you'd sleep 'til noon, considering I kept you up half the night."

"I think you've got that backward," she quipped, walking over to the coffeemaker. After turning it on to brew, Breanna turned around with a smirk. "It's me who kept up you."

"Get over here." His arm hooked around her waist, and pulling her to his chest, he kissed her.

Good morning, indeed.

With the familiar feeling of worn flannel beneath her fingertips, she stepped out of his hold and went to get her coffee. "Where's Francie?"

"Haven't seen her," Sinjin answered, sticking his head in the refrigerator. He passed her a carton of cream. "I've been out in the garage making sure everything's good to go."

She stirred her coffee, tipping her head to the side.

"There's going to be a lot of snow to move later on," he said with a kiss to her nose. "Comes with living here."

"Oh." She nodded. Not that Breanna had any experience with that. It rarely snowed in Portland, and they never got any in LA.

"Why don't we do Francie a solid and get breakfast started?"

"I can make oatmeal." She grimaced at the thought.

With a stroke of his beard, Sinjin raised his brow.

"Look, I'm not much of a cook."

He opened the fridge, grabbing a pound of bacon and a carton of eggs. "I'm feeling like waffles this morning. How about you?"

"The ones you pop in the toaster?"

He chuckled. Reaching into a cabinet, Sinjin grinned and

set a waffle iron down on the counter, then turned around to fry the bacon.

Breanna just stood there, shaking her head. "Sinjin…I…"

"Scrambled okay with you?"

…*can't.*

She pulled up Google on her phone. *How to make waffles.*

"Yeah, sure," she agreed, getting milk and butter from the fridge. "Give me two of those eggs, will you? And where do I find flour, sugar, baking powder, and salt? Hell, I'm going to need a bowl, too."

"Pantry." Smirking, he tipped his chin. "You need to learn your way around your own kitchen."

"It's not mine," Breanna insisted. "It's Francie's."

Sinjin turned away from the stove. Glancing down at her, his eyebrows pulled together, and he folded his arms across his flannel-clad chest.

"Is that what this is about?"

"Maybe." He shrugged. "And maybe I just want you to make me waffles."

Ted wasn't kidding. There had to be more food on the shelves in this kitchen within a kitchen that Sinjin called a pantry, than Hank had in his entire store. *Good grief.* Luckily, Francie had everything neatly organized, and after finding the items she needed, Breanna carried them out to the island.

She opened up the recipe on her phone and blew out a breath. Whistling as he fried the bacon, Sinjin didn't so much as glance her way. *Here goes nothing.* Breanna mixed the dry ingredients before adding in the milk. Cracking an egg on the edge of the bowl, a chunk of shell fell in along with the slobbery mess, and she muttered, "Shit."

"Potty mouth." He snickered.

"Shush you." Breanna giggled too. "Unless you'd rather wear your waffles instead of eating them."

Sinjin came up behind her. Kneading her shoulders while she picked out the shell and stirred the batter, he kissed the skin beneath her ear. "See, princess? You've got this, so don't ever let me hear you say you're not much of *anything*." He swatted her bottom. "And I'd much rather be eating you."

As Breanna poured the last of the batter onto the hot iron, Sinjin set platters of eggs and bacon down on the polished stone, and Ted, Francie coming along right behind him, joined them in the kitchen. "You made breakfast? Is it my birthday or something?"

"Good morning, Auntie," he greeted her with a kiss on the cheek. "Think we need a special occasion to spoil you a little?"

"Well, I can't remember the last time anybody cooked for me." Francie looked at her husband. "And this looks delicious."

"Shall we bring this to the morning room or eat right here?"

"Let's stay here," she said, settling into a seat. "As long as we're going to be cooped up in here for a while, I figured I'd start decorating for Christmas today. I wasn't going to bother this year, but I thought about it, and Valerie would've wanted me to, especially being Breanna's here."

"Yeah, she'd have had the house all decked out already." Sinjin's gaze seemed to travel somewhere in the past. He smiled, but there was a touch of sadness to it. "I'll bring everything up after breakfast."

"Your grandmother sure loved decorating for the holidays," Francie said, clasping onto her hand. "You can help me if you'd like."

"I would." Smiling, Breanna nodded.

Smiling back, Francie cut into her waffles. "Oh, dear, these are wonderful."

And smirking, Sinjin winked.

Thank you, Arien Brooks—whoever you are.

"Found a recipe on a blog is all." Breanna shrugged like it was no big deal. "It said using warmed milk and melted butter in the batter makes all the difference."

"Mm, I'll have to remember that," she said, devouring another forkful.

"After you finish helping your aunt, I could use some out in the garage." Licking the syrup from his thumb, Ted looked over at his nephew. "Have to get the blowers gassed up and ready for the storm."

"Already done, old man." Sinjin grinned. "Got the power shovels charging, too."

"Well, dang it." Reaching across the island, Ted speared another waffle onto his plate. "Nothing for me to do now 'til it's time to move some snow."

"I've got something you can do, Mr. Keeler." Francie elbowed her husband in the ribs.

"Oh, yeah?" He waggled his eyebrows. "And what's that, Mrs. Keeler?"

"Help me clean this kitchen."

Sinjin held her hand, taking her down the stairs to the walk-out basement. Cut into the slope of the mountain, Breanna looked through a wall of glass to a patio, covered by the first-floor deck above, and the panoramic view beyond it.

"Beautiful, isn't it?"

"It is." But the word didn't accurately describe it. "Have you always lived here?"

"Pretty much. Between here and Sacramento." His arm around her shoulders, he led her down the hall. "My mom grew up in the village."

"Francie did too, then."

Nodding, he opened a door. "Their father—my grandfather—was also an attorney."

"For the Daltons?"

"Of course." Snickering, Sinjin began pulling red plastic totes down from a shelf. "Your family and mine go way back."

So I've heard.

"What's down here?"

"Didn't my cousin give you the grand tour?" With a roll of his eyes, he waved his hands around the large room filled with row upon row of metal shelving. "Storage mostly."

"There has to be more here than that. This space is massive."

"We don't use these rooms often during the colder months. Except for the gym. I work out a lot." Returning to his task, he shrugged. "There's a wine cellar, an old bowling alley that no one's used in decades…"

"How come?" Breanna asked, looking up at him.

"I don't know." Sinjin smiled at her, dropping another tote down to the floor. "The pinsetter is broken, I think."

"We should get it fixed." Holding onto him, she bounced on the balls of her feet. "I love bowling."

"Know what I love?" His arms came around her waist, and he pulled her to his chest.

"What?"

Is it me?

Whiskey eyes searing into hers, Sinjin held her face in his hands and kissed her.

Maybe it is.

His cell phone began vibrating in his pocket, but he ignored it and kept right on kissing her. Lips nuzzled into her neck, and Breanna melted in his arms. Safe. Secure. Wanted.

The vibrating stopped only to begin again.

Annoyed, Sinjin looked at his phone. "What the fuck does he want?"

"Who?"

"Derek. I should answer it. He won't stop calling until I do." He handed her one of the lighter totes. "Here, take this to Francie. I'll be up with the rest in a minute."

"Okay."

Out of his line of sight, Breanna paused outside the door, listening to the hubris in his voice.

"It's not happening, motherfucker."

And she smiled to herself, making her way back down the hall.

Chapter Twenty-One

Ian kissed Breanna's forehead, then watched her disappear around the corner before he answered the call. "What?"

"Good morning, cousin." Amused by his annoyed tone, Derek chuckled. "How's our lovely Miss Dalton? Has she signed the documents yet?"

"No."

And she isn't going to.

"That's not what I was hoping to hear." He released a heavy sigh. "We have investors waiting, Ian, and they're growing impatient. You need to convince her."

"It's not happening, motherfucker." Cocksure, Ian propped his booted foot on a tote and leaned back against the wall.

"Make it happen," Derek clipped, his voice low.

"Can't. That isn't Valerie's Will."

"So? Breanna will never know that."

"No? Explain to her then, how your father witnessed the execution of a document from his grave, you stupid fucking fuck." Pushing off the wall, Ian raised his voice. "Hope you like it up the ass, cousin. You're going to end up disbarred and in prison."

And I won't be able to save you, even though I'll try.

Derek laughed him off. "You're so dramatic, Ian. Just a minor oversight. Thanks for catching it, though. I'll be sure everything is in perfect order before it's filed with the court."

"You've lost your fucking mind."

Maniacal laughter came through the phone.

"Hardly. We're finally going to get what's coming to us, cousin. Everything that, rightfully, should have been ours all along." After a long pause, Derek asked with a snicker, "Tell me, have you fucked her yet?"

He answered with silence.

"You forget how well I know you, cousin." Hearing his devious-sounding chuckle, Ian had no trouble picturing the shit-eating grin on his face. "It's all right, you know I don't mind sharing."

Oh, I know you don't…

And he knew it all too well.

In the early days of Derek's relationship with Miranda, Ian was often invited to join them in their bed, and what twenty-three-year-old guy would say no to that? Sometimes there'd be another girl there, too. His cousin would direct their sordid scenes, commanding the woman to eat out his girlfriend's cunt, or fist her, while they enjoyed the show, and took turns fucking them both afterward. Derek got off having power over her, and Miranda handed it over to him. But then, she'd do anything he asked if it meant getting a ring on her finger.

…but know this, asshole, I do mind. You're not touching her.

"I'll be back on Friday. Now, it doesn't matter to me how you do it, just get her to sign."

"And if I don't?"

"Pussy's that good, eh?"

Once again, Ian refused to give him the satisfaction of an answer.

"Well, if you don't, then by *any* means necessary, I will."

Breanna wasn't waiting in the kitchen when he finished hauling the red plastic totes upstairs. Neither was anyone else. The living room sat empty. So did the sitting room, the morning room, the billiards room, the library, and every other fucking room on this level of the house.

Gazing up at the black antlers suspended from the ceiling, he shook his head and climbed the stairs. For Breanna to survive his cousin, and for him to have a snowball's chance in hell of keeping her, Ian knew he'd have to tell her everything, and sooner rather than later. Because there wasn't all that much time left.

He knew the key code to her door but knocked anyway.

She opened it, and without a word, her fingers threaded in his hair, hands cradling his face, as she slipped that sweet tongue inside. And it was everything. Breanna took what she wanted and gave him what he needed. Willingly. Lovingly. Enthusiastically.

"Look, baby, I got all of you in me this time."

Fuck, it had taken everything in him to keep from coming when she said that.

Breanna was what Ian had always longed for in a partner, but never hoped to find.

He felt this gravitational pull to her the instant he saw her. She did, too. One look inside those blue, fairytale eyes of hers told him that.

With a rush of blood flooding toward his groin, Ian grabbed the back of her thighs and wrapped her legs around him. He shouldn't be thinking about fucking her right now when hell was closing in on them. But with his appetite for her insatiable, his veins filled, pulsating with blood, like snakes slithering beneath the skin that stretched taut around his dick.

"Does my princess need another fucking?"

"Is that bad?" Biting her lip, Breanna glanced up at him and grinned.

"Never." Sliding his hand inside her jeans, Ian's fingers sought her warm, wet pussy. She hissed. "Are you sore?"

"A little."

"A soak in the hot tub will fix that." Dropping his forehead to hers, he smiled.

"That sounds heavenly, except it's thirty degrees outside."

Trust me, you won't even notice.

"What happened to Christmas?"

"I don't know." She quirked a shoulder. "When I got upstairs, the kitchen was clean, and they were gone."

Chuckling, Ian carried her into the living room.

"What?"

"Mr. and Mrs. Keeler must be, uh…busy." He winked.

"No way." Pulling her head back, Breanna wrinkled her nose as if what he just implied was utterly ridiculous. "They're too old to…you know."

"Think sixty-year-olds don't fuck?"

"I just can't picture it, and I don't think I want to," she said with a shake of her head.

"Then picture this." Ian nipped at her lip with his teeth. "I'm going to be fucking this pretty pussy right here when I'm sixty, eighty, and God willing, when I'm a hundred."

"Think so, do you?"

"I know so," he said with the utmost confidence, easing her feet to the floor. "But right now, you and me…" He waved his finger back and forth between them. "…we've got some searching to do."

Taking advantage of an opportunity to go through Valerie's rooms with Ted and Francie otherwise occupied, Ian took Breanna to the third floor. Rather than chance his aunt or uncle alerting Derek without meaning to, he figured it was best to be discreet about what they were doing up here.

She stood at the unlit fireplace. He watched her gaze flit from the carpets to the walls, seeming to take in the room.

What is she thinking?

He wondered.

Because taking everything in stride so far, Breanna hadn't reacted at all as Ian expected her to.

He picked up the photo of the teenage girl from the mantel. Red bikini. White polka-dots. Pink ice cream. "How old were you here?"

"Summer before junior year, so, nineteen—almost twenty," she said, turning around. "What are we looking for, Sinjin?"

"Papers."

Blue eyes narrowing, her brows pulled together.

"Your grandmother's Will, for starters—the original one." *Trust documents I'm almost certain exist.* "Even a certified copy will do. They have to be here somewhere."

"Wouldn't your uncle have kept copies at his office?"

"Without a doubt."

Breanna tugged on his arm. "Let's just go to Sacramento and get them, then."

"Have you forgotten that's where Derek is?" If they found nothing here, however, Ian would gladly risk it. "Besides, it's to our advantage if we let him believe he's holding all the cards."

"How do you figure?"

"Because I have a plan." Running his fingers through her hair, he kissed her brow. "But we need those documents."

They went through every closet. Skimmed the pages of every book. Opened every drawer. Together, they looked high and low but found nothing.

"Where else could they be? Downstairs in the study?"

Ian shook his head. "I use that room all the time, so I think I would've seen them, but we can check."

"A secret safe?" she offered.

He chuckled.

"What if Derek already has them?"

Then we're well and truly fucked.

If Valerie stashed her copies anywhere else, that was entirely possible. But knowing her as he did, Ian believed the documents had to be here. Somewhere. They just had to find them.

"He doesn't have access to the third floor. No one does. I have the only key."

"Why you?" she asked with a slight cock of her head.

Ian placed his arm around her shoulders, and drawing her closer, he smiled. "Your grandmother and I were close. She trusted me."

"Over Francie?"

"She loved my aunt." He paused, and Breanna steered them down the hall toward her father's apartment. "Look, what I'm trying to say is Valerie liked her privacy, and she trusted me to respect that. If the doors to the stairway were locked, that meant your grandmother wanted to be left alone. And Francie is the kind of person who always has to be doing for others—it's her nature. She tends to hover."

"Yeah, I can see that." She watched him punch the code into the keypad, then glanced up at him. "How did she die?"

"Peacefully. In her sleep."

"How do you know her death was peaceful?"

"She appeared to be." Tucking her hair behind her ear, Ian shrugged. "I'm the one who found her."

With a nod, Breanna wet her lips. "I'm afraid to touch anything in here."

"Why?"

"Because everything is just as he left it," she said, fingertips tracing over the photo of a family that never got to be. "That is what you said, isn't it?"

"Yeah. No one was ever allowed in here, though I think your grandmother would have made an exception for you." He squeezed her shoulders. "You know, we won't find what we're looking for in your dad's rooms, princess."

"Maybe not, but I want to look, anyway."

Going through her father's things was the closest to him she'd ever get to be, so he humored her. Ian watched the tears slip from Breanna's eyes while she smiled, sitting on Shane's unmade bed, looking at photo albums and flipping through old CDs of the music he once listened to.

"Godsmack, Alice in Chains, Queens of the Stone Age—he had good taste." Bands she no doubt knew. "Bachman-Turner Overdrive?"

"I'm thinking that one must've been your grandmother's." Chuckling softly, he shrugged. "They're from the 70s."

"Oh." Her lips pursed, Breanna got up and went over to her father's desk.

Frozen in time, with papers strewn about and books in haphazard stacks. A bulletin board, pinned with photos, Greek letters, and ticket stubs, hung over an ancient-looking computer with a tower on the floor.

Breanna sat down at Shane's desk. Ignoring the mess in front of her, she rummaged through his drawers instead. A pile of spiral-bound notebooks in her lap, she turned the pages in awe. "Look at this, Sinjin." Her voice cracked, "His writings."

Ian stood over her, rubbing Breanna's back as she opened another drawer, discovering an oblong box inside it. She lifted the lid, and there, as if waiting for someone to read them, lay a stack of typewritten sheets, some three inches high, held together with a rubber band. "Oh, my God," thumbing through the pages, Breanna squealed. "I think my dad wrote a book."

Seeing her delight, he smiled. *It sure looks like it, baby.*

"And he wasn't much older than I am now." Turning in her father's desk chair, fairytale eyes looked up at him. "Sinjin, how did he die?"

"Your mom never told you?"

Breanna shook her head, no.

Ian got down on his haunches and took her hands in his. "It was an accident."

So everyone said, anyway.

"His car slid off the mountain."

Chapter Twenty-Two

Ian stood behind her. He watched Breanna, her face upturned as she peered through the glass, waiting for a snowflake to tumble from the sky. Subdued, she'd hardly spoken since they left her father's room. He didn't get her mother's logic. What reason could she possibly have for withholding Shane Dalton's life, and how he died, from their daughter?

Breanna wasn't a child—if she were, maybe he could understand it. She was a grown woman, and she deserved to know the man her father was. The family stories that Valerie could have shared with her. Gone now. Lost forever. It made him angry she never got to hear them.

Wrapping his arms around her, Ian kissed the top of her head. "You okay?"

"Yeah, I'm fine."

He shot her a look, lifting his brow.

"No, really, I am." Breanna smiled a little, fingering the collar of his sweater. "I have his words, and you have no idea what that means to me. It's like he left a piece of himself behind."

"Words on a page live forever," he said, holding her hand to his chest.

With a nod, her smile grew brighter. "I'm going to get his novel published someday."

I know you will.

She turned back to the window. "Look, baby, it's snowing."

"So it is." Kissing her neck, Ian caressed her breasts. "Did you know every single snowflake is different? Not one is like another."

"I've heard that, but I don't understand how that can be."

"It's true," he said, his hands sliding under her sweater to feel soft, warm skin. "Even snowflakes from the same cloud will have different shapes and sizes."

He kissed her then. There would never be another like her, either. And she was his, dammit.

Hera pawing at the door, Breanna pulled her head back. "I think she wants to go out."

Ian opened the glass door, and leaving it ajar after the dog scampered off, returned to Breanna. He didn't say a word, and neither did she, as he took off all her clothes. Like the first time he gazed upon her naked and beautiful in a cabin in the storm, he wrapped her in a throw.

"C'mon."

He brought her outside, removed the blanket, and tossing it to the sofa, Ian assisted her into the steaming water.

After stripping off his clothes, he eased himself in behind her, holding her back against his chest. She looked up at the sky to watch the snow gently tumbling from the clouds. "It's so pretty."

"Each snowflake takes its own path to meet the ground. That's what makes each one distinct and uniquely beautiful."

Strumming her skin, slippery beneath the water, Ian tasted the salt on the curve of her neck. He kissed his way up the column of her delicate throat to her jaw, before she turned her mouth toward his, and he tasted the tears on her lips.

Her head falling back on his shoulder, Breanna held his hands to her breasts and squeezed. "I need you to fuck me, Sin."

Gladly. His teeth sinking into her flesh, he groaned.

"And when I scream, fuck me harder," she said, nipping at his mouth. "The only thing I want to feel is you."

He'd always give her anything she wanted, whatever she needed. Easing his dick inside, he thrust upward slow and deep. Even when he met the resistance of her body, he pressed farther.

"Fuck, yes, keep going. Just like that. It hurts," she sobbed. "But I need it to."

He didn't want to hurt her. Not like that. It wasn't what she needed. He pulled out.

"Nooo." Her nails sunk into the globes of his ass. "Put it back in me, baby. Please."

"Shhh."

Ian wrapped her in his arms and just held her. When the shudders subsided, he turned them both around and reclined against the hot tub's molded bench seat, positioning her on top of him. "I want to see those pretty blue eyes looking right at me, princess."

Her luscious pink lips turned up at the corners.

"Go on. Put me back in."

Fumbling in the water beneath her, Breanna notched him at her entrance and slowly lowered her body down.

"Fuck, yeah," he growled. "Take it. All of it. My good girl, look at us."

Her gaze flicked to where their bodies joined. She smiled, and then those pretty eyes locked on his.

Ian pulled her down to his mouth, his tongue eagerly seeking hers, as he moved in and out of her purposefully slow. Breanna might be in the dominant position, but he was the one in control. Because this wasn't going to be a fast and frenzied race to the finish.

Each delicious stroke an unhurried movement, he pushed in deep, as far as her body would allow, before gradually withdrawing until the head of his cock was the only part of him left inside her. His fingers gripped her hips, keeping her in place.

The heated water swirling around them, he did it over and over again, letting the pressure slowly build.

"Sinjin." Filled with him, she dug her nails into his flesh. "Please."

In a swift maneuver, Ian swiveled them both up from the ledge. Her legs coming around his waist, Ian stood in the middle of the steaming pool, Breanna impaled on his dick. Snowflakes landed on her face as he guided her body up and down, thrusting into her soft pussy with all his might.

"What do you feel, Breanna?"

"You. Just you," she mewled, hypnotic blue eyes locked on his. "I love—"

"I do, too, baby."

I do. I fucking love you.

She picked an ornament out of the red tote and glanced at the floor-to-ceiling glass. A minute ago, like a scene out of a Hallmark Christmas movie, the glittering snowfall made for a picturesque backdrop. Now, a mere sixty seconds later, it spun in a white whirling dervish outside the window, and as far as Breanna was concerned, there was no longer anything pretty about it at all.

The grand tree stood at least twenty feet tall, the tip of it close to touching the wood beam in the ceiling. After a delightful afternoon in the hot tub, she and Sinjin cuddled together in bed, not emerging again until dinner. When they arrived downstairs, Francie had a festive spread set out. Crisp leaves of endive topped with dill-shrimp salad, Thai meatballs, baked brie, a tree-shaped charcuterie board—all sorts of handheld foods to nosh on—along with a rich red wine punch. And Ted had erected the realistic-looking artificial tree.

That it was fake surprised her. But then maybe her grandmother hadn't seen the point in taking down a real one, only to admire it for a month before chopping its dried-out carcass into firewood.

"It looks so beautiful," Francie said in awe, setting a tray of cookies down on the coffee table. "Makes me want to put up the rest of them."

"There's more?"

Up high at the top of the tree, Sinjin looked down and sniggered. "Heh."

"At least a dozen. Ain't that right, Mrs. Keeler?"

Ignoring her husband, Francie turned toward her and shrugged. "Your grandmother just loved dressing up Dalton House for the holidays."

"We're stuck inside for the time being, aren't we?" Picking up a cookie, Breanna popped it into her mouth. "Let's do it."

"Guess I'll be dragging more shit up from the basement." Sinjin chuckled, coming down off the ladder.

He came to stand beside her, and with his hand squeezing her shoulder, whiskey eyes gazed down into hers, holding her against his side. A faint smile curved his mouth and the way he was looking at her had nerves rioting in her heart.

Staring at them, Ted cleared his throat. "Did you make any coffee to go with them cookies, Francie?"

"That's a silly question, dear," Francie said. "Course, I did."

"Bring me some whiskey to get my insides warmed up, too, will you?" Watching the storm intensifying outside the window, Ted addressed Sinjin, "As soon as there's a lull, we'll be moving some snow, I reckon."

"Yeah, and by the looks of it, we've got a foot out there already."

With a grunt, he nodded, and taking the bottle of whiskey from his wife, Ted poured Sinjin and himself a more than generous dose.

"Easy there, Mr. Keeler. I don't need you to go sliding off a roof or anything."

"No need to worry, dearie. We won't be clearing any roofs just yet."

Francie, looking wary, studied Sinjin, sipping on his whiskey-laced coffee, his arm around Breanna. "Have you spoken with Derek, Ian?"

"This morning."

"Did he mention what his plans are?"

"He'll be here Friday," Sinjin answered, rubbing Breanna's shoulder.

If that was supposed to be reassuring, it wasn't. While grateful she didn't have to face Derek alone, just the thought of having to be in the same room as him again made her body tense.

"For the weekend?"

He rested his ankle on his thigh with a shrug. "I guess so, but he didn't say."

"In that case, I'm going to call your mother. Invite her to come up for the weekend, too." Clasping her hands together beneath her chin, Francie looked her way. "My sister can help with the Christmas decorations if we're not finished by then. She's an interior designer, you know."

"No, I didn't know that," Breanna said.

"Oh, yes, Pamela had the Kimball Hotel account back in the day, and many others." "She helped your grandmother with Dalton House, in fact."

"It's certainly beautiful." Glancing over at a smirking Sinjin, he winked.

"What do you say, Ian?" Ted poured himself another shot and downed it. "Let's get this done so I can go to bed. At the rate this shit's piling up, we're gonna have to do it again come morning."

"All right, old man." Getting up from the sofa, Sinjin kissed her cheek. "We won't be too long."

Her fingertips brushing the skin he just kissed, Breanna watched him go.

"He's a liar, you know." The corner of her mouth quirking up, Francie topped their coffee with some whiskey. "They'll be out there a few hours, at least. Are you doing okay, dear? Any more headaches?"

"None, lately." Putting on a polite smile, Breanna took a sip of the potent brew. "I'm fine, thanks."

"That's good. Jordy was asking." She was quiet for a moment, her lips pursing back and forth. "You and Ian seem to be getting on rather well."

Heat rushed to Breanna's cheeks, and it wasn't because of the whiskey.

"I'm not blind, dear." Francie adjusted her horn-rimmed frames. "I love both of my nephews, but I have to say you and Ian are far better suited."

That's a no-brainer.

"Is that why you gave me the room next to his?"

"Maybe." She shrugged, wearing a grin. "And your grandmother would've approved wholeheartedly."

"She and Sin…Ian were close, weren't they?"

"They were." Francie smiled. "She adored him and he always looked out for her, especially after my brother Raymond passed."

Nodding, Breanna chewed the corner of her lip. "All of you are more connected to her and this house than I am."

Lying in bed, Hera sharing the warmth of the fire with her, Breanna stared into the flames. Sinjin wasn't back yet, and without his steadfast presence, her mind wandered to places she'd rather not go. Thinking about all this fucked-up craziness made her head hurt.

Like now.

She looked away from the fire and hugged her pillow, closing her eyes while she waited for Sinjin to come back and the Motrin to kick in.

Then the mattress dipped beside her.

Smooth lips kissed her shoulder.

Warm breath fanned her skin.

"I didn't want to wake you, so I let myself in. Is that okay?"

"It's more than okay." Breanna rolled over and palmed his cheek. "I missed you."

His fingers threaded into her hair and he gripped her nape, bringing her mouth to his. And with Sinjin's powerful arms to shelter in, everything felt all right again.

"I was hoping Derek wasn't coming back." Snuggled against his chest, Breanna rubbed his skin. "Wishful thinking, I know."

"It's going to be okay, princess," he said, strumming his thumb over her nipple. "Tomorrow, we're going to call your mom."

She lifted her head. "I don't want to."

"Your mom deserves to know where you are and that you're okay." He raised his hand to her hair, running his fingers through it. "And she might know something that can help us."

What the hell?

"They did manage your trust fund together."

"What does Derek want this mountain for?"

"Besides the obvious?" Laying her head back down on his chest, Sinjin returned to his strumming. "His father."

"His father?"

"Yeah, and he's got it in his head that there's more gold to be had here." He kissed her crown. "That's how George Dalton made the family fortune, you know."

"Is there?" Breanna bent her neck to glance up at him.

"I don't think so, but it's possible, I suppose." Sinjin snickered. "They found some near Yosemite not too long ago."

"Gold." She sighed. "Imagine that."

He rolled over on top of her, caging her beneath him. "I don't give a shit about gold."

"No?"

Greedily sucking her nipple into his mouth, Sinjin bit down on it.

"Fuck, baby, that feels good."

"You're who I care about, princess." He soothed the sting with his tongue. "I've got plans for us."

"You do?"

Raising his head from her breast, whiskey bored into blue. "I do."

"You make me feel…" *God, so many things.* "…safe, secure, wanted."

"That's how I always want you to feel, baby." And he touched his lips to hers. "Because you are."

Chapter Twenty-Three

Sinjin was gone, but Hera lay there, warming her feet. At the first sign Breanna was awake, the dog moved up on the bed, nudging her with her nose for a morning cuddle. She rubbed her thick winter coat, gazing out the window. There was nothing to see there. The world had disappeared, towering pines and grand mountain vistas obscured by streams of billowing white.

She sighed. "Guess we won't be seeing our man anytime soon, will we, girl?"

Hera blinked her ice-blue eyes, then proceeded to lick her paws.

Breanna forced herself to sit up. The room smelled of sex and Sinjin. And she missed him. The warmth of his body, his breath on her neck, his fingers tangled up in her hair.

Once upon a time, she laughed at all those lovesick girls who made decisions with their vaginas. She'd been wrong, though. Her brain might be bruised—okay, and her vagina, too—but her heart worked just fine, and there was no mistaking its message. *I love him.*

Sinjin was her only constant, an anchor amidst this churning maelstrom of uncertainty. He told her to listen to her gut, and she was. And with all of her decision-making organs in agreement, including her addled brain, Breanna got out of bed to take a shower.

The bruise on her forehead was all but gone now, only a trace of sickly yellow remained. Easy fix. As much as she loved experimenting with the latest makeup trends, Breanna preferred a natural look and went minimal with it.

Ready to get dressed, she came out of the ensuite in her underwear to find Sinjin sitting on her bed, a tray with breakfast beside him. "Goddamn, you're beautiful."

He reached for her hand, and dragging her to his lap, he kissed her.

His hair was still damp, the long ends hanging in his eyes. Wearing old, faded jeans and an everyday Henley, this was the Sinjin she loved best.

Breanna lifted the lid off the food—omelets, pancakes, and crispy hash browns. "Mm, it smells so good."

"It does, but *you* smell even better." Nuzzling his nose into her neck, he nipped at her skin. "Let's eat. Then you're going to finish getting dressed so we can call your mom."

"It's not like she can see if I have clothes on or not." She giggled.

He smirked. "We're going to FaceTime her."

"Jesus, Sinjin." She got up from his lap, dragging her fingers through her hair. "I don't want to do this."

"Why? Because you think she'll be mad at you?"

"Because I'm mad at *her*!" Breanna clapped her hand to her mouth. "I'm sorry."

"Never apologize to anyone for the way you feel, least of all to me."

"But I screamed at you. I didn't mean—"

"I like it when you scream." His head tipped to the side, and he smirked. "Course, I'd rather be naked and inside you while you're doing it."

"I'd rather you were," she said, worrying her lip. "I hate confrontation."

"No one likes it."

Right. Pursing her lips to the side, she shot him a look.

"That's different. I'm an attorney. I get paid to like it." Sinjin reached for her, pulling her to stand between his legs.

"Secrets and lies," she muttered, mostly to herself.

He glanced up at her, rubbing his fingers over the back of her hand. "Maybe she had good reason."

"Like what?"

"I don't know, baby, but it's well past time to find out, don't you think?" With a gentle squeeze of her fingers, he tugged on her arm. "Come on, it's your mom."

"Okay."

"There's my girl," Sinjin praised, as Breanna settled back on his lap. "Now, eat your pancakes."

She wiped the sweat from her palms on her leggings, rubbing her hands up and down along her thighs. Sinjin set her MacBook down on the table in front of her and sat down next to her, out of view of the camera. "Ready?"

"You're not going to change your shirt?" Breanna assessed his casual look, patting at the buttons of the cardigan she wore over her understated cami.

"No, why?" He glanced down at his chest. "Is something wrong with this one?"

Yeah, Bree, you loved him in his Henley a minute ago.

"No, it's just not very lawyerish, is all."

The sound of deep laughter bellowed from his throat.

With a flip of her hair, she said in all seriousness, "You're the one who said you'd talk to my mom as my attorney."

"I'm your man above all else, princess." He pressed a kiss to her lips and winked. "And trust me, I don't need the suit to look lawyerish. Come on, now. You're stalling."

Breanna nodded and, blowing out a breath, she pulled up the FaceTime app. "Hi, Mom."

"Bree, honey," Sarah Benjamin exclaimed, and without stopping to take a breath, kept right on talking. "Your dad already left for work and Ethan's at school. He's going to be so bummed he wasn't here when you called. He misses his big sissy."

"I miss him, too. Tell him I'll call back tonight when I can talk to him and Dad."

"You're back in class today, too, aren't you?"

"Uh, yeah." It wasn't a lie. As soon as this call was over and done with, she'd log in.

Her mom tipped her head to one side and then the other, inspecting the image on her screen. "Where are you?"

Sinjin squeezed her thigh.

"Dalton House."

What does it look like right before someone has an apoplectic fit? Because Breanna was sure her mom was about to have one. No doubt frozen in shock, not a muscle in her face twitched, and then she gave her head a little shake as if she hadn't heard her right.

"Mom, let me explain," she pleaded.

"Get your grandmother."

"I can't."

"What do you mean, you can't?" Sarah slammed her hand down like she meant business. "I want to speak to Valerie. Now!"

"You can't," Breanna said. She bit her lip, slowly shaking her head. "She's dead."

"What?" Her voice dropped to nearly a whisper and judging by the look on her mother's face, she hadn't known before now.

"That's why I'm here."

Sarah, digesting the news, stared off to the side. Whatever she might be thinking, Breanna couldn't decipher it.

"I got a letter from her attorney asking me to come here," she continued. "I thought Valerie wanted to see me and—"

"Which attorney?" Refocused, her head turned back to the camera.

Quickly glancing at Sinjin, Breanna answered, "Derek St. John."

"Let me guess, Raymond's son?"

"Yes."

"Breanna." Her mom expelled a breath, raking her fingers through her long blonde hair, making a mess of it. "Why didn't you tell me?"

"I learned not to talk about my father or his family a long, long time ago." It felt like a cotton ball was stuck in the back of her throat. Breanna picked up a bottle of water from the table and took a drink. "Any time I asked about him, it always made you sad, so I just didn't."

"I loved Shane and…" Pausing, Sarah traced her fingers back and forth along her collarbone. Her blue eyes filled. "I still don't understand why you went there by yourself or why the attorney didn't contact *me*."

Secrets and lies. It was time to get everything out in the open. No matter how painful it might be, this conversation was long overdue.

"Oh, I don't know, Mom. Maybe because I'm Valerie's granddaughter. Maybe because Derek knew you'd keep it from me, just like you have everything else."

"That's not fair, Breanna. You don't know—"

Not fair?

She smirked. "I didn't, but I do now."

"How long have you been there?" Her eyes narrowing, Sarah crossed her arms over her chest.

Breanna lifted her chin, looking her mom right in the eye. "I left Portland the day after classes let out for Thanksgiving break."

"I thought you were with Kayleigh. You lied to me."

"*You* lied to me."

More like she withheld the truth from her, but isn't that the same thing?

After a moment of tenable silence, her mother blinked and tipped her head to the side. "Wait…you drove there?"

"Yeah. I got into a little accident, but it's okay. I'm fine and my car's being fixed. Sinjin helped—"

"Who the hell is Sinjin?" She was yelling now.

"I am." He scooted over, and under her mother's watchful gaze, his arm came around her shoulders. "Hello, Mrs. Benjamin. Ian Maynard. Remember me? We spoke on the phone."

What in the actual fuck?

Breanna's head snapped up. She glared at him. Sinjin and her mother talked? When? What for? And why had he never mentioned it?

Sarah nodded. "Can you tell me what happened, Mr. Maynard, and please, start at the beginning?"

"Certainly," he said, his tone business-like. "Valerie suffered a stroke and passed away in September."

"Are you sure about that?"

"Quite sure. An autopsy was done." Sinjin glanced her way. "She named Breanna as executor of her estate, and so, Mr. St. John contacted her and asked her to Dalton House. I imagine he didn't want to convey the sad news of her grandmother's passing by telephone."

"No one contacted *me*," her mother reiterated once again.

His mouth curved into that smirk she was all too familiar with. "Breanna's an adult."

"And I'm her mother. Valerie and I co-manage the trust fund her father left for her."

"Yes, I'm aware." Fingertips pressing into her shoulder, Sinjin tipped his head. "Breanna, however, was not."

"I didn't spend any of my daughter's money, if that's what you're implying."

"I know you didn't. You couldn't even if you wanted to."

"Both your grandmother and I had to authorize any withdrawals," Sarah explained, looking at her daughter. "We both agreed to help you with the down payment on your car, and your tuition, of course. You'll control your own money when you graduate, get married, or turn twenty-five—whichever comes first. Valerie wanted you to grow up like every other average kid, and not some spoiled princess. I agreed with her."

Pffft.

Breanna rolled her eyes. "You didn't even like her!"

"Not always, no, but when it came to you, she had your best interests at heart." Nodding, her mother worried her lip.

She still didn't understand, and that only made her angrier. "Then why did you keep us apart?"

Her mother sighed. "To protect you."

"Protect me?"

"Valerie and Lawrence were afraid for you." A tear snaking its way down her cheek, Sarah wrung her hands. "See, they knew they'd never be able to prove it, but your grandparents swore your father's death was no accident."

"And you were the only Dalton left," Sinjin murmured, as if suddenly it all made sense. "What did they think happened?"

"Lawrence suspected someone tampered with the car," she said, swiping at the wetness on her face.

"Who?"

Her mom shrugged. "I don't know, but Valerie never

trusted Raymond. She told me so. Of course, Lawrence didn't want to hear it."

"They were close. Longtime friends." His finger rubbing over his upper lip, Sinjin nodded.

"I know all about it." Sarah sniggered, the timbre of her voice venomous. "The Daltons and St. Johns go way back."

"This is all so fucked up." Shaking her head, unbidden tears rushed from Breanna's eyes.

Sinjin's fingers swept through her hair. "Shhh, everything's going to be all right, princess."

Her mother's eyes widened. "Valerie kept Breanna away from Dalton House for a reason, Mr. Maynard. I need to know my daughter is safe."

"Ian. Please," he insisted, and gazing at Breanna tenderly continued to stroke her hair. "Raymond died three years ago. You don't have to worry about him."

"And yet Valerie still feared for her, *Ian.*"

He looked at her mom then. "I've got her, Mrs. Benjamin—"

"Sarah."

"Breanna is safe with me, *Sarah*," Sinjin assured her. "I promise."

"I'm going to hold you to that." She didn't seem convinced.

Breanna held her hand up. "Mom, enough."

"I'm going to talk to your dad when he gets home. We can fly up as soon—"

"No. Don't. I'll be fine. I can handle this." Vehemently, she shook her head. "Besides, I'm coming home for Christmas."

"I hate seeing you so upset, honey." Wringing her hands some more, her mother bit into her lip.

Breanna sniffled and took in a breath. "It's just that I grew up thinking my grandmother didn't care to even see me…"

"She saw you." Closing her teary eyes, her mom softly smiled. "Once."

"When?"

Her eyes opened. "Remember the summer we went up to Tahoe?"

"She was there?"

Sarah nodded. "At the pool. She came by and gave you and your brother a strawberry ice cream cone."

With Sinjin squeezing her hand, Breanna closed her eyes and tried to pull the memory of it from her subconscious. She came up blank.

"I'm so sorry, honey."

Yeah, I am too.

Chapter Twenty-Four

Ian glanced at her from across the room. Headphones in, Breanna concentrated on the screen as she scribbled away in a notebook. He had to give her credit for her self-discipline, her commitment to her studies. Without being forced to sit in a lecture hall, as he had in college, he sure as hell wouldn't have had the wherewithal. But that was just it. More than her beautiful face or her luscious body, her strong-willed nature was what attracted him to her.

She'd spent most of the week combing through Valerie's things, even going through every nook and cranny of the study while he worked, to no avail. Just as he'd predicted, the documents weren't there. Still, Breanna resolved to find them. "I know they're here somewhere. I feel it in my gut."

And time was running out.

Derek was expected to return today.

He was going to have his hands full dealing with him, keeping him away from Breanna without rousing too much suspicion. Ian was just a kid when her father's car careened off the mountain, but even then he'd heard the whispers. A clear September day. No other vehicles involved. It couldn't have been an accident.

Shane was born and raised on this mountain. He knew the pass like the back of his hand, every twist, turn, and curve of it. Same as Ian did. Maybe his brakes failed. Who knows? But it surprised him to learn that, like many of the villagers, Valerie and Lawrence also believed there was foul play regarding their son's death. While he knew she wasn't particularly fond of his uncle, she'd never mentioned her suspicions.

Raymond couldn't be that deranged, so hellbent on revenge, could he? What happened with Sharon was ancient history. And he and Breanna's grandfather were like brothers, or so it appeared, anyway. The man was broken after his son's death. A shell of his former self, Lawrence Dalton died five years later, at the age of fifty-eight.

"The Daltons owe this family, son. Don't you ever forget it."

Then again, maybe he was. He'd heard those words often enough at the office, Uncle Raymond drilling it into Derek's head any chance he got. At the time, Ian thought little of it. His cousin would just roll his eyes behind his father's back and snicker. Then, after six months in Sacramento, he went to Dalton House at Valerie's request—not that he minded.

Ian adored her, and she him. From the time he was a young boy, scampering around Dalton House alongside his mom while she and Valerie redesigned its grand interior, he thought of her as he would a grandmother or a kindly older aunt. His allegiance, his loyalty, was hers, and hers alone. And now it belonged to her granddaughter.

So gazing at the girl he found himself in love with, Ian vowed to right his cousin's wrongs—and his own, if he were to be honest. His princess never deserved the disdainful opinion he once had of her. How he wished Valerie had confided in him before she died. If she had, he could've outsmarted Uncle Raymond and Derek. Then she might've felt it was safe enough to build a bond with Breanna.

We all fucked up. What a fucking waste.

He shut his laptop, got up from the sofa, and crossed the room to the oversized chair Breanna was curled up in. With those headphones on, she didn't notice his approach, and leaning over her from behind, Ian swept her hair to the side to kiss the skin beneath her ear.

She giggled.

The humming of Christmas carols in the kitchen ceased. He glanced up to find Francie grinning. Having deemed her a trustworthy ally, Ian winked.

"You about done here, princess?" His fingers slid through her silky hair. "Mom and Derek should be here soon."

Breanna wrinkled up her nose. "Yeah, I need to go up and change."

Dressed in leggings, fuzzy socks, and a Portland State sweatshirt, Ian thought her perfect. "Why? What you have on is fine."

"For studying, maybe." She tipped her head back and puckered her lips, so he kissed her. "But I will not be looking like a bum in front of your mother."

"I told you, you're fine."

"Yeah?"

"Yeah." He smiled.

"I'm going to change, anyway." She snapped her laptop shut. "Be right back."

With a shake of his head, Ian chuckled, and watching Breanna sprint up the stairs, he strolled over to his aunt. "I'll never fully understand the way the female mind works."

"Nothing to it, dear. I mean, look at you in your chinos and cashmere. My sister is always impeccable, and Derek?" She harrumphed. "Well, you know Derek. Breanna is the lady of this house now. About time he knows it, too."

"She doesn't need to impress *him*, my mother, or anybody else."

"It's not about that, Ian," Francie said, glancing up from the potatoes she was peeling. "How would you feel walking into court in jeans and a T-shirt?"

"Totally out of place." Not that he'd ever do that.

"The suit makes the man, eh?"

"This isn't court, Auntie, it's her home."

With an arch of her eyebrow, she shot him a look.

"Okay, yeah, I get it."

"Breanna's a wonderful girl, Sinny."

Though everyone called him Sinjin as a kid, his aunt hadn't used the nickname Pamela gave him in a very long time. These days, she saved it for when she was especially meaningful or showing him affection. Ian figured in this instance, it was a little of both.

The corners of his mouth rose, and he softly agreed, "Yes, she is."

"I see so much of Shane in her." Biting on her lip, Francie choked, "He and Valerie would be so damn proud."

Hugging his aunt, Ian sighed. "Yeah."

"You've got to put a stop to this, honey." She swiped beneath her glasses.

Besides him, Francie was probably the person closest to Valerie Dalton. She and Ted had been here, running the house for her, for over forty years.

"I'm trying to, Auntie."

"How can I help?" She held onto his hands.

He kissed her brow. "Right now, I need you to follow my lead and do your best to keep Derek away from her."

To say his cousin was far from happy was putting it mildly. Breanna was still upstairs when Derek charged in like he already owned the place, which he did not, and never would if Ian could help it. Of course, the bastard cornered him the first chance he got. "Did you get it done?"

"Told you, cuz." He poured himself a bourbon. "It's not fucking happening."

"I guess we're doing things my way, then." And with a smirk, Derek turned toward their aunt. "What's for dinner, Francie?"

"Creme Fraiche salmon, escarole salad, potatoes Anna, beef tenderloin, and I baked us a chocolate caramel pecan tart for dessert."

Now, in the sitting room with said pecan tart, Breanna safely tucked between him and Pamela, Ian watched Derek return with a tray of brandy, obviously miffed, judging by the pinched expression on his face, that he had no choice but to sit with Ted and Francie.

His mother snickered, taking a snifter from the tray. "What a difference a week makes, eh?"

"And just what is that supposed to mean, Pamela?" Derek's nostrils flared. "I wasn't aware you were joining us this weekend."

"Hm, perhaps because my comings and goings are none of your concern, dear." She sipped on her brandy with a smile. "I'm here to help Francie and Breanna with the holiday touches."

"I see."

"Why are you here?" Pamela asked, as if she didn't already know.

"For Miss Dalton, of course."

"Shouldn't you be…oh, I don't know…at a dinner party somewhere or spending the weekend in Tahoe with Miranda? That's what you usually do, isn't it?"

"I have more important matters to attend to here," Derek said, his sights on Breanna.

She ignored him, asking his mother instead, "Who's Miranda?"

"His fiancée, darling. They've been engaged for years."

Inwardly, Ian chuckled.

Wrinkling her nose at him, Breanna looked at Derek like he was the equivalent of pond scum.

"Not anymore. We, uh, ended our engagement."

I call bullshit.

"Oh, no. I'm so sorry to hear that, dear." Shaking her head, his mother patted her nephew's hand. She was quite the actress when it was called for.

"It was for the best." Derek placed his hand on top of hers, effectively putting an end to her patting, and returned his gaze to Breanna. "Besides, I've discovered my interests lie elsewhere."

For fuck's sake.

"And what might those be, dear?" Not that Pamela gave him a moment to answer. "A new hobby is just the thing after a break-up. An ex of a friend of mine took up racquetball when they separated—or was it squash? Neither here nor there, I suppose. The point is to find an activity that invigorates the body as well as the mind."

"Exactly my thought." He smirked.

"Racquetball?"

"An invigorating activity." Derek swept his tongue across his lip and winked.

Ted shoveled a forkful of dessert into his mouth. "This is damn good, Mrs. Keeler."

"So good," Breanna agreed. "Reminds me of those turtle candies, and they're my favorite. I think I'll have another piece."

Derek opened his mouth to speak, no doubt to chastise her for wanting seconds, but before he could utter a word, Ian cut her a generous slice of the pecan tart.

"I'd be more than happy to give you the recipe, honey," Francie offered. "It's very simple to make."

"Miss Dalton doesn't cook," Derek scoffed.

"No? She made waffles for me just the other day." Taking Breanna's hand in his, Ian grinned. "Isn't that right, Auntie?"

"From scratch, too," she said, nodding. "Best darn waffles I've ever had."

"Let's get out of here," Ian whispered into Breanna's ear, and he stood, pulling her up from the sofa with him. "Excuse us, I'm going to show Miss Dalton how to shoot some pool."

"Billiards," Derek spat.

He stood at the cue rack, watching her look out through the glass. Moonlight reflected off snow-covered peaks, painting the night sky a deep winter blue. She rubbed her arms as if she were cold, so he wrapped her up in his.

"Are you going to teach me how to play *billiards* or not?"

Ian could hear the smile in her voice. "Pick a stick, baby. I'll rack."

Breanna seemed to weigh her decision carefully. Her lips pursed, index finger rubbing her cheek, she visually sized up one cue over another, before getting the feel of her chosen stick in her hands.

"Have you ever played before?"

"Once or twice." She smirked.

"Ladies first, then." Bowing to her, his outstretched hand swept toward the table. "You break."

"All right."

She stood back for a moment, chalking the felt tip of her cue, before stepping up to the head rail. Placing the cue ball just left of center, Breanna leaned over, the cable knit sweater dress flattering her shapely ass as she lined up the shot. Relaxed, her bridge arm bent slightly at the elbow, she shattered the break, slamming two balls into the pockets.

"Impressive." Ian moved closer as she went to re-chalk her cue. "You've got solids."

"I wanted stripes, darn it."

"You fibbed, my naughty girl," he playfully chided. Tucking his tongue against his cheek, he smirked. "You shoot a mean game of pool, don't you?"

"Uh-huh." Breanna turned away from him to study the position of the balls on the table.

Ian hooked an arm around her waist, dragging her to his chest. "Care to make a friendly wager?"

"What?" The corners of her mouth turned up into a smile that was nothing less than sultry.

This girl was making him fucking insane. Waves of cappuccino and buttermilk fisted in his fingers, he kissed her. Sweet oranges infused his lungs, her decadent flavor tickling his tongue. Caramel. Chocolate. His dick painfully straining against his zipper.

"I could fuck you right here," he rasped, nipping at her lip with his teeth.

"You wouldn't dare."

"No?"

Ian took the pool stick from her hand. Gripping it firmly, he trailed it between her breasts, over her sweater, to rub between her thighs.

Panting, Breanna licked her lips. "Derek could walk in."

And right now, he wouldn't give a shit if he did.

"Fuck him." He snickered, sliding the cue back and forth against her covered lips. "Though maybe you'd like to. Would you?"

"No," she protested, limpid blue pools locked on him.

Ian leaned into her. Pressing her against the table, he held the stick snugly against her cunt, running it across the telltale wetness, saturating the gusset of her tights.

"He wants to fuck you, princess."

"Sinjin," she whimpered. "Please."

"I'd die before I ever let him touch you." He growled, and

pushing her onto the table, Ian tugged the thin barrier of a garment down her thighs. "You're mine, understand?"

"Yes." Her breath hitched with a gasp as he inserted the thick butt end of the stick several inches into her sopping-wet hole.

"You're *my* princess…my dirty girl." Mesmerized by the sight of the cue in her pussy, he withdrew, just to watch it slide back inside her again. "Only mine."

"Fuck." Her teeth sank into her pillowy bottom lip.

"Like that?" Ian kissed the skin beneath her ear. "You're so perfect."

"Oooo," she keened when his fingers fell to her clit, the cue stick moving in and out.

Screaming with her orgasm, he removed the stick from her pussy. Coated in her sweetness, Ian smeared it across her lips. Grabbing it out of his hand, Breanna sucked the stick into her mouth, like she would his cock, and then licked it.

Jesus.

Overcome, he shoved his fingers inside her. "Whose little freak are you?"

"Yours."

"And who does this pussy belong to?"

"You, baby," she cried, her fingers reaching for her clit. "Only you."

That's right.

Ian tossed the stick, then lifting her into his arms, he carried her up the stairs.

Chapter Twenty-Five

I t came out of nowhere. This urgency inside him. A primitive need to claim her, mark her, make her his, and only his, in every conceivable way.

Ian carried her to his room and laid her down atop soft linen sheets. He took the boots off her feet, then the tights that were caught around her knees, before lifting the hem of the cable-knit dress and sliding it over her head. Bathed in moonlight, Breanna looked up at him with an expression on her face he could only describe as beatific.

And with his gaze never leaving hers, he rid himself of his clothes.

Gathering her in his arms, he placed a tender kiss on her lips. The urgent need growing ever stronger, Ian couldn't hold back, and knowing his princess, she wouldn't want him to.

Fingertips skating down her spine, he deepened their kiss. They traversed across her hip, up her side, and down again. Her movements matched his own. Soft hands roaming over his skin, Breanna pressed him closer to her.

Wet between her thighs, Ian ran his fingers through her folds. He dipped two inside her tight, hot cunt, his thumb pressing hard into her clit, and Breanna whimpered.

"Yes, yes, yes…baby…please…fuck me." She held onto his wrist and spread her legs wider. "Make it hurt."

"Want my fist?" he asked, shoving four fingers inside her.

"God…that feels so good." Her hips lifted off the bed. "More."

He did as she asked. Fucking her with his fingers, he rubbed her clit. Cum squirting from her hole, he tucked his thumb against his palm and pushed his way inside. "Look, baby. I got all of me in you this time."

Her thighs shaking, tears streaming down her face, Breanna glanced down to see his hand was inside her, up to his wrist. "I fucking love you, Sinjin."

"And I love you so fucking much." Her pussy clamping down on his hand, he carefully turned his wrist from side to side. "Is this okay, baby? Am I making you feel good?"

"God…yes," she moaned, her fingers seeking her clit. "I'm gonna come."

"You will not scream. I'm going to make you forget how to breathe." And ruining her pussy with his fist, he licked the cum from her fingers on her clit.

Ian lay beside her after, rubbing her cum into her skin, trailing it up the split of her ass, kissing every inch of skin his lips could reach. Breanna embodied everything he ever wanted in a partner, in bed and out. She was it for him. He thanked Fate, the universe, the mountain—whatever put her in his path that day. God, he never realized he could love someone as intensely as he loved her.

Languidly, and it felt like heaven, she stroked his aching dick. "I need everything, Sinjin, and I can take it. Promise you won't ever go easy with me."

His baby liked it rough, and that's the way he knew how to give it. Tender kisses. Hard fucking.

"Never."

Kissing his pec, Breanna whispered, "I'm brave enough now."

Brave enough?

His fingers continued their strumming. "What is it, my dirty girl?"

"I love that." Tipping her head back, she glanced up at him.
"What?"

"That I'm your dirty girl." And she squeezed his cock.
"Fuck my ass, baby. Please, I want you to."

His finger slipped inside her unfucked hole.

Breanna mewled.

Ian rolled her onto her tummy, and rubbing the globes of
her ass, he parted them.

"Mine."

And heaven help the bastard who tried to take what was
his.

Caught up in tangled sheets and twisted limbs, he opened
his eyes to see the most beautiful girl in the world sleeping
next to him. Nothing could be better than starting every day
like this, and as much as he wanted to stay in this bed and
love on her some more, Derek was in a room on the other
end of the hall.

Ian kissed her brow, carefully extricating himself from the
bed so as not to wake her. Naked, he strolled over to the window and looked out at an overcast sky. They weren't expecting
snow today, but flurries blew from the trees, dancing to the
tune of the wind. Maybe that would be enough to convince
his cousin to hightail it back to Sacramento, but somehow, he
doubted it.

In front of the fireplace, Hera stretched out her paws,
then walked over to the door. He patted her and opened it,
watching her scamper off into the snow. Warm lips kissed his
back, her arms wrapping around his middle. "It's still early,
baby. Come back to bed."

Right then, there wasn't anything Ian wanted more. He

closed his eyes and, wrapping her fingers around his morning wood, saw his fist disappear inside her pussy, his dick sinking into her ass. "I have to get rid of him."

"Shhh." Breanna stroked him.

He placed his hand on hers, stilling her movement. "We need to go downstairs."

"And do what?"

"You are going to decorate Christmas trees with Francie and my mother," Ian said. And turning around, he kissed her. "I'm going to buy us some more time."

"I love you." She rubbed her head on his chest.

He smoothed her hair down her back, tucking a wisp behind her ear. "I'm keeping you. You know that, right?"

"I know." Breanna smiled against his skin.

His hand dropped to the sweet place between her thighs and he cupped her pussy. "My babies are going to come out of here."

"I'm not ready for that yet."

"I know."

She looked up at him, her blue eyes locking on his. "Someday."

Nodding, he kissed her forehead. "I love you."

They were all in the morning room having breakfast when Ian came downstairs. All except Breanna, that is. A naked tree stood in the center of the windows, waiting for the women he loved to dress its branches in holiday finery, hanging lights and baubles and bows.

"Good morning, darling," Pamela crooned from where she sat beside her sister, sipping coffee. "Sleep well?"

"I did." With a smile he couldn't hide, he took a plate from the sideboard. "Looks delicious, Auntie."

"Your mom did the cooking this morning." Francie grinned, bringing a napkin to her mouth. "She insisted."

"Made your favorites. It's not every day I get to spoil my only son."

Eggs Benedict topped with crab, roasted asparagus, savory breakfast potatoes, and croissants. Ian would never hurt her feelings, but Breanna's waffles were his favorite now.

"I see that," he said, filling his plate. "Love you, Mom."

"Love you, too, dear. Where's Breanna?"

His face hidden behind a newspaper, Derek snickered. "She'll be down shortly, I'd imagine."

"Good, because we have business to attend to." His cousin tossed the paper to the table. "Perhaps she's in her right mind now."

Ian wrenched out a chair, and cocking his head, he glared at his cousin.

"What?" Derek rolled up his sleeves with a smirk. "We are all aware Miss Dalton suffered a terrible concussion and hasn't been able to make a sound decision since. Headaches. Delusions. Mood swings. I have plenty of witnesses that can attest to it."

Fucking bastard.

"It's *you* who's not right in the head, cousin." Leaning across the table, Ian got in his face. "Breanna sent the papers to her mom to look over, and their attorney, so, for now, she's not signing."

So what if he fibbed a little, right?

"I gave you one simple task, Ian," he said through gritted teeth.

Francie looked up from her plate. "What papers?"

"Your darling nephew here concocted a shitload of phony documents bequeathing the entirety of Valerie's estate to Dalton Trust Development Opco—which happens to be Derek, by the way."

"Nooo, it's *all* of us. And Breanna gets a million."

"How generous of you." Ian rolled his eyes.

If it wasn't for his mother and his aunt, he'd wipe the haughty smirk off Derek's face. With his fist.

"I thought so, considering she hasn't earned her rightful place here."

"Through no fault of her own," Pamela said, throwing down her fork.

"Derek." Francie held her hands to her cheeks. "Think about what you're doing, honey."

"Fraud, forgery, embezzlement, misappropriation of funds." Ian cut into his eggs with a shrug. "Shall I keep going?"

"This isn't at all what Valerie wanted," Francie said, as if her saying so would make any difference.

"Why should you care what that old bitch wanted? It was our family who helped make the Daltons rich from the very beginning and she stole it from us." Crossing his arms over his chest, Derek tipped his chin at their aunt. "Come on, look at you, nothing more than a servant who wasted her life cooking and cleaning for that woman."

"No one forced me to care for Valerie and this house." Raising her voice, Francie tore the napkin from her lap and threw it on the table. "Mr. Keeler and I met here. We built a life we love here, and this is where I want to be."

Francie never yelled. The silence that followed, then, was deafening.

Ian glanced around the table. His arm around his wife, her kind eyes filling behind her glasses, Ted stared daggers at Derek. The callous fucker shrugged, indifferent to the fact he'd shown no regard for Francie's feelings.

"Apologize to your aunt," Pamela seethed. "Now."

Though it's unlikely he would have, Derek never got the chance to. Breanna came in, and reading the tension in the room, quietly said, "Good morning."

"Miss Dalton." *Thank fuck.* As he stood, Ian pulled out a chair for her between him and his mother. "Can I fix you a plate?"

"Uh, sure." Her gaze flicking around the table, she tentatively sat down. "Thanks."

Offering Breanna a half-hearted smile, his mother cleared her throat. Still trying to collect herself, Francie stared down at her half-eaten plate. The ringing of Derek's phone was almost a welcome intrusion. He picked it up and silenced it.

"It's Miranda, dear." Peeking over his shoulder, Pamela smirked. "You probably want to take that."

"Excuse me a moment," Derek said with a huff, and left the room.

Sitting down with Breanna's breakfast, Ian grazed her back with his fingertips. "How much of that did you hear?"

"Enough." She picked up her fork, silently tucking into her food.

"I'm sorry."

Her lips parted to speak, but then Derek came back in. "My apologies, but I have to return to the city."

"Is Miranda all right, dear?" Pamela asked, feigning concern with a shit-eating grin on her face.

Derek ignored her.

"Take care of Miss Dalton in my absence, will you?" Slapping him on the back, he bent down and leaned into his ear. "One task, cousin. You better get it done." Then he kissed Breanna's cheek. "Be a good girl and listen to Mr. Maynard. I'll be back soon, sweetheart."

"What do we do now, Sinjin?"

"We keep looking for the documents." Ian glanced at Francie. "You wouldn't happen to know where Valerie might have kept them?"

"No," she said, worrying her lip.

He sat back and exhaled, lacing his fingers behind his head. "I'm going to Sacramento on Monday, then. I can slip into the office after hours, get the files, and slip back out."

"It isn't just about money for him, I'm afraid. The root of it goes much deeper than that." Pamela pursed her lips and sighed. "Like his father, he'd love nothing more than to wipe out the Dalton name."

"Why?" Breanna asked, putting down her fork.

"Revenge." She paused, her bottom lip disappearing behind her teeth. "Once, there were four of us, you see. My sister, Sharon, was the eldest. The summer she graduated from high school, she came up here to help the former Mrs. Dalton, your great-grandmother. Lawrence was home from college for the summer. Sharon was always going on about him. Your grandfather was quite handsome when he was younger, and quite the catch, too." With a bob of her head, Pamela's lips curved into a soft smile. "Anyway, she fancied herself in love with him, and one thing led to another, I suppose. Summer fling, you know? School started up again in the fall, and that was the end of that."

Ian knew this story, of course, but Breanna didn't. His arm went around her shoulders, hugging her to his side. *No more secrets, baby.*

Still smiling, his mother continued. "I was only eleven, but I remember watching Sharon get ready for the Thanksgiving open house. She was so excited to see him again. You see, she believed Lawrence was in love with her, too."

"But he wasn't?"

"No, as it turned out," Pamela said with a shake of her head. "They were, you know, typical kids with raging hormones. She wasn't quite nineteen that summer and Lawrence was just a couple of years older."

"What happened?" Breanna asked, her attention rapt.

"We walked into the grand foyer, and there was your

grandfather, looking as handsome as ever, with Valerie Kimball on his arm." She blew out a breath. "They announced their engagement at dinner."

"Oh, no." Her fairytale eyes going wide, Breanna gasped. "How awful for her."

"She was devastated, to say the least."

"I remember that and I was only five." With a nod, Francie finally spoke. "Sharon ran out of there in tears."

"No one could console her. Not even my brother, and she and Raymond were extremely close. Two days later, Sharon came out of her room smiling as if she didn't have a care in the world. Told my father she was going shopping, kissed his cheek, and said she'd be back before dinner."

Pamela wasn't smiling anymore.

The eyes behind her glasses pained, Francie shrugged a shoulder. "But she never came back."

"They found what was left of her car the next morning," his mother recounted, staring out at the mountains through the window. "She drove herself right off the pass."

"On purpose?" Her jaw slack, Breanna gazed up at him with a look of disbelief on her face.

Pamela nodded. "And Raymond never got over it. He blamed your grandfather for her death."

"Because he broke her heart?"

"There's so much gray to every story, dear. Nothing is ever black and white. I don't know this to be fact, but supposedly, Sharon was three months pregnant with your grandfather's baby when she died."

"Oh, Jesus." Breanna covered her mouth with her hand. "Wait, weren't Raymond and my grandfather good friends?"

"You know the old saying, don't you? Keep your friends close and your enemies closer." She pursed her lips to the side, then released a heavy breath. "Look, I loved my brother, and while I understood his grief for our sister, as the years went by, he became more and more unhinged. Drove his wife to divorce him. Infected Derek with his crazy nonsense, too, it seems."

Ian glanced down at Breanna. She seemed a bit shaken. Hugging her to him a little tighter, he kissed her crown.

"Everyone knows Shane's death wasn't an accident." Pamela got up from the table and grabbed a bottle of whiskey from the liquor cabinet. "I always suspected my brother had something to do with it somehow."

"No, Pamela." Her lips pressed tight, Francie watched her sister pour a generous helping of whiskey into her coffee. "Raymond wouldn't…"

"Valerie thought the same." Ian nodded. At least, according to Sarah Benjamin, she did.

"I know, dear." Pamela took hold of his hand. "It's the very reason she kept Breanna far away and you close by her side."

"I take it back." Ted took the whiskey from Pamela and poured some into a glass. "I'm thinking that boy ain't blowing smoke out his ass."

No shit.

His cousin might think he was smart, but Ian was smarter. He had the girl.

Now he was going to put an end to all this bullshit. And maybe, if it wasn't too late, he could save Derek from himself.

He just wasn't sure exactly how.

Chapter Twenty-Six

S
he sat down at her father's desk with a sigh. Touching the things he'd once touched, Breanna closed her eyes as if that would bring him back somehow. After breakfast this morning and finishing the Christmas trees this afternoon, she just needed some time to herself.

What kind of sordid, mixed-up shit had she been born into? *Secrets and lies.* "God, I sure hope that's the last of them."

Because if there were any more skeletons in the proverbial family closet, she feared she might lose it.

Not wanting to think about cars plunging off the face of the mountain for one more minute, Breanna sifted through the stack of notebooks sitting beneath her fingertips. Her father's novel, each word painstakingly written in his own hand. Placing them in sequential order, she packed the notebooks, along with other writings that she'd found, into a box. As long as she was here, she'd start transcribing his manuscript onto her laptop, where it could be kept safe in the cloud forever.

Cold hands. Kneading her shoulders, Sinjin bent down to kiss that place beneath her ear that tickled. Breanna giggled, jumping in her seat. "Were you outside? Your fingers are like icicles."

"Want to warm them up for me?" He swung her chair around, and crouching on his haunches, shoved his hands beneath her sweater. "There. That feels nice."

"That's cold, baby."

"Just give it a minute." Sinjin kissed her on the nose, warming his hands on her skin. "What are you doing in here?"

"Organizing." She nodded to the box on the floor. "I'm going to take those to my room."

"I'll bring it down for you." He stood and hefted the box onto his shoulder.

Falling into place beside him, Breanna paused at the doorway. "Hey, I just had a thought. We haven't looked in here. Do you think Grandmama could've stashed the papers here somewhere?"

"It's possible, but I don't think so. Valerie kept these rooms like a shrine. No one ever came in here—not even Francie," Sinjin said, glancing around her father's living room. "She wanted everything to remain just as Shane left it."

"Where the fuck are they, then? And why hide them so they can't be found?"

"Good question." Holding the box on his shoulder, his free arm came around her. "It's okay. I'll get them from the office."

"But what if Derek's already destroyed them or they aren't there?"

Because that was a distinct possibility, now wasn't it?

Gazing down at her with a shrug, Sinjin blew out a breath. "Then we're fucked."

Not if I can help it.

And it wasn't about the money, though admittedly, having it wouldn't suck. Her family's legacy, this mountain, the house they built, is what mattered. That, and she couldn't let Derek get away with this. Breanna would not let him win.

"I'm guessing if she didn't trust Raymond, then she didn't trust his son very much, either." Glancing up at him, a lightbulb went off in her head. "She hid those papers where she thought Derek would never think to look, but *you* would."

"Maybe, but where?"

"Come on." She tugged on his arm. "We haven't been looking in the right places."

Sinjin put the box he carried down on Valerie's coffee table. Shaking his head, he raked his fingers through his dark hair, then pulled her into his arms. "Breanna, we've already scoured every square inch of these rooms."

"And I'm telling you, we haven't."

"We've gone through the pages of every book, ransacked the closet, her drawers…"

"Those are the obvious places." Her fingers wrapped around his biceps, and she gazed up at him, trying to make him see. "Let's try some not-so-obvious ones."

"Like?"

I don't know… "You have to think like she did, Sinjin, and you knew her better than most."

He paced around her grandmother's living room, eyes combing the shelves they'd already searched. Sinking into a chair facing the unlit fireplace, he stared straight ahead.

"Ice cream." Abruptly, Sinjin stood and walked over to the mantel. "Strawberry ice cream."

"I'm not following…"

"Didn't your mom say that's what Valerie gave you at the pool when you were in Tahoe?" he asked, the photo of her at Venice Beach in his hands.

"Yeah, but…"

"What are you holding in this picture?"

"A strawberry ice cream cone." Out of nowhere, tears rushed to fill her eyes. "Sinjin, you don't think…"

Breanna watched him carefully remove the backing from the frame, and there, behind the photo, was a key taped to a letter.

"Just like her to leave instructions." Passing her the handwritten note, he chuckled. "I knew it. The bulk of the estate is in a trust. The original documents are in a safe deposit box in Sacramento."

"What made you look there?"

"You told me to think like her." He shrugged. "Your grandmother would sit in this chair every day and look at that picture of you."

And the tears that filled her eyes broke free.

"Shhh, it's okay." Rubbing circles on her back, Sinjin held her. "Everything's going to be all right now, princess."

After a quick stop at River City Bank, and then the courthouse, Dalton House was safe from Derek. And so was Breanna. With the probate and trust documents filed, they were a matter of public record now, and there wasn't a thing his cousin could do about it.

Ian glanced at the white bakery box in the passenger seat and smiled. He'd stopped at Hank's, getting one of his wife's banana cream pies to bring home to her. He checked in on her car at the shop, too. Looking better than new, they told him she'd be good to go by the end of the week. What would Breanna do then? Stay? Go to LA? Portland? He understood she had another semester to go, but her graduation in May seemed so far away.

She was in the kitchen with Francie, watching her wrap a nice tenderloin in puff pastry. "Beef Wellington, Auntie?" he asked, kissing her on the cheek.

"Mmhm, and there's truffle mashed potatoes, arugula salad, green beans, and fresh-baked bread to go with it." Francie didn't even bother glancing up when she asked him, "Everything go okay?"

"Yeah, it's done."

"Thank goodness," she replied, letting out a breath.

"Stopped at Hank's." With a wink, Ian kissed Breanna's cheek and set the bakery box on the counter. "Picked up dessert."

"Is that a banana cream pie?"

"Could be." He grinned. "Checked on that damn girly car of yours, too. It should be ready by the end of the week."

"Oh." Pressing her lips together, she nodded. "Good. That's good."

"You've got another hour before dinner's ready." Glancing up at them, Francie smiled. "I'm guessing the two of you have some talking to do."

"Yeah." And lacing his fingers with Breanna's, he kissed his aunt on the cheek. "I suppose we do."

Once inside his living room, loosening his tie with one hand, Ian tossed his briefcase to the sofa with the other.

"I take it back," she said, looking up at him from beneath her lashes. "You do look lawyerish."

"Oh, yeah?" Grabbing her hand, he pulled Breanna to his chest and held her there.

"Yeah." Smiling, her fingertips smoothed over his lapels. "And I like it."

He kissed her then.

Tightening his hold, Ian pressed her into him closer, his embrace engulfing her entire body. And for a moment, time stood still. Tasting her soft, candied lips. Inhaling citrus from her hair. The feel-good chemical cocktail she incited released into his veins. He savored the feeling.

With a feather-light sweep of his lips on hers, Ian's thumb grazed her cheek, and he turned toward the glass. Going over to it, he got out of his jacket and tore the tie from his neck, throwing them both to the floor.

Then, as he gazed upon the snow-covered peaks, with her

face pressed into his back, Breanna wrapped her arms around his waist. "Are you okay?"

Not really.

With a sarcastic snicker, he exhaled. "I'm no better than Derek."

"What are you talking about?"

"I knew what he was planning to do." Squeezing her hand, Ian rubbed it up and down his chest. "Not the how of it, but the why, and when Valerie passed, I didn't give two shits."

The woman had cared for him as she would a favored grandson, gifting him generously over the years for doing a job she could have easily managed herself. He just couldn't abide someone—anyone—who didn't appreciate Valerie Dalton for the wonderful, selfless human being that she was.

"Because from what I could tell, you never gave a shit about her." He turned around, whiskey eyes locking on blue. "And I despised you for it."

With a sudden intake of breath, Breanna gasped at the harshness of his words.

He angled his head, stroking her pretty hair. "In my mind, you were nothing more than an entitled princess who only cared about Valerie's money." Pausing to exhale, Ian wet his lips. "But then I met you."

"Your perception changed, then?"

He nodded. "I was on my way to Sacramento when I ran into you at Hank's. See, Derek told me you were coming. I didn't want to see you, and I didn't want any part of what he was doing. That doesn't absolve me, though. Knowledge makes me just as culpable. I should've put a stop to it…"

"But you did." Her fingers holding onto his biceps, Breanna shook him. "Maybe I should doubt you, but I never have. I gave you my trust in blind faith, and that's how it's going to stay."

God, I don't deserve her, but thank you.

"I didn't plan on falling in love with you—or anyone— that's for sure. But I did. From the moment I saw you in your deathtrap of a girly car, I think." Shaking his head, he chuckled. "And you're trading that thing in, by the way. I need to know you're safe."

She nodded, giggling through her tears. "Okay."

"Because you're *my* princess, and I love you."

"I love you, too."

You're mine, all mine.

He kissed her again. "I have to go back to Sacramento."

"Why?"

Rubbing the furrow that appeared between her brows with his thumb, Ian explained, "I still want to get those files from the office."

"Derek can't do anything with them, can he?"

"Don't worry, he can't touch the estate. Everything is filed with the court, just as it should be." He held his lips to her forehead. "But he's still my cousin, baby, so in case he's tempted to try, I need to destroy those documents before he incriminates himself."

Pulling back, Breanna nodded. "What do you think Derek is going to do when he finds out?"

"That I betrayed him?" Ian snickered.

"You didn't."

But I did.

"That's how he's going to see it."

Chapter Twenty-Seven

On the other side of the mountain, the predawn sky was just beginning to lighten. Bathed in fog and shadows, the view outside her window appeared ominous. At dinner last night, Ted informed them a monster storm was on the way. "They're saying we're gonna get eight to ten this weekend."

"Inches?"

"Nooo, Breanna." He chuckled at her naïveté. "That would be eight to ten feet."

"Oh."

"Remember when I explained what an atmospheric river is?"

Kind of. She nodded.

"Well, there's one headed straight for us."

That's when Francie advised her that if she hoped to make it to LA for Christmas, she'd best be off the mountain, heading south on 395, before the first snowflake fell. Breanna thought she'd at least have another week. She didn't want to leave. Not yet. Her plan was to go home, come back to ring in the new year with Sinjin, and then return to Portland to start her last semester, dammit.

After dinner and a glass of brandy, Ted and Francie bid them goodnight, then she and Sinjin went upstairs. The door had barely closed behind them when he grabbed her, kissing her and tearing at her clothes like he might never see her again.

And they'd been going at it like rabbits ever since.

Her pussy was raw, and her nipples tender. Breanna was certain that once it was light enough to see, she'd find bite marks and fingerprints coloring her skin. But then, she was sure she'd find them on him, too.

"Damn, princess, how is it you're still so wet?" The sheets beneath her soaked, his fingers were inside her once again.

Breanna curled her fingers around his erection and squeezed. "How is it you're still so hard?"

"Fuck," Sinjin groaned, his teeth sinking into her neck.

He smoothed over the sting with his tongue, kissing up the column of her throat and along her jaw until their lips met. The ache in her pussy flaring, Breanna gave in to the feeling. She never could resist his magic fingers or those decadent kisses.

So she didn't.

Jagged lightning erupting through her belly, a rush of fluid seeped down her thighs. Caught off-guard, she choked on air, the orgasm striking without warning. She couldn't breathe for a moment, and when, at last, she could suck in a breath, tears were flowing from her eyes.

The pads of his fingers pressed into her flesh, stroking up and down her thigh. "Shit, baby, did I hurt you?"

"Don't be silly."

"You're bleeding." His gaze flicked up from between her legs.

"I am?"

"Look."

Twilight casting the room in gloomy shades of gray, Breanna glanced down to where his palm rested on her tummy. Blood stained the fingers that were just inside her.

Crimson smeared her thighs and the once pristine sheets beneath her.

Well, hello, Aunt Flo.

"It's my period, Sinjin." She swallowed, wiping the wetness from her eyes. "Looks like I'm not pregnant after all."

"Are you sad?" he asked, brushing the hair back from her face.

Was she?

"Yes. No. I don't know." Breanna shrugged. "You put the thought in my head and…"

"If you want a baby, we'll make one, okay?" Rubbing her back, Sinjin pressed his lips to her forehead.

She sniffled. "Maybe someday."

"Whenever you're ready."

"Okay." And nodding against his chest, Breanna smiled.

He tipped her chin up, bringing her lips to his. "Come here."

"I have to take a shower." She kissed him. "And these sheets need to go in the trash."

"I said, come here."

His arms in a vise-like grip around her, Sinjin took her mouth. Stole her breath. And for just a moment, Breanna forgot there was a mess between her legs, that the expensive linens they laid on were ruined, that the seed he planted in her head hadn't taken root in her belly. She should be relieved, and mostly, she was, so why all the tears?

Teeth skimming down her throat, Sinjin licked the sweat from her neck and between her breasts. He held them in his palms, his tongue slowly snaking on a path toward her tummy.

Her fingers caught in his hair, Breanna pulled. "Sinjin, what are you doing?"

"Loving you," he murmured into her skin, his lips kissing lower and lower.

"What part of *'I've got my period'* did you not get?"

"Oh, I got it, princess."

His whiskey eyes burning black, she felt the faint curve of a smirk on her flesh, and undeterred, his wicked tongue laved between her lips.

Holy fuck.

She should be mortified, and she would have been, except his mouth on her bleeding cunt felt glorious. Sinjin devoured her. Lapping up period blood commingled with their cum. Sucking on her clit as he pressed his fingers back inside. Wrung out, Breanna didn't think she had another orgasm left in her.

She was wrong.

He willed it from her.

Fingers holding onto his sweat-dampened hair, hips coming off the bed, she spasmed. Sinjin growled, but Breanna couldn't make a sound. Bit by bit, she melted onto the bed, and gasping for breath, inhaled life back into her lungs.

Caressing her quivering flesh, Sinjin kissed his way up her tummy and nuzzled between her breasts. "Did you really think I'd care about a little blood?"

Unable to speak, Breanna rubbed her fingers through his hair.

"It's a part of you." He kissed her skin. "And I love all your parts."

After weeks at Dalton House, she finally left the mountain. In the back of Jordy's truck, Breanna peered through the window, craning her neck to see up to the top, but clouds obscured her view, so she couldn't.

"Bet you're glad to be gettin' your car back, Miss Dalton." Bobbing his head, the sheriff grinned a dopey grin in the rearview mirror. "Especially with snowmageddon comin.'"

"Yeah." She wasn't, though.

"Francie tells me you're leaving us in the morning."

"I'm going to my mom's for Christmas," she said, her smile tight, trying to appear somewhat amenable to her impending departure. "Then I have to get back to school in Portland."

"We're sure gonna miss you around here."

"She'll be back." Beside her, Sinjin squeezed her hand. "Won't you, princess?"

As fast as I possibly can.

And if another damn atmospheric river messed up her New Year's Eve plans, she'd return once she was settled in the routine of a new semester—the last one. Breanna had an editing practicum to complete this coming term, and she already had a project in mind—her father's novel.

"Of course I will."

They drove past the original house George Dalton built, and then around the curve, the sleepy little hamlet came into view. Quaint, it was even prettier in the daylight. Aged brick. Wrought iron. Shops adorned with twinkling Christmas lights. Breanna was certain she'd come to love it here. Sacramento wasn't all that far away, and San Francisco was just a couple of hours beyond that, for when she had a craving for someplace bigger.

They pulled in at the garage. Turning his face toward hers, Sinjin kissed her cheek. "Wait in here with Jordy while I get the car."

He was out the door, sprinting over to see the mechanic before she could blink an eye.

Glancing her way, the portly sheriff inclined his head. "As long as it's just the two of us here, I, umm…I want to tell you I'm sorry for misleading you back at the cabin."

"You lied to me, Jordy." She couldn't be mad at him for it, though. With a shake of her head, Breanna smiled. "Thought I might've lost my mind there for a while."

"On account of Derek, Ian thought it best. He was so concerned about you." Chewing on the inside of his cheek, he nodded. "And I agreed with him. That boy ain't been right in the head since his father died. I don't wanna see you go, but I'm glad you won't be anywhere near here when he finds out he's been bested."

"What about Sinjin?"

Breanna worried because he'd have no choice but to deal with the fallout of his cousin's wrath. And as much as she cringed at the prospect of ever seeing Derek again, Sinjin shouldn't have to do that on his own. She was perfectly capable, ready, and willing to stand at his side.

"Ian knows how to handle Derek," Jordy assured her, patting her hand. "You'd never know it now, but those two were closer than brothers as kids. Where one went, the other was always sure to follow."

She wasn't convinced. Her teeth sinking into her lip, Breanna glanced at the garage office. With her car keys in his hand, Sinjin waved from the doorway.

"I don't think I'll get to see you again before you go." The sheriff leaned in for a hug. "You take care now, Miss Breanna."

"I will, Jordy," she said, kissing him on the cheek.

He glanced out the window. "He loves you, you know."

Sinjin opened the passenger door. "Ready, princess?"

248

Stepping out of the truck, Breanna looked back at Jordy. "I know."

"Safe travels, dear."

"Thanks again, Jordy." Smiling, she gave him a little wave. "For everything."

Sinjin kissed her crown and, holding her to his side, they went over to her car. "See? Good as new."

"God, I love this car." Her fingertips skimming the polished white hood, Breanna caressed it. She'd worked so hard, saved every penny, just to get it.

Little did I know, I didn't have to.

But by withholding the privilege her father had left for her, Grandmama taught her a valuable lesson she might never have learned otherwise. *Wise woman.* She appreciated that car because she'd earned it.

"Even so, you're trading it in." Sinjin opened the passenger door for her. "I can't have you sliding off the goddamn mountain."

"Or smashing into it?" Arching her brow, Breanna smirked and got in.

"Or that." He chuckled, buckling her into her seatbelt. "C'mon, let's go home."

"Can we stop at the drugstore first?" Scrunching her shoulders, she pursed her lips to the side. "I need to pick up some things."

Tampons, specifically. She only kept a couple in her purse.

"Of course we can." He closed her door and came around to the driver's side. "How about we take a walk down Main Street? I'll show you around a bit and we can grab a bite to eat."

"Yeah, okay." Breanna giggled, watching Sinjin trying to adjust his seat in her little, girly car. "I'd like that."

She studied the details of the old buildings as they walked past, noting the year of construction embedded into the wall. 1887. 1921. "This is so cool."

"Datestones. They used to do that back in the day," Sinjin explained, coming to a stop in front of the drugstore. "The Daltons and St. Johns pretty much built this town together. Our families were never divided—at least not until Sharon died."

"But that's in the past now, isn't it?"

"Yeah, princess." He kissed her brow. "We made sure of that."

Sinjin opened the door for her, escorting her inside. Scoffing at the Plan B pills she hadn't needed sitting on a shelf next to bottles of KY Jelly, Breanna proceeded down the aisle and dropped a box of tampons—super absorbency because Aunt Flo's a goddamn bitch—into the red plastic shopping basket. At the checkout, she threw in a big bag of chocolate-covered pretzels. Raising his brow, Sinjin smirked, so she added a tube of Burt's Bees coconut lip balm for good measure.

"Got everything you need, princess?" With a chuckle, he handed his card over to the cashier.

As long as I've got you. She nodded.

Out on the sidewalk, Sinjin asked, "Hungry?"

"Aren't I always?" Besides, Aunt Flo turned her into a ravenous beast.

"Come on." He chuckled. "I better feed you, then."

After scarfing down a burger at the same bar she'd seen the old men walk into the night she came here, they headed back up the mountain. With Sinjin driving, she could take in the village as it disappeared behind them, the hairpin curves of the pass, the harrowing drop-offs into nothing. *Jesus.* She swallowed. Her heart was in her throat even now. This road with her name on it had claimed two lives that she knew of already. Breanna squeezed her eyes shut at the thought of it taking another.

As if reading her thoughts, Sinjin reached across the console, and taking her hand, he held it on his thigh. "You'll get used to it, and soon, driving the pass will seem as natural to you as breathing."

Somehow, she didn't think so.

He parked the Miata beneath the shelter of the porte-cochère. She went to gather her things, grabbing her shopping bag from the floorboard and the charger she'd left behind the night of the storm. Breanna heard the ping from his phone but didn't give any thought to it.

Sinjin read the text, pocketed his phone, and glanced over at her.

"He knows."

Chapter Twenty-Eight

He told her not to worry.

But in between pacing around her room and packing up her things, she did.

"What did Derek say?" she'd asked as he led her up the stairs. "How do you know he knows?"

Pausing at her door, Sinjin huffed out a breath. "He said I'm dead to him."

"That doesn't mean…"

"That's exactly what it means." He nodded, tucking Breanna's hair behind her ear. "It's okay, baby. I planned on telling him once you left for your mom's, anyway."

"What do you think he's going to do?"

"Nothing he can do, baby. So don't worry."

Her packing skills weren't even close to being on the same level as Kayleigh's. *Fuck it.* She'd take only the clothes she couldn't do without and leave the rest of them here. The plan was to come back in a few weeks anyway, right?

Right.

And tonight was her last night with Sinjin until then.

She wasn't about to ruin the hours they had left together all worked up over Derek St. John. "He can go straight to hell."

Breanna zipped up her duffel bag, and tossing it onto a chair, went into the ensuite. A long, hot shower would make her feel better and clear her head. She stripped out of her clothes, admiring the marks Sinjin left on her body as she gazed at her reflection. Addicted to him now as she was, being apart was going to be torture.

Steam rose from the shower, hot water raining down on her skin. Heavy-handed with the soap, Breanna lathered herself. She always felt dirty when she had her period, no matter how much she scrubbed. Maybe that was silly. Aunt Flo sure didn't put Sinjin off, after all.

She giggled to herself, making a mental note to keep some towels handy so she wouldn't ruin another set of sheets.

After showering, fluffing, and buffing, Breanna sat cross-legged at the vanity, wearing the teal bra that made her breasts look bigger, applying her makeup. A smoky eye and subtle lip were just the look for tonight.

"There." Pleased with herself, she spritzed her face with setting spray. "That's perfect."

"You're fucking gorgeous, Miss Dalton."

His face half hidden in shadow, Derek emerged from the hall. Still in his 'uniform,' as Sinjin would say—tailored suit, crisp white dress shirt, and tie—he must've rushed over here straight from the office.

"But I think you're well aware of that."

"Sinjin reset the key code. How'd you get in here?" She eyed his reflection in the mirror.

"It's Sinjin now, is it?" Derek made the name sound like a curse word, and coming closer, he smirked. "You left the door to the deck unlocked."

Again? Fuck.

"I'm not dressed, so I'm going to need you to leave."

"I think not." Cool hands clamped down on her shoulders. "Put on a pretty dress. I'll wait."

"Derek, please, just go."

"My own blood fucked me over..." His fingers painfully curled into her skin. "...for *you.*"

"That's not true." Her chest heaving with every breath, Derek lowered his hands to fondle her uplifted breasts. Swatting at him, Breanna shouted, "Don't touch me... Sinjin!"

"Ian's not coming. He already got what he wanted from you. I warned you about him, didn't I?" He snickered. "My turn."

Derek ripped the teal satin. He molded her flesh like modeling clay, squeezing and pinching the already tender tissue.

She smacked his hands. "Stop it."

He stopped, but in a swift move that surprised her, Derek yanked her out of the chair, his open palm slapping her face.

"You're going to be a good little girl and do whatever I tell you to do." Taking her by the throat, Derek pushed her toward the closet. "See, you've left me no other choice. You and I are going to take a little ride."

"I'm not going anywhere with you."

"No?" Maniacal brown eyes leering at her, he tipped his head to the side and smirked. Something hard, hidden in his jacket pocket, pressed into her side. He didn't have to tell her what it was. "Bet I can change your mind. Now, get moving. The Marriage Bureau in Reno closes at eight."

"What?"

A creepy grin appeared on his face. "Happy wedding day, Mrs. St. John."

Oh. Hell. No.

"You're fucking nuts if you think I'm marrying you."

"Breanna?"

He's here. Fuck you, asshole.

"Sin—"

His hand covering her mouth, the crazed fucker

slammed her against the wall. Pure hatred. It was there in his eyes.

Her gaze darted to Sinjin, who cautiously approached. "Let her go, Derek."

A husky laugh tumbled from his throat. "Fuck off, Ian."

"Come on, man. You were never going to get away with it. I saved your ass." For a brief moment, Sinjin locked eyes with her. It seemed as if they were trying to tell her something, but she didn't know what. "You're just making this worse for yourself."

Derek lowered the hand in his pocket and turned around. "I told you, you're dead to me."

"Get dressed, baby," Sinjin prompted her with a tip of his chin.

"Yes, and hurry it up, Miss Dalton." Derek snickered. Breanna could hear the menacing smirk in his voice. "Tick tock, tick tock."

"Gun," she mouthed to Sinjin, patting her side.

Fingers trembling, Breanna pulled her leggings on and grabbed a tank top and hoodie while she looked for a pair of boots. Her knit ankle booties would have to do. They were house slippers, but whatever.

"*You* are going to take that mangy mutt of yours and go back to your party house in Sacramento. Your services are no longer required here or at the firm, either."

Gun, gun, gun!

Frantically, Breanna waved her arms in the air and scrambled to put the booties on her feet.

"I expect you to be gone before Miss Dalton and I return."

She could hear voices coming down the hall. "I'm telling you, I haven't seen him, Miranda."

Francie. *Thank fuck.*

"His car's in the driveway. Where's Ian?"

Derek moved toward the door.

Sinjin's eyes pleading with hers, he whispered, "Run."

Fuck, fuck, fuck. Why didn't I take my keys?

Panting. Cold. Out of breath. Breanna raced along the deck to the stairs, holding onto her phone. At least she'd had the sense to grab that. But then it was sitting right there on the bed. The keys to her car were in her purse.

On the ground level, once Breanna was certain no one was following her, she hid behind a tree and took out her phone. Her voice quivering, she choked on the words. "Jordy, it's Breanna. You've got to come quick."

"Calm down, sweetie. What's going on?"

"Derek's here and he's got a gun." Crying, she wiped the snot from her nose.

"Where's Ian?"

"In the house with Derek. He told me to run. Please, hurry." Afraid the tree couldn't hide her for long, Breanna hung up the phone.

And she ran.

Thankful the moon was hidden behind a thick veil of clouds, she scurried through the snow to the caretaker's cottage and pounded on the door. But Ted wasn't there. The unmistakable sound of a gunshot came from the house. Sinking to her knees, Breanna glanced up at her bedroom window and covered her mouth to stifle her scream.

Please be okay, baby. Please be okay. Please, please, please.

She couldn't stay here.

Ted had to be in the garage. She ran toward it.

Under the porte-cochère, the fucker's Jag blocked her car

in. Breanna couldn't have gotten away even if she had brought her keys.

Locked tight, the garage door wouldn't budge. She closed her eyes, trying to remember the numbers Sinjin punched into the keypad the day he showed her the mountain, but she couldn't. Banging on the door could be a risk. Someone might hear it, but desperately, Breanna banged, anyway. It was a wasted attempt. No one answered. Wearing only a hoodie, her knit booties sopping, she sagged against the door, unsure of what to do or where to go.

Frozen to the bone, uncontrollably shaking, Breanna tried to think. The cabin was too far, not that she'd find it in the dark with only the sobbing gurgle of the mountain stream to guide her. Should she sneak back inside the house? Surely, she could find a place to hide until Jordy got there. Because she certainly would not make it out here.

As Breanna doubled back the way she came, footsteps crunched on the icy walk.

Shit!

Ducking behind her car, she prayed it wasn't locked.

"I know you're out here, Breanna." Derek laughed, and it was eerie. "I'm going to find you, sweetheart. You left me your footprints in the snow."

She watched him walk toward the garage and slowly reached for the door handle. As soon as he was far enough past her, she tried opening it. *Thank you, God.* Sinjin hadn't locked it. She slipped inside, then quickly and quietly closed the door.

Now what? Her car wasn't the safest place to hide. He'd only follow the footprints she hadn't thought to hide—not that she could have, anyway—and find her here.

Makes an excellent weapon should you need one.

"The flashlight." What did she do with it after Sinjin rescued her? "Please be here."

She reached inside the glove compartment and breathed a sigh of relief. "Thank you, Daddy."

Then, armed with the flashlight ready in her hands, she waited.

A deep breath in.

A slow exhale.

Her gaze darted left and right, then left again, the sound of that gunshot echoing in her head.

Sinjin's okay.

Inhale.

Exhale.

Where is he then?

Inhale.

Exhale.

Please be okay.

Inhale.

Exhale.

Hurry, Jordy. Please.

Inhale.

Exhale.

And the door wrenched open. "Gotcha."

She didn't even look when she swung.

Whack.

Breanna climbed over the console, bolted out the passenger side door, and didn't look back. Then, running down the driveway, she collapsed with relief at the first sight of blue flashing lights.

An engine revved.

Jordy sped by, her gaze following the truck.

Another gunshot exploded, reverberating off the trees.

But this time, squeezing her eyes shut, Breanna screamed.

So. Fucking. Loud.

With the acrid scent of spent gunpowder tainting the

crisp winter air, she opened her eyes. Headlights were coming toward her. Francie stood on the walkway, a rifle at her side. Too exhausted to get up, she sat in the snow, watching Derek's Jag fly past her.

Jordy scooped her up and half-carried, half-dragged her over to Francie.

"Sinjin?"

But Francie didn't answer, shouting instead, "Get her a blanket."

"Hey, Randall. We're gonna need another unit up here." The static of a two-way radio. "For Breanna. No, she's not shot."

She didn't see it, but she heard it.

Bang.

Bang.

Bang.

Crash.

BOOM.

"What was that?" She heard someone say.

"Not sure, honey. Can't worry about that now."

"Where's Sinjin?" Why wouldn't anyone answer her, goddammit?

Sirens blaring, flashing red lights raced up the driveway. Medics jumped out, sprinting with a stretcher toward the door. "Up the stairs and to the right, Randall. Ted's with him."

"Sinjin?" Her tears falling, Breanna gazed up at Francie.

"Shh. Everything's going to be all right."

Nooo.

He looked so pale. Ted walked beside the gurney, his shirt and hands dyed red.

Blood.

"Sinjin." But her voice came out barely a whisper.

"We heard what sounded like an explosion."

"Yeah, we saw it." She thought maybe it was Randall talking, but she couldn't be sure. "A vehicle skidded off the pass."

The shrill scream of a woman pierced through the air. Breanna didn't know who it was. But then maybe it was the ambulance driving away with the only man she would ever love that she heard.

Sinjin.

Francie held her.

Tears froze on her face.

And the world went dark.

Chapter Twenty-Nine

He didn't remember much after the bullet struck his flesh.

Derek standing there.

Francie rushing through the door.

Was Miranda there, too?

Ian wracked his brain, but everything was still so foggy. He blamed it on the morphine, or whatever the fuck they were pumping into his veins. With heavy eyelids, his gaze traveled up the tubing to the bag dripping the drug into a chamber.

He tried counting the drops.

Drip.

Drip.

Drip.

"Sinjin. Baby, wake up."

"Princess?" His eyes focusing, he squinted. "Oh… Mom…where's Breanna?"

"I told you, dear." Pamela leaned over the bedrail to kiss his brow. "She went to the airport to pick up her folks."

"But I need her." He did. Every minute of every day for the rest of his life.

"Breanna's been with you the whole time, baby. She hasn't left your side," his mother said, her fingers combing through his hair. "Let's raise your head and sit you up a little, yeah?"

"Ah, fuck." It felt like his insides were ripping apart.

"I'm going to ring for the nurse."

"No, don't." He gritted his teeth, snatching Pamela's hand so she wouldn't press the call light. "They'll just shoot me up with some more shit I don't want."

"A bullet blasted through your liver. Take the damn medicine."

Ian glanced down at the bandage covering his chest and snickered. "That's going to leave a good scar, isn't it?"

"It isn't funny. Do you have any idea how lucky you are?" She squeezed his hand to emphasize the point. "You almost died."

"But I didn't."

Mother and son. She looked at him and he looked at her. Neither one of them said it, but Ian was sure they were both thinking about Derek.

"Sinjin, don't."

He let out a breath. "What?"

"There's nothing you could have done. Your cousin put himself on a path of self-destruction." She glanced out the window, diverting her gaze for a moment. "Francie even tried to stop him and couldn't."

"Maybe I could have."

"I doubt that. Valerie wanted you at Dalton House, but Raymond and Derek allowed it for a reason." Pamela caressed his cheek. "The blame rests with my brother. He's the one who started this all those years ago."

No, they all shared the blame—Lawrence and Sharon, Valerie, Sarah Benjamin, Aunt Francie, his mom, and himself. Any of them might have prevented this tragedy from ever happening.

"What day is it?"

"Sunday." God, it'd been three days already.

"When can I go home?"

"Your surgeon said you need to stay a few more days," Pamela informed him, adjusting his pillow. Unlike her sister, his mother wasn't usually a hoverer, but considering the circumstances, Ian figured her hovering was justified.

"So, Wednesday?"

"Maybe. If they're done clearing the pass by, then." She shrugged. "They've got six feet up there already, I heard, and it's still coming down heavy."

Snowmageddon.

"Ted's going to need help."

"Already taken care of. Don't worry."

Jordy saw to it, he was sure.

"Why don't we comb your hair and wash your face, hm? I wouldn't want you to scare off Breanna's family when they get here."

"That bad?"

She made a face, her head tipping to the side while she scrunched her shoulders.

Too late, Mother.

"Hey, princess." His lips curved into a smirk, but as she tiptoed into the room, Ian couldn't contain it. He grinned so widely it hurt his face.

Breanna smiled back, and it was the most beautiful sight he'd ever seen.

She hurried to his side and, combing her fingers through his hair, softly kissed his lips. "Finally. You're awake for real this time."

"I wasn't before?" He chuckled.

"You opened your eyes now and then. Otherwise, you've been out of it."

"Come here." Ian patted the narrow space beside him.

Pamela winked, and smiling, she said, "I think you two need some time alone."

He looked on as she went to the doorway to greet Breanna's parents, who were standing with a blonde twenty-something girl.

He waved. The trio waved back.

"Is that Kayleigh?"

"Yeah, she insisted on coming when I told her what happened, but I think she just wants to check you out. Their flights were only fifteen minutes apart, too."

"How convenient." He smirked. "This is not how I planned on meeting your folks."

"You saved me, so you're their hero."

He didn't, though. Breanna saved herself.

"That's pretty fucking good the way I see it."

His fiery princess. He *was* lucky, and not just because he was alive. Ian got to be the man who loved her.

"Potty mouth."

"You love it."

"I do." He smirked, waggling his brows. "Now, come here."

"I don't want to hurt you."

"Don't care. I need you next to me." Careful not to pull on his IV, Breanna climbed onto the bed. He kissed her, soft and sweet. "I love you, princess."

"I love you, too, baby."

Caressing her cheek, Ian gazed into fairytale eyes. "Let's get married."

"Are you proposing?"

It's not how he planned to do it, but then life is too short to wait, right? "Yeah."

"You haven't even asked me out on a date yet."

"I think we're past that part, aren't we?" Ian raised his brow.

Breanna grinned, her forehead touching his. "Never."

"So, if I buy you flowers and take you to dinner, then will you marry me?"

"There's a very good chance I will." She giggled.

I know you will, princess.

"I'm going to take that as a yes."

Epilogue

Five years later.

Ian gazed at his princess, his beautiful wife, nursing their three-month-old son.

She did marry him. The day he got the green light from his physician, he drove to Portland and took her on that date. And a year after they met, as snow softly fell on the lantern-lit deck, they spoke their vows to each other.

Breanna got that internship with Penguin and published her father's novel, just as she said she would. She wrote the foreword herself. It was a *New York Times* bestseller. Posthumously, Shane achieved what he'd always aspired to be.

Ian leaned over from behind her, gently stroking his son's dark hair, he kissed Breanna's crown. "Everyone's waiting for us."

"I know." She smiled up at him. "He's about finished."

"Good, because Daddy's starving." He winked.

"Oh, yeah?" Handing him the baby, Breanna stood. "Well, so is Mommy."

Oh, how I love my wife.

And his son.

His entire life.

They descended the stairs together. His mother and hers, all their family and friends, gathered together in the grand foyer. Some things should never change. Everyone came to Dalton House on Thanksgiving, just as it had always been.

Jeanine Fellows made her way to them before anyone else could. "Let me see that baby."

"Would you like to hold him?" Breanna offered, proud mama that she was.

The old lady's smile beamed. "Ohh, may I?"

"Of course."

"Poor kid's gonna get passed around like a bag of chips, ain't he?" Jordy chuckled.

"Heh, sure looks like it."

"Hello, baby Shane." She sniffled. "You sure named him right. He looks just like your daddy."

"Yeah?"

Ian disagreed. Shane Dalton Maynard resembled him more than anyone, but he'd keep that thought to himself.

"The Daltons and St. Johns are one family now, and there's a new generation to carry on the name, just as it should be."

Not quite. Ian was a Maynard and St. John was no more. The name died with Derek. He kept that thought to himself, too. It didn't matter, anyway. He and Breanna could fill these rooms with a bunch of little Maynards, and they planned to, but Dalton House it would always be. What did matter was this house, with people who lived, loved, and laughed in it, was once again a home.

Later, once they'd stuffed themselves on Francie's turkey and everyone had gone home, he watched as Breanna gazed out their bedroom window. "Look, baby, it's snowing."

"It's just a few snowflakes."

"Yeah." She turned away from the glass and smirked. "And every storm starts with just one."

"Come here."

Breanna slid beneath the covers. Coiling his arm around her middle, Ian held her back to his chest and tucked her head beneath his chin. With his fingertips stroking her stomach, he whispered, "I love you."

And he did.

He always would.

Fate and a snowstorm brought him to her.

His beautiful princess.

The End

Acknowledgments

Let it snow! I finally typed 'The End'. I never realized just how much snow they got in the Sierra Nevada until I did my research for this story. I didn't make those numbers up. They get a LOT! But I have an inkling that Breanna and her Sinjin don't mind it a bit!

The Pinterest board and the playlist for *Whiteout* on Spotify and YouTube are open. We're going back to the ranch! *The Hardest Part*, Book 2 in *Brookside* is coming, as well as Matt's story, *Rhythm Man*, Book 7 (yes, I said Book 7!!!) in the *Red Door* series. And after that? We'll see where the muse takes me. I tend to get ahead of myself, so I'm going to leave it at that.

As always, I have a ton of people to thank. 9 books in 4 years—I couldn't have done it on my own, you know. I say this every time, I'm going to try to keep this short and sweet. No, really, I am.

My loves—Michael and Raj, Charlie, Christian, Josie Lynn and Josh, Zach and Sam, Jaide, Julian, Olivia, Jocelyn, and baby Jalina. Fate brought me you, and I love you. It's really just that simple.

Michelle Morgan, who helped me out with the editing of this story. Breanna got her dream job from you! And I love you! xoxo

The amazing Linda Russell and the fantastic team at Foreword PR. What can I say that I haven't already? I love you and get that whip ready—we're doing it! xoxo

My Cover Queen of Hearts, and my gorgeous Aussie

babe, Michelle Lancaster. Your amazing talent and beautiful art never ceases to amaze me. I saw an image of Eric Guilmette and immediately knew he was who I wanted for this cover. I have to say, I couldn't have chosen better. My thanks and much love to you both! xoxo

Lori Jackson did it once again! Another flawless cover! I keep telling you—she makes magic. I love, love, love working with her, but then I just love her, so…until the next one, Lori! xoxo

Ashlee O'Brien, my girly—did y'all see that freaking (Why can't I drop the F-bomb when my characters do?) fantastic alternate cover? She did that! And all the graphics, the trailer. I don't tell her a thing. She just reads the story as I'm writing it and comes up with all this fabulousness. I'd be lost without her, and she knows it. I love you the mostest, book daughter, but you already know that! xoxo

Stacey Blake—only the best formatter on the planet! I cut this one down to the wire, and despite that, she patiently waited for me to finish. The pages inside have to be as beautiful as the cover, and no one does it better than she does. So thank you, Stacey—I love you! xoxo

Mark Barrett of Dark Art Designs. He drew the amazing and hot NSFW scene from Chapter 7! *fanning self*

My beta team—Charbeee Balderson, Jennifer Bishop, Heather Hahn, Kim Lannan, Marjorie Lord, Lee Ann Mathis, Anastasia Meimetas, Melinda Parker, Sabrena Simpson, Trisha Sparks, Rebecca Vazquez, and Staci Way, together with my ARC Team—as always, thank you for being my ride or dies! Much love to all of you! xoxo

Bloggers, Bookstagrammers, and Booktokkers—I appreciate everything you do, every day, for me and every indie out there. Thank you isn't nearly enough, but thank you!

My Redlings who hang out with me *Behind the Red Door*.

Y'all know how to hype a girl up and I love you for it! If you'd like to hang with us too, you can find the group on Facebook. We'd love to have you join us!

And as always, my lovely readers. Thank you for reading the twisty stories that come out of my head. I sure hope you had fun playing in the snow. Now saddle up, we're going to play with some cowboys next!

Until next time...
Much love,
Dyan xoxo

Sneak Peek of *Rhythm Man*—Red Door #7

The doorbell rang.

"About time."

After a late night at the club, he was fucking starving.

Wearing only a pair of grungy old sweats, Matt opened the door. A girl stood on the other side of it. Long dark hair in a ponytail, her eyes a mix of sable and green, she cocked her hip, his pizza in her hand.

He licked his lips. "You're not Luca."

"Nope." Shifting her eyes, she scanned his bare torso and made a face.

"Who are you?"

"The pizza girl." She smirked, shoving the box into his hand. "It's gonna get cold."

Then, turning around, she skipped down the porch steps.

He was tempted to chase after her, but he didn't.

"Hey, you got a name, pizza girl?"

"Doesn't everyone?"

What the hell?

Her ponytail swinging, she glanced back at him from over her shoulder. Shaking his head, Matt took a step back inside the house.

"Gina."

She'll be back.

And closing the door behind him, he grinned.

Books by
DYAN LAYNE

Red Door Series
Serenity
Affinity
Maelstrom
The Other Brother
Drummer Boy
Son of a Preacher Man
Rhythm Man (coming soon)

Brookside Series
The Third Son
The Hardest Part (coming soon)

Standalones
Don't Speak
Whiteout

About the Author

Dyan Layne is a nurse boss by day and the writer of twisty sensual tales by night—and on weekends. She's never without her Kindle and can usually be found tapping away at her keyboard with a hot latte and a cold Dasani Lime—and sometimes champagne. She can't sing a note, but often answers in song because isn't there a song for just about everything? Born and raised a Chicago girl, she currently lives in Tampa, Florida, and is the mother of four handsome sons and a beautiful daughter, who are all grown up now, but can still make her crazy—and she loves it that way! Because normal is just so boring.

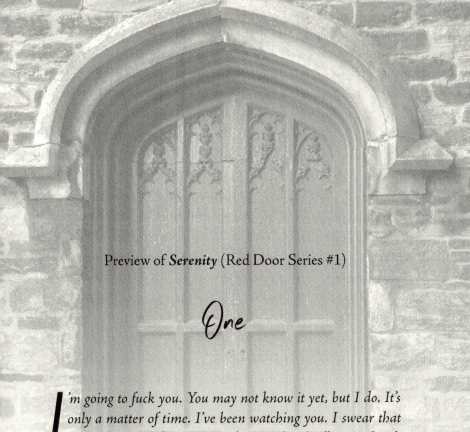

Preview of *Serenity* (Red Door Series #1)

One

'm going to fuck you. You may not know it yet, but I do. It's only a matter of time. I've been watching you. I swear that you've been watching me too, but maybe it's all in my head. No matter. Because I've seen you, I've talked to you and I've come to a conclusion: You are fucking beautiful. And I will make you lust me.

The words danced on crisp white paper. Her fingers trembled and her feet became unsteady, so she leaned against the wall of exposed brick to right herself, clutching the type-written note in her hand. She read it again. A powerful longing surged through her body and her thighs clenched.

Who could have written it? She couldn't fathom a single soul who might be inspired to write such things to her. Maybe those words weren't meant for her? Maybe whoever had written the note slid it beneath the wrong doormat in his haste to deliver it undetected?

Linnea Martin, beautiful? Someone had to be pulling a prank.

Yeah. That's more likely.

She sighed as she turned and closed the solid wood front door. She glanced up at the mirror that hung in the entry hall and eyes the color of moss blinked back at her. Long straight hair, the color of which she had never been able to put into a category—a dirty-blonde maybe—hung past her shoulders, resting close to where her nipples protruded against the fitted cotton shirt she wore. Her skin was fair, but not overly pale. She supposed some people might describe her as pretty, in an average sort of way, but not beautiful.

Not anything but ordinary.

Linnea slowly crumpled up the note in her hand. She clenched it tight and held it to her breast before tossing it into the wastebasket.

Deflated, she threw her tote bag on the coffee table and plopped down on the pale-turquoise-colored sofa that she'd purchased at that quaint secondhand store on First Avenue. She often stopped in there on her way home from the restaurant, carefully eyeing the eclectic array of items artfully displayed throughout the shop. Sometimes, on a good day when tips had been plentiful, she bought herself something nice. Something pretty. Like the pale-turquoise sofa.

Linnea grabbed the current novel she was engrossed in from the coffee table and adjusted herself into a comfortable position, attempting to read. But after she read the same page three times she knew she couldn't concentrate, one sentence blurred into the next, so she set it back down. She clicked on the television and scrolled through the channels, but there was nothing on that could hold her interest. The words replayed in her head.

I'm going to fuck you.

Damn him! Damn that fucker to hell for being so cruel to leave that note at her door, for making her feel…things. The words had thrilled her for a fleeting moment, but then the excitement quickly faded, replaced by a loneliness deep in her chest. Love may never be in the cards for her, or lust for that matter, as much as she might want it to be.

Once upon a time she had believed in fairy tales and dreamt of knights on white stallions and handsome princes, of castle turrets shrouded in mist, of strong yet gentle hands weaving wildflowers in her long honeyed locks—just like the alpha heroes in the tattered paperbacks she had kept hidden under her bed as a teenager. She thought if she was patient long enough, her happily-ever-after would come. She thought that one day, when she was all grown up, that a brave knight, a handsome prince, would rescue her from her grandmother's prison and make all her dreams come true.

Stupid girl.

Her dreams turned into nightmares, and 'one day' never came. She doubted it ever would now. It was her own fault anyway. She closed her eyelids tight, trying to stop the tears that threatened to escape, to keep the memories from flooding back. Linnea had spent years pushing them into an unused corner, a vacant place where they could be hidden away and never be thought of again.

It was dark. She must have been sitting there for quite a while, transfixed in her thoughts. The small living room was void of illumination, except for the blue luminescence that radiated from the unwatched television. Linnea dragged herself over to it and clicked it off. She stood there for a moment waiting for her eyes to adjust to the absence of light and went upstairs.

Steaming water flowed in a torrent from the brushed-nickel faucet, filling the old clawfoot tub. She poured a splash of almond oil into the swirling liquid. As the fragrance released, she bent over the tub to breathe in the sweet vapor that rose from the water and wafted through the room. Slipping the sleeves from her shoulders, the silky robe gave way and fell to a puddle on the floor.

Timorously, she tested the water with her toes, and finding it comfortably hot, she eased her body all the way in. For a time serenity could be found in the soothing water that enveloped her.

You may not know it yet, but I do. It's only a matter of time.

At once her pulse quickened, and without conscious thought her slick fingertips skimmed across her rosy nipples. They hardened at her touch. And a yearning flourished between the folds of flesh down below. Linnea clenched her thighs together, trying to make it go away, but with her attempt to squelch the pulsing there, she only exacerbated her budding desire. And she ached.

Ever so slowly, her hands eased across her flat belly to rest at the junction between her quivering thighs. She wanted so badly to touch herself there and alleviate the agony she found herself in. But as badly as she wanted to, needed to, Linnea would not allow herself the pleasure of her own touch. She sat up instead, the now-tepid water sloshing forward with the sudden movement, and reaching out in front of her she turned the water back on.

She knew it was wicked. Lying there with her legs spread wide and her feet propped on the edge of the tub, she allowed the violent stream of water to pound upon her swollen bud. It throbbed under the assault and her muscles quaked. She'd be tempted to pull on her nipples if she wasn't forced to brace her hands against the porcelain walls of the clawfoot tub for leverage.

Any second now. She was so close.

I'm going to fuck you.

And he did. With just his words, he did.

Her head tipped back as the sensations jolted through her body. The sounds of her own keening cries were muffled by the downpour from the faucet. Spent, she let the water drain from the tub and rested her cheek upon the cold porcelain.

Prologue

"Aidan, baby."

His mother took him by the hand and pulled him along behind her as she hurried out of the kitchen. He'd only eaten half of his grilled cheese sandwich and some grapes when the banging started. It startled him and he knocked over his juice. By the time she went to the front door to see who it was, the banging noise was coming from the other side of the house.

"You can't keep me out, bitch."

It was a man. He was yelling. He sounded angry. Aidan didn't recognize his voice.

His mother seemed to, though. Her eyes got real big and she covered her mouth with her hand. It was shaking.

There was a hutch in the living room that the television sat on. It had doors on the bottom. He hid in there sometimes. His mother opened one of the doors, and tossing the toys that were inside it to the floor, she kissed him on his head and urged him to crawl inside.

"We're going to play a game of hide and seek from the loud man outside, okay, baby?" his mother whispered.

Aidan nodded.

The banging got louder.

"You have to be very, very quiet so he doesn't know you're here." It sounded like she was choking and tears leaked out of her eyes, but she smiled at him.

"Like at story time?"

Aidan's mother took him to story time at the library every Saturday, and afterwards if he'd been a good boy, she would let him get an ice cream.

"Yes, baby. Just like that." She nodded with tears running down her face. "Now stay very still and don't speak a word until I tell you to—no matter what, okay?"

He nodded again. "Okay, Mommy."

"I love you, Aidan."

"I love you, Mommy."

Everyone said the place was haunted. The kids at school. The people in town. It didn't look scary, but nobody ever went anywhere near the two-story white clapboard house that was set off by itself on the cove.

It was to be her home now.

Molly stood at the wrought-iron gate with her mother, holding onto her hand. She clutched her *Bear in the Big Blue House* backpack, that she'd had since she was four, with the other. A boy with sandy-blond hair sat on the porch steps. Aidan Fischer. He didn't pay them, or his father unloading their belongings from the U-Haul, any mind. He had a notebook in his lap and a pencil between his fingers. It looked like he was drawing.

The boy chewed on his lip as he moved the pencil over the paper. Even though he was in the fifth grade, and three years older than her, Molly knew who he was. Everybody did. He was the boy who didn't talk. And six days from today, when her mother married his father, that boy was going to be her brother.

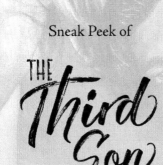

Sneak Peek of

THE
Third Son

C oming out of the bathroom, Arien stubbed her toe, close to taking a tumble over a stack of forgotten boxes in the hallway. "Ouch. Motherfu…"

She held onto her foot, hopping the rest of the way to her bedroom in the small townhouse apartment she shared with her mom. It was all packed up, cartons neatly labeled, identifying the contents inside. Bed stripped. Closet and drawers emptied.

It wasn't like she had a choice.

A moving van was parked outside.

Holding her towel closed, her back against the wall,

Arien sat cross-legged on the bare mattress. She had exactly thirty minutes to put on some makeup and get dressed. It would only take her ten.

This is so not fucking fair.

She blew out a breath. A week ago, her room was pretty and her life wasn't packed away in cardboard boxes. That all changed when her mother and her boyfriend—if that's what you call a man in his forties—took her out with them to dinner.

And that alone should have told her something was up.

Jennifer Brogan had been dating Matthew Brooks for about six months now, but Arien didn't know him all that well. A real cowboy, her mother said. He had two sons and lived on some ranch up in Wyoming, an eight-hour drive from Denver. He'd come into town for business, and to see her mom, a few times a month.

He was the one to break the news to her. "Arien," he said with a smile, taking her mother's hand in his. "First off, I need you to know I love your mama very much. So much, I've asked her to marry me."

She about choked on her green-chili cheeseburger.

Her mom held up her left hand, waving the huge diamond glittering on her finger. "I said yes."

Okay.

Arien was seventeen, soon-to-be eighteen. She'd be going away to college at the end of summer anyway. Her mom deserved some happiness, right?

Swallowing down the cheeseburger, she put on a smile. "At least you won't have to change your monogram. When's the wedding?"

"Next week," her mother announced, biting her lip. "I'm pregnant."

"Three months already," Matthew said proudly, patting

his new fiancée on the shoulder. "I'm coming back with the boys. We'll get married and have you all moved in before Thanksgiving."

What? To Wyoming? Nope. Not happening.

"Wait. You want me to move, to change schools during my senior year?"

"I'm sorry, sweetie."

"You're going to love Brookside." Her soon-to-be stepfather patted her on the hand. "We have a superior private school there. The ranch. The mountains. You can take lots of pictures."

"There's mountains right here."

Isn't thirty-six too old to have a baby anyway? Apparently not. And what happened to all those lectures her mother gave her about having sex, taking precautions, and all that stuff? She should've listened to her own advice. If she had, Arien wouldn't be going to a courthouse wedding to leave Denver, and the only life she'd ever known, behind.

Only for a little while.

True. She had her acceptance letter to UC. She'd be back.

"Sweetie, are you ready yet?" her mother asked from downstairs. "Matt and the boys are here."

Dammit.

"Almost," she answered, plucking through her makeup bag.

Clearly a lie. She hadn't even begun.

Holding a compact mirror in one hand, Arien applied mascara with the other, the towel slipping away from her.

She couldn't say for sure what made her look up. A feeling she was being watched, maybe.

Two boys—no, these weren't boys, they were hot-as-fuck men—stood smirking in her doorway.

"Who the hell are you?"

"I'm Tanner." The man smiled, and taking a step inside her room, he hitched a thumb behind him. "That's Kellan."

"And I'm naked." She snatched up the towel, covering herself.

Kellan snickered.

Tanner came closer. "Well now, that's a mighty fine hello, little sister."

Character Index

Breanna Dalton—daughter of Shane (deceased) and Sarah Benjamin

Derek St. John—attorney for the late Valerie Dalton, cousin to Sinjin Maynard

Ethan Benjamin—Breanna's younger brother

Francesca "Francie" St. John Keeler—housekeeper/cook, wife to Ted, aunt to Derek and Ian, youngest sister of Sharon, Raymond, and Pamela

George Dalton—a 19th-century pioneer who built the original Dalton House

Hank—proprietor of the general store

Hera—Ian's Husky

Ian "Sinjin" Maynard—attorney and property manager for Dalton House, cousin to Derek St. John

Jeanine Fellows—old lady from the village

Jordy—sheriff

Kayleigh—college friend and roommate of Breanna

Lawrence Dalton (deceased)—father to Shane, husband to Valerie, paternal grandfather to Breanna

Miranda—Derek's girlfriend

Nathan Benjamin—stepfather to Breanna

Pamela St. John Maynard—mother to Ian, aunt to Derek, sister to Sharon, Raymond, and Francesca

Randall—paramedic

Raymond St. John (deceased)—father to Derek, uncle to Ian, brother to Sharon, Pamela, and Francesca

Sarah Benjamin—Breanna's mother

Shane Dalton (deceased)—father of Breanna

Sharon St. John (deceased)—eldest sister to Raymond, Pamela, and Francesca. Romantically involved with Lawrence Dalton before her death

Ted Keeler—caretaker/handyman, husband to Francie

Valerie Kimball Dalton (deceased)—paternal grandmother of Breanna

About the Author

Dyan Layne is a nurse boss by day and the writer of twisty sensual tales by night—and on weekends. She's never without her Kindle and can usually be found tapping away at her keyboard with a hot latte and a cold Dasani Lime—and sometimes champagne. She can't sing a note, but often answers in song because isn't there a song for just about everything? Born and raised a Chicago girl, she currently lives in Tampa, Florida, and is the mother of four handsome sons and a beautiful daughter, who are all grown up now, but can still make her crazy—and she loves it that way! Because normal is just so boring.

Made in the USA
Columbia, SC
24 September 2024

42285787R00188